STARLESS

A Medieval Romance

By Kathryn Le Veque

Book Three in the Executioner Knights Series

KATHRYN LE VEQUE NOVELS

The Dragonblade Series:
Fragments of Grace
Dragonblade
Island of Glass
The Savage Curtain
The Fallen One

Great Marcher Lords of de Lara
Lord of the Shadows
Dragonblade

House of St. Hever
Fragments of Grace
Island of Glass
Queen of Lost Stars

Lords of Pembury:
The Savage Curtain

Lords of Thunder: The de Shera Brotherhood Trilogy
The Thunder Lord
The Thunder Warrior
The Thunder Knight

The Great Knights of de Moray:
Shield of Kronos
The Gorgon

The House of De Nerra:
The Promise
The Falls of Erith
Vestiges of Valor
Realm of Angels

Highland Warriors of Munro:
The Red Lion
Deep Into Darkness

The House of de Garr:
Lord of Light
Realm of Angels

Saxon Lords of Hage:
The Crusader

Kingdom Come

High Warriors of Rohan:
High Warrior

The House of Ashbourne:
Upon a Midnight Dream

The House of D'Aurilliac:
Valiant Chaos

The House of De Dere:
Of Love and Legend

St. John and de Gare Clans:
The Warrior Poet

The House of de Bretagne:
The Questing

The House of Summerlin:
The Legend

The Kingdom of Hendocia:
Kingdom by the Sea

The Executioner Knights:
By the Unholy Hand
The Promise (also Noble Knights of de Nerra)
The Mountain Dark
Starless
A Time of End

Contemporary Romance:

Kathlyn Trent/Marcus Burton Series:
Valley of the Shadow
The Eden Factor
Canyon of the Sphinx

The American Heroes Anthology Series:
The Lucius Robe
Fires of Autumn
Evenshade

Sea of Dreams
Purgatory

Sons of Poseidon:
The Immortal Sea

Other non-connected Contemporary Romance:
Lady of Heaven
Darkling, I Listen
In the Dreaming Hour
River's End
The Fountain

Pirates of Britannia Series (with Eliza Knight):
Savage of the Sea by Eliza Knight
Leader of Titans by Kathryn Le Veque
The Sea Devil by Eliza Knight
Sea Wolfe by Kathryn Le Veque

Note: All Kathryn's novels are designed to be read as stand-alones, although many have cross-over characters or cross-over family groups. Novels that are grouped together have related characters or family groups. You will notice that some series have the same books; that is because they are cross-overs. A hero in one book may be the secondary character in another.

There is NO reading order except by chronology, but even in that case, you can still read the books as stand-alones. No novel is connected to another by a cliff hanger, and every book has an HEA.

Series are clearly marked. All series contain the same characters or family groups except the American Heroes Series, which is an anthology with unrelated characters.

For more information, find it in **A Reader's Guide to the Medieval World of Le Veque.**

Author's Note

Welcome to Achilles and Susanna's story!

This is a very interesting story in that it marks something I've never done before – writing the love story of a couple who had their "first meeting" in another tale. Part of writing a romance novel includes the first meeting and then developing the story from there, but Achilles and Susanna met in *The Mountain Dark*, Book Two of the Executioner Knights series, and readers were begging for a continuation of their story from the outset.

So, here we are!

This novel essentially picks up right after the last chapter of *The Mountain Dark*, but instead of Kress de Rhydian and Cadelyn of Vendotia's story, we continue on with Achilles and Susanna. You don't need to read *The Mountain Dark* to understand this tale, but it helps. It gives it much more dimension.

Interestingly enough, originally I hadn't meant Susanna for Achilles. He had an entirely different story planned, but after the (several) combative encounters these two had, I knew I couldn't give Achilles any other heroine. Susanna was made for him. And that makes this story a heck of a lot of fun.

This series originally started off as just a trilogy – the stories of Maxton of Loxbeare, Kress de Rhydian, and Achilles de Dere, men known as the Executioner Knights: The Unholy Trinity. However, the series is growing the more I introduce cool new characters. Now, the Executioner Knights is beginning to encompass the entire stable of knights that serve William Marshal as special agents and spies – and this would include characters like Sean de Lara (*Lord of the Shadows*) and Garren le Mon (*The Whispering Night*) among others. The Unholy Trinity is the "original" three of this series – the OG knights – Maxton,

Kress, and Achilles. Characters like Alexander de Sherrington are close friends of the Unholy Trinity, but not official part of them. They do, however, all work together.

In the first three books in the series, knights have rotated in and out – knights we have met in previous books – Gart Forbes, Christopher de Lohr, David de Lohr, Bric MacRohan, Dashiell du Reims, Cullen de Nerra, and Sean de Lara to name a few. This particular book happens to have Kevin de Lara, brother to Sean de Lara who played a major secondary role in *Archangel*, also playing a major secondary role here as well. This book also contains a major plot point for *Lord of the Shadows*, by the way. It's part of Sean de Lara's backstory. Like an Easter egg, you'll need to find it!

So many books are related to the Executioner Knights series, books that aren't actually part of the series but connected to it. Those titles are *Rise of the Defender, Steelheart, Archangel, The Promise, Godspeed,* and *High Warrior* to name a few. The heroes all serve William Marshal within the same twenty-year time frame, so they rotate in and out of these tales. It's a small world in my early 13th century England universe.

Fun things to note – since I have quite a universe of characters and locations, I want to point out to readers that Susanna's ancestral home of Aysgarth Castle first appeared in the novel *Fragments of Grace*. That's one more book to tie in to this series! That de Tiegh family comes about ninety years after this one, descendants of Susanna's brother.

Now on to Achilles – he's got a lineage in the Le Veque Universe! His parents are Tyren and Valeria from *Of Love and Legend*. Surprise! If you haven't read that novella, make sure you do. It gives you a little insight into Achilles' parents. His older brother is none other than Brickley de Dere, a major secondary character in the de Lohr novel, *Steelheart*. Achilles is the baby of the family, born several years after his eldest brother, Brick (whom I loved in *Steelheart*). I didn't list the offspring of Valeria and Tyren when I wrote the novel, so here it is:

Antonia

Cecelia

Brickley – (served the Earl of Canterbury, Lyle Hampton, later served the Earls of East Anglia – father of Dashiell du Reims)

Benedict

Tobias

Achilles

Richmond Castle in Yorkshire plays a role in this tale and I must say that Richmond is one of my all-time favorite castles. If you ever have a chance to visit it, or use Google Maps to see it, do. It's absolutely enormous – and beautiful – and has quite a history, some of which is part of this storyline.

A few things to note – real places versus fictional:

Real:
Richmond Castle
Skipton Castle
Whorlton Castle (and the family that owned it is the actual family in this novel, de Meynell. Whether they held the views expressed in this novel are purely a figment of my imagination for plot purposes)

Fictional:
Aysgarth Castle
And, the usual pronunciation guide:
De Tiegh – duh TEEG
De Dere – duh DARE
Aysgarth – ACE-garth
De Meynell – duh mayNELL

And to answer your questions, YES – Alexander (Sherry) and a new character introduced in this book, Caius d'Avignon, will be having their own stories told soon. I will also be working in a story for Kevin de Lara – finally, Sean's little brother will have his own tale.

Whew! That was a big author's note. This is a fast-paced story, and very different from most I write, so I sincerely hope you enjoy it. Achilles and Susanna are a total match made in heaven.

Love,

Kathryn

"I suppose we all hope to meet that one person who makes us spark."
– *Lady Susanna de Tiegh to Achilles de Dere from Book Two, The Mountain Dark*

PARTIAL EXCERPT OF THE FIRST MEETING

From the novel, The Mountain Dark

May, Year of Our Lord 1206

~ First encounter between Susanna de Tiegh and Achilles de Dere ~

*W*ILLIAM MARSHAL HAD *told them that Lady Cadelyn had a female bodyguard, he suspected who the woman was.*

"You are the bodyguard The Marshal told us of," Kress de Rhydian said to the woman. "Susanna de Tiegh, is it?"

Susanna nodded. "Aye, my lord."

"Where are you from?"

"My father was Baron Coverdale of Aysgarth Castle in Cumbria."

"I have heard of it," Kress said, his gaze lingering on her. "But you... a lady bodyguard? How did this come about?"

Susanna met his gaze steadily and Kress found himself looking into fine features and eyes the color of a sapphire. She wasn't unattractive in the least, but her hair was uncombed and her dress slovenly. She almost had a masculine way about her, tough and seasoned in a world of men who would not accept that from a woman.

Any woman.

If Kress could guess, the woman had to be closed to thirty years of age, and obviously unmarried. No husband would permit his wife to assume duties that Susanna had assumed, and if he did, then he would be a poor excuse of a man.

She was quite an oddity.

"My father had two children, twins," Susanna said, breaking into his train of thought. "My brother and I were inseparable. Anything he did, I did, and that included fostering. We both went to Exelby Castle to foster years ago, but I did not want to learn what fine ladies learn. I wanted to do what my brother was doing. Lord de Geld, the lord of Exelby, was not a very firm man. He let me do as I wished, against the advice of the knights. As it turned out, I was better than most of their recruits."

She was making a statement of fact, without gloating in her manner, but the distaste the men felt at the thought of a woman thinking she could possibly be as skilled as they were was evident. Achilles de Dere, part of Kress' contingent and seated next to her, spoke up.

"Then Exelby must have had a good many weak men parading as warriors," he said, doubt in his voice. "Were you knighted?"

Susanna turned to look at him, a warrior who was a good deal younger than his bald head would suggest. "Nay," she said, lifting an eyebrow. "Were you?"

Kress fought off a grin at her saucy reply but he could see that Achilles found nothing humorous about it.

"By men better than anything you have ever stood against," he growled. "A woman who does not know her place in life is an insult to every man who has ever lifted a sword."

To her credit, Susanna didn't openly react to his offense. She kept her composure. "I would be happy to demonstrate just how much of an insult I am," she said. "Say the word and I shall meet you with my sword wherever, and whenever, you wish."

Achilles' eyes narrowed. "I would not lower myself to such a thing."

Susanna shrugged. "As you wish, my lord," she said, returning her attention to Kress. "Do all of your men fade from such a challenge? Mayhap they are not up to the task of escorting Lady Cadelyn to her betrothed. That task requires men of courage."

Before Kress could reply, Achilles was going for his sword and Susanna, seeing his movement in her periphery, vaulted from the bench and ended up several feet away, her skirts up around her waistline to reveal that she was wearing leather breeches and a broadsword strapped to her waist underneath. Her hand was on the hilt of her sword and the gemstone eyes were fixed on her opponent.

(And with that, the stage was set…)

CHAPTER ONE

ET TU MORIERIS IN GLADIO
(YOU SHALL DIE BY THE SWORD)

The Horse's Arse Tavern
Skipton, North Yorkshire
Three Months Later

"ARE YOU WELL? Do you need anything to make you more comfortable?"

The words sounded rather anxious, coming from Achilles as he spoke to Susanna. She was dressed just like him, wearing clothing that suggested she was far more a warrior and far less a lady. Over her heavy mail coat she wore a tunic with the blue and black shield of the House of de Winter, while Achilles wore the yellow and green split shield of the Earl of Pembroke, William Marshal. It was one of the most recognizable standards in all of England.

But to his concerned words, she eyed him impatiently.

"I do not need anything," she assured him. "If I do, I will ask."

"Are you certain? Can I get you food and drink?"

"Aye, you can get me food and drink. But, Achilles?"

"Aye?"

"Stop hovering or I will kill you."

He broke into a weak grin. "Do you flirt with me, Sparks? You know how talk of killing arouses me. Say it again."

Sparks. That was something he'd been calling her because of something she'd said to him recently, a term of endearment that made her cheeks flush every time she heard it. But in seeing that her threat had backfired, she shook her head at him.

"God's Bones, you are an uncouth man," she muttered.

He started laughing. "But that is what you like about me," he said. "Admit it. That is what has drawn you to me and has you begging for a lock of my hair."

Considering he was bald, that was a ridiculous statement. Susanna looked at him sharply, frowning as he grinned and pointed to his shiny head. He looked so comical, and so adorable, that she couldn't help but laugh at him. But she turned her head quickly so he couldn't see.

"Imbecile," she muttered.

Achilles snorted, greatly humored. Their small party had just finished a long day of travel, a journey that had started in a small village south of Chester and would end at Susanna's ancestral home of Aysgarth Castle in Yorkshire. On this night, they'd ended up in a rather large, one-storied inn on the edge of the village of Burnley, one with mossy stone walls on the exterior and a leaning dirt floor in the common room that had a rather vertiginous feel.

But none of that mattered to Achilles. All that mattered was that Susanna had a warm, comfortable place to stay for the night.

He was concerned for her.

But it wasn't concern that she appreciated, for Susanna wasn't like a normal woman. She was as tough as the steel broadsword she carried. When it came to fine manners or polite responses, they were rather lost on her.

Living in a world of men, she tended to behave like one.

"Food and drink are coming." The third knight in their party joined the table, sitting heavily as he pulled off his leather gauntlets. Sir Alexander de Sherrington, a handsome man with black hair and a trim black beard looked straight at Susanna. "I secured a room for you so that you may rest tonight in comfort. How are you feeling after today's journey?"

Susanna showed more patience with Alexander than she had shown with Achilles. "I am well," she said. "Truly, you two needn't worry so much. I am perfectly fine."

Seated at her right, Achilles snorted. "If you are, then you have healing powers none of the rest of us have," he said. "Three weeks ago, you took a sword to your belly. No man – or woman – is perfectly fine from that a mere few weeks later."

Susanna looked at him, feeling a little more tolerance because he wasn't trying to antagonize her. He was quite serious and his concern was very sweet, even if it was difficult for her to both admit it and accept it. She'd never been fond of a man in her life until Achilles came along. The man had started out as her mortal enemy but, as of late, that wasn't the case. Still, the mere fact that he was starting to show some affection for her was quite alien.

She had no real idea how to show it in return.

"I am much better than I was," she said. "You really needn't worry so much."

He looked at her. "Would you truly prefer if I did not care?"

"I am simply saying you need not worry. If something is wrong, I will tell you."

He curled his lip. "Ungrateful wench. Do you not know when someone is trying to show you kindness?"

"You have been doing it since I became injured."

His eyebrows lifted as if that statement had somehow grossly insulted him. "And you are opposed to this?"

Across the table, Alexander could see something brewing. But, then again, something was *always* brewing between the pair. For two people who were attracted to one another, he'd never seen anything so awkward in his entire life. They liked one another; it was *clear* that they liked one another. But neither one of them had the ability to really show it.

It was going to be a long night.

The food and drink began to come. The innkeeper and his daughter, a freckled lass with hair the texture of straw, delivered bowls of *ricque-manger*, or eggs and apples fried in butter, a big trencher of vegetables that had been boiled in wine, and plenty of bread and butter. Achilles made sure Susanna was served before he even considered taking a bite of his own food.

"We should be at Aysgarth Castle tomorrow," he said, mouth full of eggs and apples. "I shall find someone this night to take a message on ahead. When was the last time you saw your brother?"

Susanna was buttering her bread. "It has been two years," she said. "Serving William Marshal, I can only go where he sends me. For the past several years, I was the stationed in Norfolk, as you know. I was commanded to stay close to a certain Welsh princess."

The name of the Welsh princess was not to be spoken aloud, not these days. Not when she and her knight had fled into hiding. It was a secret the knights were sworn to protect. They had only just come from that particular assignment, now returning to normal after a harrowing adventure involving the princess and a faction that had threatened her. But it had been more than that; so much more than that.

It had been part of Susanna's life for a very long time.

"And you did your job well," Achilles said as he shoved food into his mouth. "But during that time, you left your assignment to return to Aysgarth from time to time, did you not?"

Susanna nodded. "The Marshal had me return home on occasion to see what my brother was doing," she said. "He wants to make sure Samuel is not doing something he should not be doing. Or allied with someone he should not be allied with. As Baron Coverdale, he has a considerable army and my brother has not sworn allegiance to the king, nor has he sworn allegiance to the king's enemies. My brother is an enigma that makes The Marshal nervous."

"Then returning home to recuperate will also find you educating yourself on your brother's recent activities," Alexander said quietly, his gaze intense over the tabletop. "Now that the Welsh princess has married a man who can take great care of her, you are no longer needed by her side. That must feel strange after having been with her for so long."

"Strange, indeed."

"Do you miss her?"

"I probably should not, but she was not only my assignment, she was my friend as well."

"Then this will be a time of change for you as you return to your brother's home and assume a new assignment."

"Only until The Marshal decides to send me elsewhere."

They all knew that was the case, as men and women who served the Earl of Pembroke were pawns in his great political and military game. It was simply their way of life and they accepted that. The conversation soon lagged as the food was consumed at an alarming rate by the knights while Susanna thought back to the task she'd been charged with for almost ten years.

It was still difficult to believe it was all over.

The Welsh princess they were speaking of, Cadelyn of Vendotia, had been a rarity. With royal blood on both sides of her family, she had been afforded special protection from William Marshal. Cadelyn had been betrothed to an English earl, but she'd ended up falling in love with one of the knights in the escort assigned to take her to her wedding. Susanna had never seen the woman happier, even if she had married a warrior who was known as an Executioner Knight.

Chewing on her bread, Susanna looked at the men she was seated with. They, too, were Executioner Knights. There were three men who carried that reputation officially, four of them unofficially. Maxton of Loxbeare had been the leader, but he'd married well and was now holding the southern end of the Welsh Marches from the property he'd acquired from his wife. Susanna had never met him, but she'd heard plenty about him. The second man, Kress de Rhydian, had been part of Cadelyn of Vendotia's escort and was now in Scotland where he'd taken his wife into hiding from her Welsh enemies.

The third man was Achilles.

He was more of a follower than a leader, but he was the perfect follower. Bright, with precise instincts and flawless obedience, he had a youthful edginess to him that was quite dangerous. Tall, broad, and handsome, he was a very big man with an uncontrollable temper when aroused, and oddly pious when the mood struck him. There was something of a mystery in everything about him.

Lastly, there was Alexander, or "Sherry" as everyone called him. He was the unofficial fourth member of the Executioner Knights. Alexander had worked with the Executioner Knights in The Levant, a tremendously skilled assassin that mostly preferred working alone. Even so, they didn't come any greater or any smarter than Alexander de Sherrington, and his camaraderie with Maxton and Kress and Achilles was unbreakable.

Susanna found it utterly fascinating to be around men with such reputations. Their very presence smacked of power. She'd seen them in action, most notably in the fight that had left her with a wound in her belly, as Achilles had mentioned. It had been a fight that had allowed Cadelyn and Kress to escape to safety from the Welsh who had been pursuing Cadelyn, but it had been a bloody skirmish.

Susanna was only now able to move around with some ease.

Truth be told, she was far more exhausted and in pain than she let on, but she was trying desperately not to cause trouble. Achilles and Alexander were escorting her back to her brother's castle so she could recuperate fully there and she didn't want to be a burden.

So, she kept her mouth shut as they'd ridden for hours and hours over the past three days, feeling agonizing pain in her gut and in her back from her healing wound. Even now, as she ate her bread and her eggs, all she wanted to do was lie down and rest. It was genuinely becoming too much for her.

But she didn't want to tell them.

She wanted them to think she was as strong as they were.

"Where will you be returning once you leave me off at Aysgarth?"

she asked simply to make conversation. "Will you be returning directly to London?"

Achilles' mouth was full of food so Alexander answered. "We are returning to Chester," he said. "We are to meet Bric MacRohan and Christopher de Lohr and return with them to London. Unfortunately, we must all report to William Marshal and explain the disaster that was the betrothal between Cadelyn of Vendotia and the Earl of Ellesmere. I have repeated what to tell the man over in my head a thousand times but I fear that I will need de Lohr there to support my position that one of my knights ran off with the lady."

Susanna knew that; after the fiasco of the failed betrothal, there was the not-so-small matter of reporting all of that to William Marshal. Christopher de Lohr, the powerful Earl of Hereford and Worcester, had been peripherally involved in the situation and, even now, remained with Ellesmere, along with another Marshal knight, Bric MacRohan, to help the earl regain control of his earldom after a threat perpetrated by the same Welsh who had threatened Cadelyn. It was all quite complicated, and quite tense, but de Lohr would have to face The Marshal sooner or later, as would they all.

It was something no one was looking forward to.

"It was not your fault that Cadelyn and Kress fell in love," Susanna said after a moment. "You cannot take the blame for it."

"But it was *my* escort. I was the commander."

"Can you command emotions away, then?"

Alexander wasn't going to let her console him on this matter. "The fact remains that a knight under my command absconded with a woman meant for Tatius de Shera," he said. "That *was* my fault. But what was not my fault was the fact that the earl's brothers were conspiring with Welsh rebels to take Tatius' earldom from him and use Cadelyn to inspire their rebellion. They had the entire de Shera army convinced that Tatius was a weak and ineffective earl, and now that the brothers are dead, Tatius has a good deal of rebuilding to do. De Lohr and MacRohan are helping him do that."

"Will they help you rebuild trust with The Marshal when you tell him what has happened?"

Alexander smiled thinly. "Mayhap. But I shall face The Marshal's wrath without fear. This was my command and my responsibility."

Susanna's thoughts lingered on everything that had happened over the past several weeks. It seemed like a lifetime ago, yet it seemed as if it were only yesterday. So much had happened in a very short amount of time.

Maybe when she was stronger, she would be more willing to reflect on the situation that had brought her to this point in her life but, at the moment, her fatigue had the better of her. Taking a final drink of her wine, she gathered her saddlebags and her broadsword, and stood up wearily.

"I would like to rest," she confessed. "Which chamber is mine?"

Alexander pointed down a darkened corridor that branched off from the common room. "Down there," he said. "Last door on your left."

"Where will you and Achilles be?"

"In the chamber directly across from you."

As Susanna turned to leave the table, Achilles was on his feet. "I will escort you."

She paused. "That is not necessary."

He gave her a look that suggested he was going with or without her permission, so she pursed her lips wryly and turned to follow Alexander's direction. At least, that was her intention until the door to the inn slammed back on its hinges and men began to filter in.

Knights bearing blue and yellow tunics were entering the smoky room. They were loud and brash, pushing patrons out of the way as they searched for a suitable table.

It wasn't an idea situation. Too many knights from different factions in one small room created something of a tense situation and this was no exception. Achilles didn't recognize their standards right away, but there was a crowd of them and they were aggressive, which didn't bode well in any case. At the sight, Achilles sighed heavily.

"Go to your chamber," he said quietly. "Hurry, now. Do not let them see you."

Susanna was eyeing the knights. "I will not leave you and Sherry alone," she said. "Who are they?"

"I am not sure. Do you recognize them?"

"The standard is familiar, but I cannot place them. Retrieve Sherry and let us retreat to our chambers at the same time. You have eaten your meal. It is time to retire."

Achilles counted seven knights. He turned to look at Alexander only to see the man staring at the newcomers as a hunter would sight prey. Alexander's intense black eyes had a way of striking fear in the hearts of men and seeing that the man was already highly attuned to what was going on, Achilles returned his attention to Susanna.

"Do as I say," he said quietly. "Go to your chamber. I will gather Sherry."

Susanna nodded, her focus on the knights as she headed towards the darkened corridor where her rented room was located. But entering the mouth of the corridor was as far as she got before she heard the knights as they began to bang on the table, demanding food and drink.

Something told her not to go any further.

Sinking back into the shadows, she watched the common room from her vantage point. Mostly, she was watching Achilles and Alexander, wondering if Achilles was really going to force Alexander to leave the table and not particularly surprised when Achilles simply sat down next to Alexander, watching the knights across the room.

Frustrated, she shook her head at the pair, men who were fearless in all things. In fact, she knew that Achilles rather enjoyed a fight. If there was one to be had, he was always in the middle of it. Perhaps he wasn't looking for a fight tonight, but he wasn't going out of his way to avoid one, either. Worse still, he was staring at the knights much in the same way Alexander was.

Waiting for someone to make the first move.

Quickly, Susanna made her way down to the end of the corridor and to the room indicated by Achilles. Opening the door, there was already a fire in the hearth. The chamber was tiny, with a tiny bed, but it was enough for her needs. She slung her saddlebags onto the bed and unsheathed her broadsword, which was rather plain by most standards. Most knights carried adornment of some kind, gold at the very least, but Susanna had a sword that was perfect in every way even if it was rather bland.

And it was sharp enough to split hairs.

Sword in hand, she returned to her place in the shadowed corridor, watching the room and realizing that in the time she'd been gone, the knights had noticed the two Pembroke knights as they sat over near the hearth. It was enough attention that the innkeeper was already trying to clear out the room.

This was not going to end well.

It started with the knights making rude comments about William Marshal as Achilles and Alexander sat there and calmly drank their ale. Food arrived for the loud men and they were ill-mannered about it, going so far as to pass around the serving wench, trying to kiss her as she resisted.

When they grew bored of that, they began to insult everyone around them, driving patrons out into the night simply to get away from them. The innkeeper didn't dare ask them to behave. The man had taken his daughter, and the abused serving wench, and disappeared into the kitchen, leaving his patrons to fend for themselves.

Then came the moment Susanna had been dreading.

The dark-eyed knight who had been making the most noise finally stood up from the table, cup of ale in his hand. His eyes were on Achilles and Alexander as he spoke to his men.

"Some men should stay in their own village," he said loudly. "Would you not concur?"

His men rumbled loudly in agreement and he continued. "If a man does not stay where he belongs, then is it not correct to assume that he is looking for trouble?"

More agreement, more rumbling, and some laughter. That caused the dark-eyed knight to turn towards Achilles and Alexander. He meandered towards their table casually.

"Is that what you are doing here?" he asked them. "Looking for trouble?"

Susanna held her breath. Achilles wasn't one to hold his tongue and she waited for him to launch himself over the table. That was his usual reaction to a challenge. To her surprise, however, he looked away as Alexander replied.

"No trouble," he said. "We will not bother you if you will not bother us."

The dark-eyed knight grinned, looking pointedly at their tunics. "Pembroke," he muttered in disgust. "You are very far north, Pembroke. Are you coming to visit your brothers at Richmond Castle? 'Tis a travesty that Pembroke has command of the place. Like vermin on a dog, they should be washed away."

Alexander didn't rise to the insult. "As I said, we will not bother you if you will not bother us."

"What *are* you doing here?"

"Minding my own business. As should you."

The smile faded from the knight's face. "It was a civil question. Since you are in my territory, I expect an answer."

Alexander eyed him. "Who are you?"

"De Meynell," he said as if that should mean something. "Lord of Whorlton Castle."

Alexander returned to his wine. "Now I understand," he said. "South of Richmond, your much bigger and much more enviable neighbor. It is at least a two days ride from here."

"We can make it in a day."

It was a boast and Alexander remained unimpressed. "It is still far to the north. Therefore, this is not your territory. We are in Skipton's territory now and his soldiers are loyal to William Marshal. Shall I send for him so you can tell him this territory belongs to de Meynell?"

The smile vanished from the knight's face. Glaring at Alexander, he took a swig of his ale, contemplating what to say next.

"Since you serve a contemptable man, you must be contemptable yourselves," he snarled. "Tell me what underhanded and despicable things you have done today, knights. Well? I wish to be entertained."

"I would not provoke them if I were you."

The decidedly female voice came from the corridor as Susanna stepped into the common room. She was without fear as she moved, brave beyond measure, but for the sake of a quickly deteriorating situation, she felt the need to intervene. One more insult and seven knights could quite possibly be missing heads. Never mind that it was seven against three; those seven knights had no idea just who their opponents were.

Susanna intended to educate them.

"Did you hear me?" she asked. "It would be best if you did not provoke them."

At the sight of her, the de Meynell knight's eyes widened. "A wench with a sword?" he said, aghast. "And she wears the colors of de Winter."

"Indeed, she does."

"The man has a cow serving him!"

As his friends laughed uproariously, Achilles flinched but Alexander threw out an arm, preventing the man from attacking. Susanna, looking over the de Meynell knights, joined them in their laughter.

"He does!" she agreed, forcing loud laughter. "And your lord has swine serving him, so I suppose our lords are even in that regard."

The laughter ended abruptly and the de Meynell knights seated at the table stood up, insulted by the wench bearing the de Winter tunic. As they stood up, Achilles and Alexander stood up, and the situation was about to become critical. Susanna held up a finger to the de Meynell commander to emphasize a point.

"Since we understand one another now, I want to explain my comment when I told you that you should not provoke these men," she said.

"I am doing you a favor."

The de Meynell knight eyed her with contempt. "I do not need your favors, cow."

Susanna shrugged. "It was for your benefit," she said. "I simply wanted to point out that these two knights are not ordinary knights."

"They look ordinary enough to me."

She smiled, humorlessly. "That is where you are wrong," she said. "Have you heard of the Executioner Knights? If not, then you should have. They earned their reputation in The Levant because if there was a dirty job to be done, these men would do it. They are warriors, spies, and assassins in every sense of the word. You even asked them what despicable things they had done today, so surely you know yourself what men serving William Marshal are capable of."

The de Meynell knight cast Alexander and Achilles a long, if not disbelieving, gaze. "Capable of nothing more than the rest of us, I am sure, only less honorable and less skilled."

He was mocking them and Susanna continued. "The Muslim commanders could not kill them," she said. "Years with King Richard could not destroy them. They are men so skilled, so deadly, that you would be stupid to tangle with them, for they shall end your life without effort. If you do not believe me, try them. You shall find out soon enough."

The de Meynell knight was still looking at Achilles and Alexander with great disdain, but he wasn't so foolish that he didn't take some measure of her words seriously. The seeds had been planted. After a long moment, his focus returned to Susanna.

"And you?" he said. "Don't tell me you were in The Levant, too."

She shook her head. "Blackchurch."

That brought a strong reaction. "*You* trained at Blackchurch?"

She nodded. "The Lords of Exmoor run the finest training school in England and I was there for three years, learning my craft. And before you scoff in disbelief again, know that they take women if they are particularly talented. If you do not believe that I am, I would be happy to demonstrate."

The knight stared at her as if trying to determine if she was jesting or not. After a moment, his smile returned and he extend his hand back towards his table of men.

"It would be a pleasure," he said.

One of his men placed the hilt of his sword in his open palm. Susanna wasn't entirely sure she was ready for combat considering she was still recovering from her gut wound, but she was willing to give it a go. She certainly wasn't going to back down.

"First one to be disarmed or fall loses," she said.

"And first blood?"

"If you are on your feet, it makes no difference."

The de Meynell knight snorted. "You are going to be very sorry, cow."

"And you are going to look like a fool when I am done with you."

As Susanna assumed a defensive stance, she caught movement out of the corner of her eye. She turned in time to see Achilles flying at the de Meynell knight, so fast that he was nothing more than a blur. The de Meynell knight received a sword in his gut. As he fell to the floor, the entire room erupted in chaos.

Alexander was charging the entire table of de Meynell men, throwing punches as well as swinging his sword, no easy feat, but he made it look effortless. Enraged that Achilles disrupted what she considered a personal fight, Susanna leapt into the fray, attacking a man who was engaged in a battle with Achilles. While he was distracted with Achilles' big sword, Susanna took him out by the knees, severing the tendons that controlled both of his legs.

Screaming, the man went down. Before she could go after another man, Achilles grabbed her by the arm.

"Get out of here," he roared. "You cannot take another wound!"

Susanna flatly ignored him. A de Meynell knight charged her and she deftly stepped aside, sticking out a foot and shoving the man to the ground at the same time. When he tried to rise, she clobbered him on the head with the heavy hilt of her broadsword, knocking him unconscious.

Very quickly, six of the seven de Meynell knights were down. Three of them were badly wounded and the other three were unconscious. The last remaining knight standing lifted his hands, letting his sword fall to declare his surrender. As quickly as the fight started, it was over, and as Alexander took care of the remaining knight, Achilles grabbed Susanna by the arm again and dragged her away from the carnage.

She let him.

They were down the corridor and into her chamber without a word spoken. Instead of yelling at her, as Susanna had expected, Achilles' simply pointed at her saddlebags.

"Collect your things," he said in a low voice. "We must leave in a hurry."

His command was not meant to be disobeyed. Susanna did as she was told, picking up her possessions and following Achilles back out to the common room, where some of the dazed de Meynell knights were beginning to come around. When Alexander saw Achilles and Susanna emerge, he quickly went to them.

"I do not think we should be here when they regain their wits," he said, looking at the man Achilles had gored as one of his comrades knelt over him. "Let's move on to Skipton and seek lodgings for the evening there."

Achilles didn't say a word. He simply collected his possessions, as did Alexander, and the three warriors headed out into the moonlit night with the destination of the safety of Skipton Castle.

So much for a restful evening.

CHAPTER TWO

HE WAS ANGRY.
Susanna knew that Achilles was angry for the simple fact that
he wouldn't even look at her. Since leaving The Horse's Arse, he had
not said a word on the short ride to Skipton Castle, lit up like a beacon
against the night as it overlooked the darkened landscape. With its six
enormous drum towers and magnificent walls, the powerful fortress
was a welcome sight.

It was held by descendants of the family who built it, de Romille,
but it was commanded by a seasoned knight by the name of Amund de
Bermingham. De Bermingham welcomed Alexander and Achilles
congenially, as vassals of William Marshal, and extended Skipton's
hospitality. Susanna was barely introduced to the man before Achilles
was asking for a chamber where she could rest and de Bermingham was
most accommodating.

Almost immediately, Susanna was whisked away by two older serving women in aprons and tight wimples. One woman had each arm and
Susanna was coming to think that she couldn't have pulled away from
them had she tried. They had quite the iron grip. One was speaking of
food and water to wash with, while the other was speaking about fresh
linens for the lord's bed.

Susanna had no idea what they were talking about until they wound
their way up a steep flight of steps that took a sharp turn to the left.

There was a door in front of them and the women ushered her straight through those doors, straight into a large chamber with a large, four-poster bed.

It smelled of smoke and the pungent musk of a man. Susanna had been around enough of them to know what they smelled like when they hadn't washed for weeks on end. Once inside, the women let her go and went to work. One of them stoked the fire, bringing about a nice blaze, while the other one went rushing off through an alcove, only to return with linens for the bed. Stripping off what was there, she replaced them with the stiff, slightly scratchy linens, including a coverlet that she proudly announced had just been washed and dried in the sun.

All the while, Susanna stood in the middle of the room, watching the fuss and feeling very awkward about it. She wasn't used to people fussing over her and she wasn't entirely sure she liked it, but she let the women do whatever they needed to do. She didn't want to seem ungrateful but, in truth, the longer she looked the bed, the more exhausted she became.

With the fire roaring and the bed freshly tended, food was brought to her along with a bucket of steaming water than smelled of rosemary. The serving women were very solicitous and offered to help her wash, but Susanna politely declined. She couldn't help but notice the disappointed and even disapproving looks as the women left the chamber and shut the door. Susanna could only imagine what they thought of the lady wearing a mail coat and the de Winter tunic, and who didn't need help washing.

It was all quite scandalous.

Finally alone in the borrowed chamber, Susanna took a brief moment to observe her surroundings. The chamber beyond the reach of the firelight was rather impressive with pewter plate on the mantel and a big tapestry on one wall. But there were no windows and she realized it was because the big tapestry hung over the openings that faced out over a small inner courtyard.

It was a room she could have taken a good deal of time exploring but all she wanted to do was sleep. It had been a long day and an eventful evening, and the bed with the fresh linens was calling to her.

She was anxious to heed the call.

Setting her saddlebags on the floor by the bed and propping her broadsword against the wall where she could get to it quickly, Susanna began to remove her clothing. Belts came off before the tunic, both ending up on a nearby chair. The mail coat was a little more difficult, but she'd been dressing herself for years, so she managed to get that off with little problem. Underneath, she wore two more tunics, including a padded one, so she proceeded to strip down until she was nude in the middle of that big, borrowed room.

But God's Bones, it was a relief.

Over on an elaborately carved table near the hearth, the tray of food and the bucket of warmed water continued to steam. Susanna padded across the cold wooden floor, which only had animal hides near the bed, and headed straight for the warmed water. She very much wanted to wash her face and hands, but as she came upon the water, she saw that the serving women had left her two clean rags to wash and dry with, and a white bar of lumpy soap that smelled heavily of the same rosemary that was in the water.

It was heavenly.

Taking one of the rags, Susanna proceeded to wash herself from her head to her toes. The soap was milky and slimy, but it cleaned the grit from her face and body, a luxury she didn't often have.

Or maybe it was because she never really took the time.

Being raised as a warrior meant she dressed like a man and often smelled like one. The entire time she had been Cadelyn's bodyguard, the woman had constantly been trying to coerce her into being a bit more feminine.

But the truth was that she didn't know how.

Or perhaps she was simply too stubborn and embarrassed to learn. It wasn't something that concerned her in the least until the advent of Achilles. Now, she thought about it constantly.

Drying off with the other rag, Susanna came across the puckered, purple scar on her body where the sword had punctured her. It was near the left side of her pelvis, almost on the bone, and she'd been very fortunate that although she'd lost a good deal of blood, the wound hadn't festered. She ran her finger over it; it was tender, but certainly nothing like it had been. It could have been deadly.

But Achilles wouldn't accept that fate.

Thoughts of Achilles flooded Susanna's mind. Even as she dunked her head in the soapy, warm water and used more of the soap to scrub her hair, her thoughts lingered on the enormous knight who had once been her greatest enemy. She smiled as she thought of the insults they'd slung at each other and the actual fist fight they'd once had at a tavern called The Nag's Head.

It had been quite a brawl.

Days of insults and hostilities had come to a head, and the two of them had slugged it out for quite some time before being separated. Bric MacRohan, the big Irish knight who served the House of de Winter as well as William Marshal, had broken it up along with Alexander. Achilles had been dragged away by Alexander while Bric had remained with Susanna to ensure she didn't try to follow. Susanna had come to like Bric by the time their assignment had finished because he was one of most skilled knights she'd ever seen. He was also as mean as a rabid dog, a personality trait she had a healthy respect for.

But her respect for Achilles was greater even than that.

He'd nurtured her through a very bad wound, tending her as closely as a mother would tend a child. Odd how a man who had antagonized her so should be so caring. He was aggressive, annoying, and reckless, but he was also a man who felt deeply and had a great deal of loyalty to his friends. She'd seen that from the outset. There was nothing restrained about him when it came to his personal feelings or his emotions, and she found that fascinating. Knights were taught to control their emotions, to think clearly in every situation, but Achilles threw the control of his emotions to the wind. He seemed to use them to feed his drive in a unique way.

With Achilles, one always knew where he, or she, stood.

Wringing out her wet hair, Susanna began to dry it off with one of the rags, going over to her saddlebags and pulling forth a long sleeping shift. It was her one and only guilty pleasure, given to her by Cadelyn. She wore breeches and tunics as her main staple, but when she slept at night, it was in the only feminine thing she had. It was soft and warm against her skin. Pulling the rumpled, slightly torn shift over her head, she went over to sit by the fire and dry out her shiny curls.

Unfortunately, she didn't last long at that. Fatigue was pulling at her and she only managed to get her hair somewhat dry before the lure of sleep was just too much. Braiding her hair tightly, she went to the bed and collapsed on it.

She was asleep before she hit the pillow.

"Susanna."

It was a voice in her dreams, calling her name, but it took her a moment to realize that it was no dream. Someone really *was* calling her name. Opening her eyes, she found herself staring up at Achilles as he stood next to the bed.

Blinking, she sat bolt upright, but Achilles grabbed her before she could pitch herself off of the bed in her haste. Gently, he pushed her down again.

"Nay," he said quietly, reaching over to pull the coverlet over her. "Do not get up. You can lay there and listen to me. I shan't take long."

He was bundling her up with the coverlet and, still half-asleep, she let him. "What is wrong?" she asked, yawning. "Has something happened?"

Achilles had a strange look on his face. "Happened?" he repeated. "Nay. Nothing has happened, but I have something to say to you."

She was a little more lucid now. "What is it?"

He took a deep breath, planting his big fists on his hips. "We must come to an understanding, you and I."

"What about?"

"I have come to a decision."

"What decision?"

"I do not want you to bear arms any longer."

She blinked in surprise, sitting up even though he'd told her not to. "*What?*" she finally hissed. "What are you talking about?"

Achilles didn't look pleased. He turned away from her, running a hand over his scalp in an agitated manner before turning to face her.

"I know you are a trained warrior," he said. "I know you serve William Marshal. I know all of this. But I do not want you to bear arms any longer. I want you to return to Aysgarth and remain there until I come for you."

Susanna was genuinely trying to understand what he was telling her, but he simply wasn't making any sense. "Come for me?" she repeated. "Why would you come for me?"

An expression of intense confusion washed over Achilles' features. "I am not doing this very well," he said. "I am trying to tell you that… you said something to me once. You said that we all hope to meet that one person who makes us spark. Do you remember?"

She leaned back against the headboard of the bed. "Of course I do," she said. "We were speaking of Cadelyn and Kress. You have called me Sparks because of it. I remember that conversation well."

He nodded. "I did not know what you meant at the time. I suppose in theory I did, but I'd never felt that kind of sensation before. I call you Sparks because of what you said, and at first I did it to taunt you, but now…" His agitation faded as a thoughtful mood seemed to take hold. "There is so much you do not know about me. I do not even know if you care to know, but if you do, I will tell you."

Susanna eyed him. "*Now?*"

He lifted his shoulders weakly. "I may not have another chance before I leave you off at Aysgarth tomorrow."

Susanna began to suspect what this might be all about, so she nodded. "Very well," she said. "What do you want to tell me?"

"Do you want to know about me? You do not have to listen if you do not care."

He was asking her to express her feelings, something supremely difficult for Susanna to speak of. She'd never had to. There was something embarrassing in speaking on her emotions, but she didn't want to upset him. She wanted him to know what she was feeling.

Or, at least trying to.

"I will listen," she said after a moment. "I want to know."

From the expression on his face, Achilles wasn't sure if she meant it, but he proceeded. "You already know I've spent time in The Levant as a special agent for King Richard," he said. "You know that I have not lived an entirely honorable life. I have fought other men's wars for profit. I have killed men's enemies because I was well paid."

"I know."

"I have also been known to pursue a pretty face."

"Did you catch them?"

He fought off a smile. "All of them."

"I have no doubt. You are handsome."

His smile faded. "Do you really think so?"

She nodded, feeling the blush creeping into her cheeks. "Did you come here to ask me if I thought you were handsome?"

He shook his head. "I came here to tell you that I have never been ashamed of my past," he said. "I have no regrets. But I have never met anyone who made me spark and I want to make sure she knows everything."

She eyed him. "I see," she said. "Have you told her, then?"

"I just did."

Susanna knew that. Or, at least, she had hoped that was where he was leading. Embarrassed and delighted, she lowered her gaze, unable to fight off the grin.

"I am not sure how you can say that I cause you to feel a spark," she said. "Our acquaintance has not exactly been smooth."

He nodded, making his way over to the bed. "I know," he said quietly. "When I first met you, I did not approve of you. That is no secret.

You aggravated me. Irritated me. I considered you an insult to the knighthood. But can you not see that something has changed?"

She kept her gaze averted, but she nodded. "I can."

"Does it displease you?"

"I am not displeased."

He suddenly plopped down on the bed, his expression intense. "Susanna, I do not want you to bear arms any longer. When you were gored those weeks ago, I realized... I realized how much it would crush me if something happened to you. I could not bear it."

She looked at him seriously. "But... being a warrior is all I know. I would not know how to be anything other than what you see."

"Would you be willing to try? Just a little?"

Susanna wasn't sure what to say. She realized that she very much wanted to please him, but at the risk giving up something she was trained to do. "I... I do not know," she said honestly. "This is not a conversation I thought I would ever have. Achilles, you and I have barely become friends. I do not even know how to speak of this... I have never been very good at speaking of personal thoughts or feelings. You must let me think on what you have said. I cannot give you an answer now."

He looked disappointed, but he nodded his head in resignation. "I understand," he said. "It is much to ask. But I do intend to return for you."

"Why?"

He lifted his big shoulders. "Because I do not want to be away from you," he said. "Didn't my actions during the time you were healing from your wound tell you that?"

She nodded, smiling at him. "You were very attentive," she said. "You never left me."

"I never will. I will return to Aysgarth to ask your brother for permission to court you, if you are agreeable."

Her smile vanished. "*Court* me?"

"Aye."

She appeared a bit bewildered by the mere suggestion. "For... for marriage?"

"Aye."

"Are you terribly certain of this?"

He sighed heavily, averting his gaze. "Certain enough," he said. "All I know is that I have never felt this way about anyone. You are strong and brave and beautiful. I would at least like to explore the possibility. Will you at least give me the chance?"

You are beautiful. Susanna had never heard that from a man, ever, and it was the most delightful shock. She truly had no idea how to respond.

"Are you certain?" she asked again.

He looked at her, then. "Aye, Sparks," he murmured. "I am certain. Will you give me the chance?"

Susanna's cheeks were back to flaming, so caught up in something she never thought she would experience. Nothing at Blackchurch had taught her how to gracefully handle a man's overture. But there only one answer she could come up with.

"I will."

Achilles smiled broadly, a rather victorious gesture. "Good," he said firmly. "But while you are at Aysgarth, I want you to promise me that you will not bear arms. Will you at least try to behave like a lady while I am away?"

"I would have no idea where to start."

"Mayhap that is something we can remedy."

Susanna had no idea how, but if he thought so, then she was willing to go along with him. "How?"

"I will find someone to teach you."

She was hesitant. "How are we to explain this to my brother? Have I become a warrior with a maid in tow?"

He smiled at her. "You are a unique creature in a unique situation. I do not know your brother, but surely he will be understanding."

"He will think it is quite strange."

Achilles' gaze lingered on her for a moment. "Not when he sees the result," he said. "Sparks, if you think I am trying to change you into something you are not, that is not the case. I do not want you to bear arms because I cannot stomach the thought of something happening to you and for no other reason than that. As for having someone teach you the finer points of being a lady, you might find them useful skills someday. And I should like to see your beauty shine through as it was always meant to be."

She was back to blushing furiously. "I have never thought about it much, although Cadelyn tried to convince me to dress like a lady and to engage in ladylike tasks."

"But you did not?"

"How could I? I was her bodyguard. I was not a friend or a lady-in-waiting. I had a job to do."

"Did you ever wonder what it would be like to be a fine lady, dressed in fine clothing and smelling sweet?"

She thought about that before reluctantly nodding her head. "I have," she said. "But I did not dwell on it. There was no reason to yearn for such a thing."

"Then I will yearn for it on your behalf."

She glanced at him. "Does it mean so much to you that I look beautiful and wear fine clothing?"

He shook his head. "Clearly, it does not," he said. "But imagine how besotted I will be the first time you wear a dress of silk, with your hair attractively arranged. With your copper-colored curls and eyes the color of a sapphire, you will outshine every woman in England."

She bit her lip, grinning. "It seems hard to imagine."

"Not for me."

He seemed convinced, which gave her confidence. "Then if you wish it, I would not be opposed to trying," she said. "I will admit that wearing something other than rough linen and wool against my skin sounds intriguing. I have often wondered what it would feel like to wear a garment as soft as butterfly wings."

He cocked his head, eyeing her as she seemed to grow more interested in what he was asking of her. "I will commission dresses to be made for you," he said. "Surely there are seamstresses near Aysgarth who will take up such a task. You can have them made while I am in London. It will give you something to do while you are recuperating. Speaking of recuperating, how are you feeling after the skirmish tonight?"

She nodded. "It was no strain," she said. "But I am very tired."

He put up a hand as if to beg forgiveness. "And I have interrupted your sleep," he said. "I am sorry, but I had to speak with you. It could not wait."

"It was worth it."

It seemed like the right moment to leave, but Achilles didn't move. He didn't want to. She was warming to him, becoming a little less awkward, and he was very glad. He smiled in reply, gazing into her lovely face and knowing that he was going to kiss her. But he also wondered if she wasn't going to punch him in the throat for trying.

There was only one way to find out.

Reaching out, he grasped her arms, looking into her eyes to see if there was any resistance. She was looking at him curiously but nothing more. Therefore, his grip tightened and he pulled her cheek very close to his mouth. Gently, he deposited the sweetest of kisses on her face and as he did so, he felt her body quiver violently. That was all he needed to grow bolder.

Without a word, his lips slanted over hers.

Pulled against his chest, Susanna stiffened in the slightest at the shock of something new and titillating but, quickly, he felt her body relaxed. She smelled clean, of rosemary, and she was warm and pliable against him. Achilles let go of her arms and wrapped her up in his enormous embrace, suckling her tender lips. It was like nothing he had ever known, and he had kissed a great many women. But this was different.

She was different.

Surprisingly, her fingers found their way onto his scalp, gripping his head as he devoured her. His tongue licked at her lips, gently prying them open, and Susanna gasped as he invaded her mouth. There was such excitement and comfort and passion to be had, sensations Achilles had never felt before, at least not on this level. It was exhilarating.

That spark she'd once spoken of… now, he fully understood it.

She had him on fire.

But the hands on his head suddenly moved to his face and she put her long, slender fingers on his lips, stopping his onslaught. When he opened his eyes, he found himself staring into big pools of blue.

"Did I frighten you?" he asked huskily. "I did not mean to. But to kiss you seemed the most natural of things."

She shook her head but her expression said otherwise. "I was wondering," she murmured. "I… I do not have to return to Aysgarth. Why can I not go back to London with you?"

He peered at her strangely. "Why would you want to do that?" he asked. "It would be a long and grueling journey. It is much better for you to rest at Aysgarth while I conduct business with The Marshal."

"You do not want me to go?"

"I want you to rest and recover. That is what I want."

She seemed to deflate a little, looking uncertain and perhaps even ashamed. It occurred to Achilles that she was trying to tell him something, but as he was coming to realize, she had a difficult time speaking on her feelings.

And he could tell by the look in her eyes that she was feeling something.

"I do not wish to be parted from you, either, Sparks," he said, leaning forward to kiss the tip of her nose. "I swear I will hurry back to you. Is that what you were worried about?"

She gave him an embarrassed little grin and looked away. Laughing softly, he pulled her against him, holding her tightly and relishing the first real embrace they'd ever shared.

It was heavenly.

"You are going to have to become better at telling me what is on your mind," he murmured. "I am not very good at reading your thoughts."

Her head was on his shoulder. "You are doing well enough," she said. "But… this is all quite new to me. While you have been pursuing pretty faces, I've not had the time nor the inclination to let a man pursue me."

"Have there been any that have caught your eye?"

She shook her head. "Men do not generally pursue a woman who can beat them in a sword fight."

"I do not hold that opinion because you cannot beat me."

Susanna lifted her head, looking at him before breaking down into laughter. "I seem to recall that the last time we were this close, it was on the floor of The Nag's Head tavern."

"I was trying not to irrevocably injure you."

"You were losing!"

Achilles' eyes glittered at her. "You think so, do you?"

"Sherry had to drag you away."

"He did it to save your life."

"He did it so you would not be humiliated."

He stared at her a moment before breaking into a grin. "You must have some magic over me that I would let you insult me so," he said. "We must be making progress because I am not trying to wrap my hands around your neck. At least, not with the intent to throttle you. You do have a nice neck."

It was the natural order of things between the two of them to be competitive and insulting, something they were going to have to work through if their feelings for one another had any hope of surviving. Susanna, as untried as she was, seemed to understand that.

"I am sorry," she said quietly. "I should not have insulted you."

Achilles shrugged. "I have come to see that we bring that out in each other," he said. "But it does not deter me. Nothing you can say any longer can deter me because I know you are a woman of intelligence and compassion, for I have seen it. We must learn to bring out the best in each other, you and I. You make me want to try very hard."

Susanna had a permanent blush on her cheeks. It was a sweet thing to say and utterly surreal. They were words she never thought she would hear, especially from him, thrilling and miraculous as they were. As she struggled to say something in return, Achilles took the opportunity to kiss her once more, a gentle and lingering kiss, before standing up.

"I will leave you to your sleep now," he said. "Sherry and I will be somewhere nearby. If you need me, send for me. I will come."

Susanna nodded again, smiling at him as he waved at her and turned to leave. Truth be told, she was rather dazed about the entire conversation and hadn't much to say as he reached the door and paused, waving to her again before closing the door softly behind him.

Alone again, Susanna put her fingers to her lips, still feeling him upon her flesh. She'd never been kissed by a man in her life and, suddenly, she understood what the fuss was about. Perhaps she'd never considered such things because she'd always assumed that they would forever be out of her reach. As she'd told Achilles, no man wanted a wife who could best him in a sword fight, but Achilles was so arrogant, he didn't think such a thing was possible.

Truthfully, Susanna didn't care.

Sliding down in the bed, she rolled onto her side, her mind lingering on Achilles and his delicious kisses. She was exhausted but, at the moment, sleep simply wouldn't come. She wasn't looking forward to being away from the man during his journey to London, but she knew it was for the best. She was looking forward to resting at Aysgarth and anticipating his return. Perhaps when he came for her, she might have a fine dress or two, and perhaps even a hint of femininity to please him. She was looking forward to the very real possibility.

At twenty years and nine, Susanna de Tiegh was to have a suitor for the very first time… and loving every minute of it.

CHAPTER THREE

Aysgarth Castle
North Yorkshire

AYSGARTH CASTLE WAS an impressive sight to behold.
A big bastion set within a narrow valley that ran east-west through Northern Yorkshire, it had not one, but two big mottes, although one motte was not quite as high as the other. It was flat and broad, surrounded by granite walls that weren't particularly tall and the remains of a moat, with an outer ward and outbuildings perched atop it.

It was the first thing visitors to Aysgarth entered after they'd passed through the main gatehouse, which was surprisingly ill-fortified. The only protection it had was a wooden gate that seemed to be somewhat old and flimsy. Beyond it, a vast yard was muddy and cluttered, sloping slightly to the south, with a muddy pool on the south end where they kept a corral with animals.

Once through the outer ward, visitors passed over a drawbridge to a second gatehouse, with no gate at all, which protected the circular shell keep. The keep was a rare type of design as far as keeps went, meaning it was literally built in a circle with apartments and a hall built against the walls, all of it encircling a small yard in the center.

Achilles had actually never been to Aysgarth Castle and although he was impressed with its sheer size of it, the gatehouses seemed ill-prepared to withstand any manner of attack and the walls of the outer bailey were shockingly low. Interestingly enough, the army wasn't housed in the castle, but down below in a field that also contained a big area for practice and mobilization. It seemed strange that there was no way for the troops below to get to the castle unless they came up the road and in through the gatehouse like everyone else.

Beneath scattered clouds on a mild August day, Achilles and Alexander escorted Susanna into this extensive ancestral home. She led the way, eager to see her brother and clearly happy to be home again, as Achilles and Alexander followed a dozen paces behind her.

"It is little wonder that The Marshal is nervous that de Tiegh is ambiguous about his loyalties," Achilles muttered. "Look at the size of this place."

Alexander was, indeed, drinking it in. "Size, aye, but protection measures seem to be lacking," he said. "Did you notice the training field as we rode in? There have to be close to a thousand men down there and not one of them English."

"How could you tell?"

"The round, wooden shields gave them away and not a recognizable tunic among them."

"You are certain?"

"I have seen shields of that type in Thuringia."

It was a surprising observation. Achilles found himself looking over to the unusual numbers of blacksmith stalls towards the south side of the outer ward. "Why so many smithies?" he wondered aloud. "There are at least a half-dozen of them."

Alexander was looking there, too. "More smithies to make more weapons," he murmured. "Clearly, there is some kind of build up going on here. The Marshal will want to know about this."

"Are you thinking what I'm thinking?"

"If you are thinking de Tiegh has himself a mercenary army, then I am most definitely thinking what you are thinking."

Those were ominous words. By this time, they were heading across the wooden bridge and over the sizeable moat. The second gatehouse was ahead, a two-storied structure that was sparingly manned. Just past that was an incline up the motte to the shell keep above and there was someone waiting for them. Susanna spurred her horse up the slope and as they watched, she practically jumped from her mount to greet the man standing at the keep entrance.

"That must be her brother," Achilles said, his gaze on Susanna.

Alexander was watching the reunion as well. "Whatever happens, do not anger the man or offend him. Be polite and respectful. We need to get out of here and back to The Marshal as quickly as possible. In fact, I should like to leave immediately."

Achilles looked at him. "Immediately?" he repeated. "As in now?"

"Now."

"But... but I was hoping to feast here tonight and then leave on the morrow."

Alexander sighed heavily. "I am not comfortable remaining here," he said. "De Tiegh knows we serve William Marshal; we are both wearing his tunic, for Christ's sake. If the man is doing something that he does not wish The Marshal to know about, then the sooner we leave, the better. My fear is that he will toss us in the vault so we cannot report what we have seen."

Achilles knew that. At least, the logical side of him knew that. The dedicated knight knew that. But the man who was reluctant to leave Susanna was trying to deny that logic. It was a struggle to keep the disappointment from his voice.

"You are right, of course," he said. "I was just hoping... I was hoping we could at least stay the night."

Alexander looked at him. He knew why Achilles wanted to stay the night and he wished that remaining would be a comforting choice, but he simply couldn't agree. Though he'd never said a word to Achilles about Susanna and the obvious attraction between the pair, he was going to have to break that stance.

The time had come.

"Achilles, I know you do not want to leave Susanna," he said. "I understand you wish to remain close to her for as long as you can before we have to meet up with de Lohr and return to London, but look around you. It is not safe for us here. I am not even sure it is safe for Susanna here, given her brother's obvious activities."

Achilles was gearing up to become defensive, to even deny what Alexander was suggesting, but he couldn't muster it. He and Alexander had been friends for a very long time and he wouldn't lie to the man.

Perhaps it was better if he didn't.

"She said it has been two years since she has been to Aysgarth," he finally said. "It looks as if her brother has been busy during that time. If you do not think it is safe to leave her here, then mayhap we should suggest it to her. She can come back to Chester with us, though the thought of her riding all the way back to London while recovering from her wound is not… ideal."

Alexander's black gaze lingered on him. "When did you figure this all out?"

"Figure what out?"

"That you were attracted to the bodyguard? Christ, Achilles, I have had to pull you two apart more than once so you would not kill one another. And now you are attracted to the woman?"

Achilles cleared his throat nervously and looked away. "She was attracted to me first. She forced herself upon me."

"Is that the truth?"

"For you, it is."

Alexander grinned. With his dark beard and big, white teeth, he had a rather brilliant smile. "You could have fooled me," he said. "Tell me this isn't some ploy to cause her to lower her guard so that you can win a fight with her."

Achilles turned to him, scowling. "If I wanted to win a fight with her, I would not need her to lower her guard in order to do it."

Alexander started laughing. "She is tough, that one. A Blackchurch-trained knight? You are lucky you survived any skirmish with her."

Achilles was still scowling at him. "Stop hooting," he said. "You sound like an idiot. Susanna's brother is looking at you and wondering what kind of fool his sister has been traveling with."

Alexander sobered instantly, looking to the keep and seeing a tall, auburn-haired man speaking with Susanna. "A fool who knows the build up of a mercenary army when he sees one," he said. "Achilles, I am sorry, but we will have to cut this very short. I want out of this place."

They were nearly to the keep. Achilles' gaze was on Susanna as she turned to him as he approached. He didn't have time to reply to Alexander, but he knew what that answer had to be.

He was starting to feel apprehensive.

He didn't want to leave her here, more than ever.

"Good knights, welcome to Aysgarth," Susanna said, sounding surprisingly jovial. "I am honored to introduce you to my brother, Baron Coverdale. Sam, these are two of the finest knights I have ever known – Sir Achilles de Dere and Sir Alexander de Sherrington."

She indicated the knights in order and Achilles found himself looking into a face that faintly resembled Susanna. Samuel de Tiegh was tall and lithe, with the same pale skin his sister had and nearly the same color of hair. They also had the same deep blue eyes, but where Susanna's were warm and caring at times, Samuel simply looked hard. The pure blue color was lost on him, becoming murky and mysterious.

Achilles didn't get a good feeling from the man from the very start.

"My lord," he greeted. "I am honored."

Samuel nodded in acknowledgement but his gaze moved to Alexander. "De Sherrington?" he said thoughtfully. "Do you have a brother, perchance?"

"Estienne, my lord."

That seemed to bring a reaction from Samuel. "Estienne de Sherrington is my good and true friend," he said and, suddenly, he was quite congenial. "He never mentioned that he had a brother."

Alexander wasn't quite so congenial. "That is because my brother and I have not seen one another since my father's death," he said. "I have been all over the known world and Estienne has remained at Broxburn Castle."

Samuel was all but ignoring Achilles and his own sister at this point. "I have recently seen your brother," he said. "He visits me regularly, in fact. As I said, we are very good friends."

"That is quite a distance from Broxburn Castle to Yorkshire," Alexander said. "You must be quite good friends for him to travel all the way from Salisbury."

"I have made my way to Broxburn many times as well."

"When you next see him, please give him my regards."

"I will be happy to." Samuel reached out and clapped him on the shoulder in an unnecessary show of friendliness for a man he'd just met. "You must feast with me tonight. Allow me to show Estienne's brother my hospitality."

Alexander wasn't enthusiastic about it in the least, but he went along with it. Achilles kept his eye on the man, seeing that he was bordering on displeasure with the entire situation, but something that Alexander had said to him kept coming back – *whatever happens, do not anger the man or offend him.*

Achilles never even knew Alexander had a brother, not in all the time he'd known him, and it was obvious that it was a sensitive subject. But Alexander was going along with his own advice – he didn't want to offend Coverdale. Furthermore, it also meant that they were to stay for the evening's feast, much to Achilles' relief. As Samuel led Alexander away, Achilles turned to Susanna.

"It seems as if your brother has something in common with Sherry," he said.

Susanna was watching the pair walk away also. After a moment, she looked at Achilles.

"Did you see the mercenaries in the field below?" she asked quietly.

Achilles grunted. "You saw that, did you?"

"They are not English, that is for certain. You must return to tell

The Marshal immediately."

"Does your brother know you serve William Marshal?"

She shook her head. "Nay," she said, indicating her de Winter tunic. "He believes I serve the House of de Winter, which has been my home for the past ten years. Though I was at Castle Rising in the course of my duties with Cadelyn and Padraig Summerlin was my commander, the castle is part of the de Winter and de Warenne holdings. You know how close those families are; they're all intermarried."

"De Warenne is Surrey and Norfolk. And de Winter sides with the king."

Susanna nodded. "I know," she said, her gaze moving to her brother and Alexander as they neared the great hall. "Come. Let us join them."

Achilles started to walk with her, but he wasn't ready to let the subject drop. "I am not sure it is safe to leave you here," he said softly. "If your brother thinks you serve de Winter, who in turn serves the king, he will not want you to return to de Winter with tales of a mercenary army at Aysgarth."

She was quiet for a moment. "Who says I am returning to the House of de Winter?" she said, putting her hand over the wound on her gut. "I can make many excuses for this wound, you know. I can tell him that I had a disagreement with de Winter and they tried to silence me. What better way to announce I no longer serve the king?"

"Is that what you intend to do?"

They were nearing the hall. "Samuel will know what I want him to know," she said. "He will know that my fealty is no longer with de Winter and that is all he need know. Mayhap it will make him comfortable enough to confide in me about the mercenaries in the field below. I can only imagine that this is the beginning of what must surely be something greater. Samuel is a good warrior, but he does not think on his own very well. He prefers that others take the responsibility for bigger decisions."

They were almost at the hall and Achilles paused, looking at her. "Then he is taking his orders from someone else?"

Susanna nodded. "There has to be more to this. Something big is going on, Achilles. I can sense it."

He eyed her with displeasure. "If that is the case, I am not certain I want you here."

Her answer was to go inside the hall in utter defiance of his wishes. With an expression of pure frustration, he followed.

CHAPTER FOUR

THE FEAST THAT evening was a loud, smoky, and sweaty affair. The hall of Aysgarth was a vast place, commensurate with the size of the castle itself, with room enough for hundreds of men. It was lavishly furnished and had two enormous hearths, one at each end of the hall, constructed with stones that were varied shades of gray so they looked like they were made of gray patchwork.

In fact, the entire hall was built of patchwork gray stones. Achilles thought it was rather interesting construction, but those two hearths fired up that hall into uncomfortably warm temperatures and his thoughts weren't lingering on the construction so much as he was thinking on what he needed to do in order to cool off.

It was becoming cloying.

Not surprisingly, it was full of men who were speaking a language Achilles had heard on the Continent when he'd returned from The Levant. During that time, he and his comrades had made a great deal of money fighting other men's battles as mercenaries themselves, and Achilles recognized the language as something he'd heard in Saxony. That meant that Alexander had been absolutely right about these men.

They were not from England.

He sat at the dais between Alexander and Susanna. Alexander sat next to Samuel and the man had been talking a steady stream since they entered the great hall a few hours ago, but only to Alexander. It was as if no one else in the hall existed. Achilles refrained from conversation with Susanna because he wanted to listen in, catching pieces of the conversation from time to time, and it was mostly about Alexander's brother and other men they were evidently friends with, including a man named Witton de Meynell.

He knew that name from the knights they'd faced back at The Horse's Arse.

It was a rather interesting bit of information.

But other than that, the conversation hadn't been very exciting, but Achilles didn't much care. He was sitting with Susanna and that was the most predominate thing on his mind. The food was plentiful, the hall was comfortable, and the serving wenches were some of the most beautiful women he'd ever seen. Surrounded by pretty girls kept the soldiers content – and a content army was an obedient army.

It was a smart tactic.

"The food is very good," he commented to Susanna, one of just a handful of comments he'd made all evening. "Your brother puts on a fine table."

Susanna was elbow-deep in a trencher of boiled beef and carrots, eating more ravenously than Achilles had seen since she'd been injured. "Of course he does," she said. "He has the de Tiegh reputation to uphold."

"And your family has a reputation for setting a fine table?"

Susanna nodded. "That is what we are known for to our friends and allies," she said, looking at him. "When I was a child, before I went to foster, I can recall feasts like this every night. The finest food and ale to be had, the prettiest serving wenches, and my mother dressed in her very best. She dressed me in my best, too."

He smiled faintly. "Did you dress as all little girls should? In finery and flowers?"

She fought off a smile. "Believe it or not, I did. Thanks to my mother, I had quite a wardrobe of clothing and she loved to dress me in the finest fabrics."

"What of your parents? What became of them?"

Her expression sobered. "My mother passed away in childbirth when Samuel and I were eight years of age," she said. "She died giving birth to another de Tiegh son. After that... after that, my father became very distant with Samuel and me. When Samuel went to foster, my father simply sent me along with him. He wanted us away from him so he could lose himself in drink and self-pity. He died several years ago, leaving the barony to my brother."

"You were not close to him, then?"

She shook her head firmly. "Nay," she said. "Not to him, but I was close to my mother. Her death was devastating to me. I have often wondered what she would have thought of the vocation I have chosen. Something tells me she would not have been pleased."

"What did your father think?"

"He did not care."

It was a sad footnote to so magnificent a woman. At least, Achilles thought so. He was coming to see that not only was she different from most other women, but beneath that strong façade, she was perhaps more vulnerable than she wanted anyone to believe.

He rather liked that side of her.

"Well," he sighed, "you are back in the place of your birth and I am sure you will enjoy your time here. Rest, eat the wonderful food Aysgarth seems to provide, and find a seamstress who will make you a few magnificent gowns."

He whispered the last few words, causing her to flush and look away. "I will," she said. "I wish I had Cadelyn to advise me on what to wear and how to wear it. It would be her dream come true where I am concerned, for she tried for years to convince me to dress properly. Surely, if she realized we were having this conversation, she would faint dead away."

He laughed softly. "Someday, you will be able to tell her of this," he said. "Someday, you will be able to show her."

"I hope so."

"I am sure of it."

A pretty wench came by with a pitcher of wine, topping off their cups and throwing Achilles a rather alluring smile. In times past, he would have quite happily taken her up on her silent offer, but as it was, he ignored her until she went away, dejected.

It was an event, however, that didn't go unnoticed by Susanna. She saw the wench, and Achilles' reaction, and a hint of a smile played on her lips.

"Are you certain you want to pass that up?" she teased, gesturing to the wench when he looked at her, curiously. "You told me yourself that you've been known to pursue a pretty face. She was very pretty."

He frowned. "Bah," he said. "I have seen dogs with better looking faces. Moreover, my days of pursuing pretty wenches are over."

"Then what am I? Not a pretty face?"

He lifted an eyebrow. "You *are* pretty," he said. "But you are the only wench in this entire hall that I can say that about. What I mean to say is that you are the only pretty *woman*. You are a woman, not a wench."

"You once called me an Amazon."

"And I apologized for it."

Susanna started giggling, trying to be discreet about the fact that they were starting to flirt with each other. It may have been rough to watch, given their unfamiliarity with it, but it was the best they could do.

"I know," she said after a moment. "I forgave you then and I forgive you now. I will not bring it up again."

"Susanna!"

Samuel was calling to her, reaching across both Alexander and Achilles to do it. She turned to look at him as he waved his hand at Achilles, motioning the man to move back so he could get a clear view of his sister.

"What's this I hear you've been injured?" he demanded.

Susanna glanced at Alexander, who had clearly told the man why they'd come. He was looking at her without any hint whatsoever of what he'd said, so she proceeded cautiously.

"Aye," she said slowly, wanting her brother to give her an indication with just how much he knew. "I took a sword to the gut, down by my hip. That is why I am here, Samuel. I have come home to recuperate but, already, I am much better. I hope I am welcome, still."

"You are always welcome," Samuel said seriously. "This is your home as much as it is mine. What happened?"

So he doesn't know how I received the wound, she thought quickly. "Trouble with de Winter," she said simply. "I would prefer to tell you privately, if you do not mind. I do not wish to shout what has happened for all to hear."

Samuel remained serious. "Trouble with de Winter?"

"You could say that."

"I was telling your brother that we found you upon the road, traveling north," Alexander said in a perfectly believable lie. "You were weak, so we thought to escort you to your destination before continuing on to ours. It was by chance, really, that we found you."

Susanna had a better idea of what Alexander had conveyed to her brother about her relationship to him and Achilles. "They have been excellent traveling companions," she said. "They could have simply left me off here, but I invited them in. I knew you would want to thank them but I had no idea that you would know Alexander's brother."

The lie, for Samuel's benefit, was being established so they all had the same story about it. Samuel didn't seem to think anything was amiss, that they weren't perpetuating a lie right in front of him. He gestured to Alexander's tunic.

"You serve William Marshal, then?" he said.

Alexander flashed that bright, toothy grin he was so famous for, the one that made him look amiable when, in fact, it hid the heart of a killer. "There is a humorous story behind this," he said. "We actually stole these."

Samuel's eyebrows lifted. "Stole them?"

Alexander nodded. "From two Pembroke knights after a fight," he said. "In fact, if you see two very angry men hunting for two knights who stole everything from them, do not tell them that you have seen us. You would be surprised how many people are willing to waive the price of a meal or the cost of a bed to sleep in for a man bearing the colors of Pembroke. It has been quite lucrative."

Samuel stared at him a moment before breaking down into laughter. "Is this true?"

"It is true," Susanna confirmed, just to make Alexander's lie believable. "They have been doing it all the way north. They are quite clever, if not the slightest bit naughty."

Samuel continued to snort. "You told me that these were two of the finest knights you had ever known," he pointed out. "I think you lied, just a little."

Susanna grinned. "It was harmless," she said. "I did not want you to think I was traveling with scoundrels. And in speaking of scoundrels, what is going on around here, Samuel? Is there something I can be part of now that I am home?"

Both Alexander and Achilles were shocked that she'd brought up the foreign army and the activity they'd seen surrounding it, but the way she made it sound came across as if she approved of it. Better still, she wanted to be part of it.

But Samuel waved her off, turning to pour himself more drink from a beautiful pewter pitcher.

"It is of no concern," he said. "These men are not mine, at least not most of them. You needn't concern yourself."

It sounded rather final and Susanna didn't push, at least not now. But she knew she would at a later time. Next to her, Achilles reached for the pitcher when Samuel was finished with it.

"Good," he said. "I am not apt to fight another man's war any time soon unless, of course, there is money involved. Pay me enough and I will fight my own mother."

For the first time, since their introduction, Samuel took some notice of him. "Something tells me you may have already done that."

"It is possible."

"Are you sworn to anyone?"

Achilles shook his head, another lie in a conversation laced with them. "Hugh de Puiset was the last man we were sworn to," he said. "I've no stomach for him, so we have been traveling ever since, fighting other men's wars until we are sick of such things. My brother is in the north serving the House of de Velt and we are heading there. He says he has a place for us so we can at least stop being transient. At our ages, it is time to find a place to rest our bones."

Alexander was nodding as if in perfect agreement with everything he was saying. "The long nights, the long days, the travel without end," he said. "It is exhausting. We have been living such a life ever since leaving The Levant. We only recently made our way home to England."

Samuel was listening intently. "De Velt at Pelinom Castle?"

"The same."

"But why not remain with me? I would be happy to accept your fealty. You are Estienne's brother, after all. Imagine his surprise when he discovers his brother is serving me."

Alexander put up a hand to beg pardon. "That is most generous, but we must decline at this time," he said. "De Velt is expecting us and we have been planning this for some time. But if it is not suitable to our tastes, then I may very well return to you and hope the offer is still open."

Samuel nodded. "For a brother of Estienne, my offer will always stand," he said, omitting Achilles from that statement. "Come, let us drink and speak of your life since leaving The Levant. Entertain me with stories of your travels."

Before Alexander could embark on what would undoubtedly be tall tales of half-truths, Susanna stood up.

"Then I will leave you to your feast and your stories, Brother," she said. "I am very weary from the long journey and this wound has been taxing. May I claim my former chamber?"

Samuel gestured towards the keep. "It is yours," he said. "I will speak with you on the morrow."

As she nodded and turned away, Achilles also stood up. "With your permission, I will retire also," he said. "We did not get much sleep last night and I find that I am weary as well. Where may I find a bed, my lord?"

Samuel put his feet up on the table, wine in hand. "Susanna will show you," he said. "There are apartments on the lower level of the keep. You know the one, Susanna – they used to be the majordomo's quarters when we were children."

Susanna nodded. "I know what you mean," she said, eyeing Achilles. "Come with me."

Achilles did. Leaving Alexander to keep Samuel occupied, he followed Susanna from the great hall at a distance, watching the reaction from the men in the hall as she walked past them. She was tall and beautiful, but dressed like a man. She was a paradox and heads turned when she walked by.

Achilles found himself fighting off a wicked surge of jealousy.

When they were clear of the hall and into the small, dark courtyard, he caught up with her as they headed to the two-storied apartments directly across the yard. Achilles came up beside her, close enough to brush against her, catching her attention. When she turned to look at him, he smiled.

"Do you think he believed us?" he asked quietly. "About stealing these tunics from some hapless Pembroke knights, I mean."

He had a rather naughty gleam to his eye and Susanna returned her focus to the apartments ahead. "I suppose he has no reason not to believe you," she said. "Poor Sherry, left to continue the lies alone."

"He is a grown lad. He can handle himself."

"Do you really have a brother with de Velt?"

"I have three older brothers and the second eldest, Benedict, does indeed serve de Velt. My mother is a de Velt, in fact."

She turned to look at him again just as they came to the heavily-fortified door that led into the apartments. "Where are the other two?"

Achilles reached out to lift the door latch, shoving the solid panel open. "Tobias serves the Earl of Wolverhampton and Brickley serves the Earl of East Anglia. Surely you must have met him before, considering how close de Winter and East Anglia are."

She came to a sudden halt just inside the door. "Brickley?" she repeated with surprise. "Brick de Dere? God's Bones, I do not know why I never made the connection. Of course I know him. A big man with brown hair?"

"And eyes that are my color."

"I never noticed, but now that I look at you, there is some resemblance. But he is a good deal older than you are."

Achilles nodded. "He is older than me by thirteen years," he said. "Benedict and Tobias are in the middle, and then I am the youngest."

She regarded him in the darkness for a moment before continuing on inside. "You are more handsome than Brick is."

"I know."

She laughed softly, rolling her eyes at his arrogant response as they came to a door, the first door in the corridor that was quite dark. Lifting the latch, Susanna pushed the panel open, revealing a good-sized chamber with at least three beds in it and windows that overlooked the courtyard. The only light in the chamber was coming from those windows, in fact, as the courtyard was lit by dozens of heavily-smoking torches. Susanna fumbled her way over to a table near the hearth, spying a taper and flint. Expertly striking the flint against stone, she lit the taper and a faint, golden glow filled the room.

Meanwhile, Achilles headed over to the windows to draw down the heavy oil cloth, blocking out a good deal of the light and blocking the view from the outside. Susanna moved from the taper to the hearth, now loading up peat and kindling to start a fire.

"Where will you be sleeping?" Achilles asked as he secured the oiled cloth.

Susanna was stacking the kindling from the depleted kindling bucket. "On the floor above," she said. "There are four chambers up there. When I was a child, I had the one in the western corner. I will sleep tonight on the same bed I slept in during my childhood."

"And that brings you comfort?"

She shrugged as she piled the last of the kindling. "As much as anything else can, I suppose," she said. Then, her movements slowed. "To be perfectly honest, I do not like to think about it because it reminds me of my mother too much."

"And that is still painful for you?"

"Still."

He came away from the windows, heading towards the hearth. "I am sorry, Sparks," he said softly. "I am fortunate in that I still have both parents. At least, I did the last time I had contact with them."

"When was that?"

"About five years ago."

She turned to look at him. "Things can change, Achilles. You should see your parents again, soon. Where do they live?"

"Blackwell Castle, south of Carlisle."

"Then it is not too far from here. Mayhap you should see them before you return to London."

Achilles shook his head, taking the flint and stone from her and striking it over the kindling, watching the sparks take root. "I cannot spare the time," he said. "It is more important that I fulfill my obligations to William Marshal right now. But mayhap when I return, we shall go and see them together."

The conversation took a decidedly personal turn, but instead of flushing violently and turning away, Susanna actually met his eye.

"I would like that," she said softly.

He smiled faintly. "I have decided something."

"What is that?"

"I am not going to court you."

Shock rippled across her features. "Why not?"

He lifted his big shoulders. "I do not want to take the time," he said.

"I will forego a courtship altogether and simply marry you."

She smiled in relief. "Are you certain?"

"Stop asking me that. I told you that I was."

She laughed quietly. "Then if that is what you wish, I am agreeable. When will you ask my brother? Before you go?"

He shook his head. "I do not think so, mostly because it would be a stranger asking," he said. "Any good brother would deny such a request and I do not wish to be denied. Therefore, during your time here and before I return, you will tell your brother about me and convince him that I am your one and only chance for a husband, and that he would be foolish to refuse my offer."

He was half-serious, half-not. Her eyes narrowed. "You are my one and only chance, are you?"

He pursed his lips distastefully. "Look at you," he scolded without force. "You dress like a man. You fight like a man. And you're *old*. How old are you, anyway?"

Her cheeks were back to flushing, tinged red because she was embarrassed. "I have seen twenty years and nine."

He snorted. "If your brother thinks you are going to get a better offer than me, he is mad." He noticed that she was hanging her head, realizing he had hurt her feelings with his harsh jesting. Quickly, he relented. "I am sorry, Sparks. I did not mean to sound cruel. I simply meant… I want you and I shall have you. You shall be my wife above all else."

She nodded, but she kept her head down. "But I *am* rather old."

"If I cared about that, I would not be here."

She peered up at him. "Are you certain?"

"Shall I prove it?"

Reaching down, he pulled her to her feet as the fire in the hearth began to grow. Orange flame threw undulating light on the walls as Achilles pulled Susanna against him, slanting his mouth over hers. It was their second kiss in as many days and, this time, there was no timidity on Susanna's part.

In fact, those sparks she'd spoken of to Achilles, once, had ignited a flame.

Fastened to his wonderful lips, Susanna moaned softly at the feel of him, hot and insistent. His arms were around her, holding her tightly, and it was the most wonderful sensation. He held her like that for a time, tasting her sweetly, before his hands move to her face, holding it as his lips devoured hers. By the time she was melting into him, giving herself over to him completely, his hands had moved from her face.

They were moving down her body.

They were fumbling at the belt around her waist, easily removing it. The belt hit the ground and Susanna was so consumed with the pleasure of his heated mouth that she was hardly aware when he pulled the tunic over her head.

Before she realized it, the clothing was beginning to come off.

Shall I prove it?

Evidently, he fully intended to.

Susanna should have put a stop to it at the very least, but she found she couldn't. She was as eager to explore him as he was to explore her, this man who had infuriated her at the beginning of their acquaintance but now turned her into a heated, malleable creature at the slightest touch. She remembered his hands on her neck as they'd fought, once. But those same hands, so strong and brutal, were now tender and loving.

Gentle.

She wanted more.

Somehow, the mail came off in between heated kisses and Susanna heard it hit the floor, too. He then went to remove his own clothing, yanking his tunic with such eagerness that he tore a seam. More pieces of clothing began coming off – undertunic, boots, and finally the ties on breeches. All of it was hitting the floor at an alarming rate and Susanna couldn't even muster the will to utter a word of protest. Suddenly, she was up in his muscular arms and he laid her upon the nearest bed. It was then that Susanna realized the extent of their naked state; flat on her back, he covered her up with his warm, muscular body.

His intentions were clear.

In fact, Achilles was going to take her. He'd already decided that. He was going to marry the woman and before he rode off to London, he was going to mark Susanna as his own. *Claim her.* He was fairly certain she had figured out his objectives at this point and thought he might ease her natural apprehension with a few well-chosen words, but he was so consumed in the feel of her naked flesh against his that the only sound coming forth from his throat was a growl.

Since she wasn't resisting, his hands roved and caressed, probed and stroked, as Susanna writhed beneath him. She was innately responsive to his touch, arching into him, squirming beneath him, and Achilles could stand no more. His mouth found her beautiful breasts and he began to suckle gently. He could feel Susanna's fingers on his scalp, holding his head against her breasts. She was so blinded by what he was doing to her that when he wedged himself between her thighs, it was as she abruptly came to her senses.

"Achilles," she whispered. "Mayhap we should not… we are not married, after all."

Achilles licked her torso, ending at a taut nipple. "It does not matter," he whispered. "You shall be my wife and I will adore you, and only you, until I die. Give me a memory to live on during my time away from you, Sparks. Already, I can hardly bear being away from you."

She shuddered violently as his fingers pinched her nipples and her eyes closed once more, giving herself over to erotic anticipation. "Nor I, you," she murmured. "You may continue."

It sounded like a command and he fought off a grin. "Thank you, my lady."

Lifting himself up, his lips descended upon her mouth once more, suckling the breath from her very bones. Susanna, swept up in the newness of sensations, moaned low in her throat. The more he kissed and stroked, the hotter she became.

Gripping Susanna behind her long thighs, Achilles pulled her knees up, winding her supple legs about his hips. Moving away from her delicious mouth, he gazed down at his engorged manhood as it pressed gently against her tender core, watching as their bodies prepared to join. It excited him beyond reason. Stroking her tender folds and feeling how wet she was, he guided his manroot to its target.

Achilles could hardly contain himself, but contain he did. It took every ounce of his self-control not to plunge into her. It was a supreme effort to move slowly, withdrawing himself and then pressing into her again, gaining headway in minute quantities. He would have been doing quite well with his controlled efforts had Susanna not bucked and sighed beneath him, fracturing his concentration. His control held firm until the unexpected happened – in a blinding flash, he suddenly found himself seated to the hilt.

Susanna yelped quietly with the shocking swiftness of the action and Achilles' eyes flew open, looking at the woman in utter surprise. He would have laughed had he not been shocked with the realization that she had thrust her pelvis forward in an attempt to force his manroot deep into her waiting body. While he was trying to be patient, she was the one who was *impatient*.

"What did you do?" he asked, incredulous.

She sighed heavily, her hands finding their way onto his buttocks. "I was tired of waiting," she whispered guiltily. "Forgive me... I was eager to be done with the pain I knew was yet to come."

He couldn't help the disbelieving grin on his face. "So you are setting the pace, are you?"

She wrapped her long legs around his hips. "Not really," she said softly. "But the anticipation was worse than the actual event. Do not be angry."

He snorted softly. "I am not," he said. "I should have expected such a thing from you. You have never met any challenge or situation without bravery, have you? You are a remarkable woman, Sparks."

"Is this all there is?"

That brought more chuckles from him. "There is much more," he said. "May I proceed?"

"Please do."

"Are you sure you do not want to do this for me?"

Her eyes narrowed and he chuckled, dipping his head down to kiss her softly and then watching her face as he withdrew from her. Then he thrust into her again, seating himself fully.

After that, he began to move.

His thrusts began to build, feeling her body draw at him. Every thrust, every withdrawal, pulled them closer together, building a world where Achilles was master and Susanna was his willing student. He knew what he was doing, and she trusted him, and the friction building was driving them both to greater pleasure. When Susanna finally experienced her first release, Achilles had to put his hand over her mouth because she was becoming quite loud about it. He put his forehead against hers, shushing her softly, before finally taking his own pleasure with her.

Then, she was the one putting her hand over *his* mouth.

It had been loud, athletic and sweaty, but oh-so-satisfying. When the heavy breathing died down, Achilles shifted his weight so he wasn't on top of her. Wrapping her up tightly in his powerful embrace, he draped a big leg over her hips, pulling her in even closer.

"Sparks," he murmured, his lips against her forehead. "I am not entirely certain I can leave you. Without you, my days will be wrought with misery and my nights will be starless. There will be no joy, no beauty. Only longing."

She was dozing in his arms, wildly content. Slowly, her eyes opened. "Starless," she whispered. "It sounds so… empty."

"It is. And I am at the thought of leaving you."

She sighed contentedly. "This is not something I ever believed would happen," she said. "I would watch Cadelyn and how men were attracted to her, and I would stand next to her like a shadow. When she and Kress began to draw closer together, I suppose that I was envious deep down. In my years at Castle Rising, I would see women marry, of course, but I always felt I was on the outside looking in. There was never any hope for me when it came to men."

Achilles pulled her closer because she sounded so vulnerable, a rare state indeed when it came to her. "I remember when I first saw you," he said. "You were dressed in skirts, like a peasant, but you tossed those skirts up to reveal breeches and a broadsword underneath. You looked like a wild, untamed creature. But in that vision, there was beauty there. Even then, I could see it."

She snorted softly. "No one else could," she said. "You are the only one. Achilles, swear to me that you will return. Swear to me that this will never end."

"It will never end. I swear to you upon my own life that I will return for you."

"Do you think… do you think that, mayhap someday, we may even come to love one another?"

He pulled back to look at her. "Do you mean to tell me that you do not love me now? Truly, Sparks, you should be far gone in love with me by now. What is the delay, Woman?"

He said it with such drama that she grinned. "Who says there is a delay?" she said. "And who says I am not?"

"You just asked me if such a thing was possible *someday*."

"Who is to say that someday is not today?"

A smile spread over his lips. "Is it true, then? Do you love me just a little?"

The flush was back in her cheeks. "It is possible."

"Tell me. Let me hear you say it."

"You say it first."

"I will not. It is your duty, as the woman, to tell me how much you love me *first*."

"You have taken charge in all things. You should be the first. I would not deprive you of that privilege."

"Tell me or I will kick you out of my bed."

She threw her arms around his body, holding on tightly. "You cannot do it."

"Can't I?"

Not surprisingly, they wrestled around until they ended up on the floor, where Achilles proceeded to take her a second time, very carefully. Knowing she was new to this, and having just lost her virginity, he didn't want to cause her any undue pain or discomfort. Susanna, to her credit, hardly cared. She relished every stroke, every touch.

In the end, he was the one to tell her first.

I love you, Sparks.

The next morning, at dawn, Achilles and Alexander thundered from Aysgarth's outer bailey as Susanna watched from the walls. Wrapped in a cloak against the cold morning, she watched them until they were out of her sight. Even then, she continued to stand there, her gaze on the last place she had seen Achilles.

She never knew it was possible to feel such longing.

His return to Aysgarth couldn't come fast enough.

CHAPTER FIVE

~ Excerpt from the epilogue of *The Mountain Dark* between
Christopher de Lohr, Earl of Hereford and Worcester, and the Earl of
Pembroke, William Marshal ~

Three Weeks Later
Farringdon House
London Townhome of William Marshal, Earl of Pembroke

W ILLIAM LOOKED AT *Christopher before snorting, an unhappy and
ironic sound. "First, I lose Maxton of Loxbeare to a woman, and
now I lose Kress. My Executioner Knights are falling away, one by one,
succumbing to the wiles of women."*

Christopher fought off a grin. "I believe they have fallen in love."

"It is the same thing."

*"Then you are not going to want to hear that I believe Achilles is
next."*

*William scowled. "De Dere?" he said. "What has he done? Tell me
this instant!"*

*Christopher started to laugh, trying not to let William see that he
thought the man's reaction comical. "He has not done anything," he said.
"But that lady warrior you sent to protect Lady Cadelyn – Susanna de
Tiegh – has the man's affection, I think."*

*"What?" William burst, outraged. "That woman trained at Black-
church!"*

"I was told that."

"She is as skilled as any warrior in my stable!"

"She is also a woman and from what I have seen, Achilles is fond of her."

William scowled. *"Where is de Dere?"* he demanded. *"He came back to London with Sherry. Where is that man, I say?"*

Christopher shook his head. *"He is waiting in an undisclosed location for word from me after I speak with you,"* he said. *"Susanna was injured in the fight at Longton and Achilles escorted her to her brother's home of Aysgarth Castle to recover before coming back to London. I am not only here to confirm what happened with Lady Cadelyn and the de Shera betrothal, but I am also here as Achilles' emissary. Will you listen?"*

William was beside himself. *"To what?"* he said. *"That he has lost his mind just like Maxton and Kress? My God, these are men who were known as the Unholy Trinity. They were the deadliest assassins the world has ever seen but, suddenly, they have become giddy squires? Appalling!"*

Christopher watched the old knight rage, his eyes glimmering with humor. *"Do you forget how you felt when you first married Isabel, William?"* he asked quietly. *"Surely you have not forgotten those feelings of warmth and adoration. I know I haven't. I feel as strongly for my wife now as I did when I first fell in love with her. More so, even. I would not be the man I am today without Dustin by my side. Surely you cannot begrudge Maxton and Kress and Achilles the same feelings. Surely you cannot begrudge them happiness."*

William wasn't in the mood to agree with Christopher even though he knew, deep down, that the man was right. He avoided looking at him.

"It has nothing to do with begrudging a man his happiness and every-thing to do with interfering with his duty," he said pointedly. *"But now that you have brought up Susanna's injury, I was told that it was not too severe and for that, I am glad. She is a fine warrior."*

Christopher was relieved that William was finally seeing reason. *"I agree,"* he said. *"Now, back to Achilles. He would like your permission to return to Aysgarth Castle to see to Lady Susanna."*

William's eyes narrowed. "Did he tell you to ask me?"

"He asked if I would, aye."

"Well, where is he?"

"I told you that he is in an undisclosed location."

William looked at him a moment before shaking his head in disgust. "He is at The Pox, isn't he?"

"I will not confirm or deny that information."

William rolled his eyes. "God's Bones, I told him to stay away from that place," he said. "Is Sherry with him? And Bric? The last time they were there, they lost money to a group of Northampton knights and in retaliation, stripped them of their clothing. I had to not only return their clothing, but I also had to pay them handsomely so they would not tell their liege that my men had ambushed them in an alley and stripped them of their dignity. When will those idiots learn not to go near The Pox?"

"Do you speak of Achilles and the others, or of the Northampton men?"

"Both, damnation!"

Christopher started to laugh, then. He couldn't help it. "I will find them and bring them back," he said. But he paused, sobering, before continuing. "Remember that in spite of everything, these are men of greatness, William. You have the finest knights in all of England sworn to you, Achilles included. He would kill for you and die for you, and even if he is fond of a woman, it is not the end of Achilles. It is only the beginning."

The Pox, a gambling establishment
Ropery Street, London, Near London Bridge

IT WAS A smoky, crowded room, jammed with men of all shapes, sizes, and classes, all of them enjoying what The Pox had to offer.

Like most gambling hells, The Pox catered to men in all financial states. Rich or poor; it didn't matter as long as one had some coinage and as long as a man was gambling steadily, the lavish feasts were provided free of charge. A man could eat from morning to night and never have the same dish twice. The wines were quite fine, from Spain and France and points east, and there were dozens of varieties.

The games were varied, as well. There were games of chance, with wooden dice, but there was also a room that was exclusively for cock fighting. The losers, if they were too injured, were cooked and eaten. Men would find anything to gamble about, including gambling over new patrons coming in to participate in the excitement. On this night, five men sat by the door, betting that an earl would enter within the hour and being disappointed when one didn't show.

On and on it went.

Achilles and Alexander were sitting at the window overlooking Ropery Street because they were waiting for someone in particular. Christopher de Lohr was meeting with William Marshal at that very moment and they expected him to show up soon to report on his meeting.

And a critical meeting it was.

Seated with Achilles and Alexander were two other knights, one of which they were particularly close with. Bric MacRohan, the enormous Irish knight with pale blond hair and eyes so blue that they were silver, sat next to Achilles with a big cup of ale in his hand. Across the table, next to Alexander, sat a knight by the name of Kevin de Lara.

Kevin was in service to the House of de Lohr, mostly with Christopher but sometimes with Christopher's brother, David, who was the Earl of Canterbury. Ultimately, however, he was sworn to William Marshal, as part of The Marshal's stable of knights. A rather short knight with the strength of Samson, Kevin was young and handsome, with blue eyes, a square jaw, and a bright smile. He had a good deal of charisma and was honest to a fault, and well liked among The Marshal's men.

The only chink in Kevin's armor was the fact that his older brother, Sean, had defected into the service of King John and, these days, had built himself a frightening and brutal reputation as a knight known as Lord of the Shadows.

Kevin adored Sean and it was no secret that he was greatly disappointed in the path his talented brother had taken even though he was well aware, as were a few of The Marshal's close advisors, that Sean's position was actually that of a spy for The Marshal. Sean hadn't really defected, but that's what he wanted everyone to think. By the man's horrible actions as the bodyguard to the king, one would have thought is defection was real.

It was something Kevin disagreed with wholeheartedly.

Therefore, no one really spoke of Sean de Lara to Kevin, even though they all knew and greatly respected Sean, because it was such a terrible subject with Kevin. Alexander in particular was a friend of Sean's, but that relationship went entirely ignored when Kevin was around.

It was a sad and touchy situation for the de Lara brothers.

It was the price they paid for serving in England's greatest spy network.

On this night, with the full moon shining over the waters of the River Thames, the four men sat at their table, having spent their time participating in various gambling games throughout the afternoon and evening, waiting for Christopher to return for them with news from The Marshal. Achilles, in particular, was anxious because he'd asked Christopher to beg permission from The Marshal to return to Aysgarth.

As he sat there and watched the moonbeams ripple over the water, Achilles had already made the decision that permission or no, he was going to return and marry Susanna. He'd made that decision the night he'd bedded her and he felt it more strongly than he'd ever felt anything in his life. That brash, bold, courageous, beautiful, and awkward woman would become his wife. They may kill each other in the end, given their history, but they were going to live and laugh and love until then.

He was very much looking forward to it.

Achilles' feelings for Susanna weren't something Kevin was privy to, however, but both Alexander and Bric were aware of it considering they'd both been an integral part of the failed betrothal mission regarding Cadelyn of Vendotia. They'd seen the building relationship between Achilles and the woman he wanted everyone to think he hated, but Alexander was even more involved given the fact that he'd accompanied them both to Aysgarth.

Alexander in particular kept glancing at Achilles, who had been unusually silent during their time at The Pox. He'd even brushed off the serving wenches that, prior to Susanna, he would not have turned away. He drank and he brooded.

Sometimes missing a woman would do that to a man.

"What do you suppose is taking so long?" Achilles finally spoke in a rare utterance. "I thought de Lohr would have returned to us by now."

Alexander toyed with his half-full cup. "He will be here," he said. "Remember that he must return for us because we must report what we have seen at Aysgarth. He is not going to even mention that to The Marshal; *we* are. De Lohr did not see what we did."

Across the table, Bric grunted. "A mercenary army," he said in his thick Irish accent. "And de Tiegh told you that it did not belong to him?"

Alexander nodded. "That was exactly what he said," he replied. "Even in our long discussion the night we arrived at Aysgarth, de Tiegh mentioned more than once that he was only housing the army for someone else, but he did not say who."

"That brings to mind something Susanna said," Achilles said. "She told me that her brother was more of a follower than a leader. She believed that there was something much bigger happening. That is part of the reason I did not want to leave her behind. She's very intelligent and I am afraid that she will try to dig deep to find out what, exactly, her brother is involved in."

"Susanna," Kevin repeated. "This was the female bodyguard for Cadelyn of Vendotia?"

"Aye," Achilles said. "Have you heard about her?"

Kevin nodded. "David and I were in the same room as The Marshal a few years ago when he received a missive from her and that was the first time I'd ever heard her name. She's the Blackchurch-trained warrior, correct?"

"Correct."

"Seems difficult to believe a woman actually trained at Blackchurch."

"She is quite skilled, I assure you."

Alexander snorted. "You should have seen how Achilles and Susanna got on in the beginning," he said. "Bric was there; he can tell you. The animosity was obvious. We were pulling them apart at every turn until we finally had to let them fight it out. Achilles had the height and weight advantage on her, but she was quite formidable. Especially when she got in behind him and started pulling his ears."

Bric started to laugh as Kevin grinned, looking at Achilles. "Did you beat her soundly for doing that?"

Achilles looked rather uncomfortable. "Hell, I did not want to hurt the woman. The Marshal would have throttled me for that."

Bric continued to laugh at the memory. "I cannot tell you the times I had to put myself in between the pair to stop their aggressions," he said. "But the fight at the tavern in Heckington was truly something to behold. There was a good deal of biting and screaming going on, mostly from Achilles."

Achilles frowned. "It was *not* me," he said. "Sparks was making all of the noise."

That statement brought a good deal of interest from Kevin. "Sparks? Who is Sparks?"

Achilles cleared his throat awkwardly, eyeing Alexander and Bric, who kept their mouths shut. This wasn't a question they were going to answer, but they both had varied degrees of mirth in their expressions.

They were very curious to see if Achilles was going to make an admission.

"That is what I call Susanna," he finally, embarrassed. "She said something to me once, something rather insightful. She was speaking of Kress and Cadelyn and said that people sometimes find a person who makes them spark. I started calling her Sparks, at first to taunt her, but then…"

Kevin wasn't stupid. He could read Achilles' body language like a book. "And this lady knight makes you spark, does she?"

Achilles' head came up, looking into the faces of his three friends. He was afraid he was in for a world of teasing, but he didn't see that in their expressions. He only saw warmth and humor in a situation that, truthfully, had a good deal of it.

There was no use in denying what they already knew.

"I suppose I cannot deny it," he muttered. "I do not know how it happened, only that it did. One moment I was fighting with her and in the next… other things were happening."

Bric leaned towards the table as if prepared to hear a juicy secret. "*What* other things?"

Achilles sighed heavily. "*Things*, MacRohan. Enough so that I plan to return to Aysgarth and marry her. I am certain you figured that out when I asked de Lohr on our return from Chester if he would beg permission from The Marshal for me to return to Aysgarth."

Bric's blond eyebrows lifted in utter astonishment. "I knew you wanted to return, but is it as bad as all that?"

"Worse. I fell for the woman, pure and simple. I never knew I had a heart until she took it."

Bric looked to Alexander in astonishment, as if the man could confirm what Achilles was telling him. Alexander nodded firmly as Kevin lifted up his cup.

"That is a rare thing, Achilles," Kevin said, his eyes glimmering. "I admire you for being brave enough to admit it."

It was a toast to courage, perhaps even to love, and Achilles fought off a grin as Alexander and Bric raised their cups as well. They were drinking deeply when movement passed by the window, catching their attentions. As they turned to the door, it was shoved open and Christopher de Lohr stepped through.

The Earl of Hereford and Worcester had arrived.

An enormous man with a crown of golden-blond hair and a trim, blond beard, Christopher *was* England. The former champion for Richard the Lionheart and a man known during Richard's reign as Defender of the Realm, Christopher was the head of one of the most powerful dynasties in England. If William Marshal was England's greatest knight, then Christopher de Lohr was England's greatest champion.

But the champion did not look pleased at the moment. As he came through the door, his gaze immediately fell on the table of the four knights near the window.

"Come," he boomed. "He is waiting for you."

There was no time to delay. Achilles was on his feet, grabbing his saddlebags and weapon as the others did the same. They were moving swiftly for the door, following the massive, blond earl out into the moonlit night.

Their time had finally come.

CHAPTER SIX

FARRINGDON HOUSE, THE townhome of William Marshal, was a structure that was part of The Marshal's world of power as much as a sword or an army.

It was a legendary place of strength and duty unto itself.

Entering through an arched and secured gate built into the house itself and protected by several guards, Achilles followed de Lohr through a tunnel that led into a damp, enclosed courtyard. To their right were stalls for the horses and a small corral, but stretching above them were four stories of an enormous stone house.

Windows faced into the interior courtyard and he could hear voices coming from the open panels – servants moving about, even at this late hour. To their left was another arched doorway, heavily-fortified, and there was another guard standing at it. The five of them entered the ground floor of the house through that arch, which included servants' quarters, a big armory, and the kitchens. It was dark and cramped. A walkway through the ground floor led to a large mural staircase, and the group took the stairs to the first floor above.

This floor was more spacious, with high ceilings and big windows. It was also the floor with the enormous solar, The Marshal's seat of power. At this hour, it was brightly lit, with a fire in the hearth and banks of fat, yellow tapers. As soon as the knights entered, they heard a familiar voice.

"Damnation, Achilles, is this true?" William Marshal was standing by the hearth, warming his old bones. "Is what de Lohr told me the truth?"

Achilles looked at Christopher, who simply motioned towards William. *Tell him.* Achilles got the message loud and clear.

"If he told you that I wish to return to Aysgarth Castle, to Susanna, then it is true, my lord," he said respectfully.

William came away from the hearth, his gaze riveted to Achilles. As he came closer, they could see that his jaw was ticking beneath his stubbled cheeks. William was tall, still powerful, with a haggard face and eyes yellowed with age.

And it was clear that he was displeased. In spite of the fact that his meeting with Christopher had ended with calm dialogue, he'd had a chance to build up a substantial rage again in the time it took Christopher to retrieve Achilles.

Now, the third knight in the Unholy Trinity had his full focus.

"Sit down," he commanded, pointing to a chair near the hearth. "Sit there and do not move. I have questions."

Achilles did as he was told, planting his big body on the chair and gazing up at The Marshal expectantly. William often reacted strongly to things involving his warriors, so this was not unexpected.

But it *was* concerning.

William, still mulling over everything he'd been told, finally turned to him. "Earlier this year, I freed you and Maxton and Kress from the dungeons of the Lords of Baux," he said. "Is that a true statement?"

"It is, my lord."

"I freed you, and paid an enormous ransom, to serve me."

"You did, my lord."

"Eleanor of Aquitaine even paid part of your ransom because your first task for me was to prevent her son, John, from being eliminated by papal assassins."

"All true, my lord."

William frowned. "I paid for three of the finest assassins money could buy," he said frankly. "Your reputation as the Executioner Knights ran far and wide, and you came highly recommended."

"Have we not performed flawlessly for you, my lord?"

William's bushy eyebrows lifted. "When it came to preventing John's death, you did," he said. "But when it came to escorting Cadelyn of Vendotia to her betrothed, you failed miserably."

"My lord, had the lady made it to her betrothed, it would have started a Welsh rebellion the likes of which we have not seen in a great while. It probably would have meant her death. It is better that the mission failed."

"Shut your lips. I will do the talking."

Achilles did as he was commanded. William glared at him for a moment before continuing.

"First, it was Maxton," he said. "He married the postulate, the one that helped us identify the papal assassins, and I lost him to the Welsh Marches. Then, it was Kress – he absconded with a bride meant for another man and now lives somewhere in the wilds of Scotland. I have lost him, too. And now you; I understand you wish to return to Aysgarth Castle because of Susanna de Tiegh."

"May I answer, my lord?"

"You had better."

"It is true, my lord. I intend to marry the woman."

Christopher hadn't known that part of it and therefore hadn't mentioned it to William. His eyebrows lifted slightly as he looked to The Marshal, whose reaction was to roll his eyes and hang his head. That seemed to bring his tirade to a pause and he turned away as if contemplating what the Executioner Knights had become. They were perfect and they were ruthless, but they were also men of flesh and blood and heart.

It was the heart that he was having difficulty with. First Maxton, then Kress… now, Achilles.

"I take it she is agreeable to this?" he finally said.

Achilles nodded. "She is, my lord."

"Will you continue to serve me if you marry her?"

"With all my heart, I will, my lord."

William sighed heavily. "And what of your wife? She has been with me longer than you have, you know. She is a tremendous asset and I hate to lose her."

Achilles hadn't really thought on all of this, on his future or Susanna's future with The Marshal, so he simply lifted his shoulders. "I will leave that up to her, my lord," he said. "If she wishes to continue serving you, I will not protest. But I will tell you that I will not be separated from her. Where she goes, I go."

William grunted. "At least I will retain you both, unlike Maxton and Kress," he muttered. "Maxton is still in my service, though I do not see him much, but Kress is long gone. I would be surprised if I ever see him again. You are the one to redeem the Unholy Trinity, Achilles. Make me at least feel as if I got my money's worth when I bought your freedom from the Lords of Baux."

"As long as Susanna and I can serve together, I will do my very best, my lord," he said. "But someday, I should like to have a home for Susanna. I would make an excellent garrison commander for one of your properties or even for Lord de Lohr."

William glanced at Christopher. "Do you hear that? He wants to push me aside and serve you at an outpost."

Christopher fought off a grin. "A wise choice."

William pursed his lips irritably at Christopher and returned his attention to Achilles. "Until the day comes that I install you at one of my holdings, you will continue to serve me as I see fit," he said. "When do you intend to return for Susanna?"

"Right away, my lord, but first, Alexander and I have information we believe you should be aware of."

"What of?"

"News from Aysgarth that does not have to do with Susanna, but with her brother and his activities. Sherry may know more, as he had a longer conversation with de Tiegh than I did. He can tell you."

William looked at Alexander, crooking a long finger at the man. "Come here."

The focus now turned to Alexander as he came away from Kevin and Bric, going to stand next to Achilles.

"My lord?"

William took a long, hard look at him. "Before we discuss Aysgarth, we are going to discuss the de Shera betrothal," he said. "You were the escort commander. It was your duty to make sure Cadelyn of Vendotia made it to Tatius de Shera. I charged you with an important task, Sherry."

Alexander had known this moment was coming and was frankly surprised it had taken so long. "You did, my lord," he said. "But as Lord Hereford has explained and Achilles has said, it was better that Lady Cadelyn did not make it to her intended. An entire Welsh rebellion was waiting for her."

William was back to being irritated. "Mayhap that is true, but you still failed."

"I do not think you would be happier if I succeeded, my lord."

William wasn't going to argue with him. He simply wanted to stress the point that Alexander de Sherrington had failed at something, even if it had turned out for the best. The entire story, as told by Christopher, had been shocking and serious, and he didn't want to hear it repeated at the moment because he was still trying to absorb what he'd been told. After a moment, he turned away from Alexander and headed over the table against the wall that contained his fine wine and pewter cups.

"What is done is done, I suppose," he said, suddenly sounding less irritated and more weary. "I am not pleased with your failure but, in this case, mayhap it was for the best. Christopher has just spent a good deal of time with Tatius trying to help the man rebuild his earldom, but we shall discuss that later. Right now, I want to know what is happening at Aysgarth."

Alexander watched the man take a healthy gulp of wine. Perhaps it was moments like this, with knights who were not doing as he wished and the world was trying to upend itself, that William needed the fortification of the ruby red liquid. Alexander was glad for it because he was fairly certain that The Marshal wasn't going to like what he was about to tell him.

He proceeded carefully.

"Susanna was injured in the battle at Longton, when the Welsh rebels made themselves known and tried to take Cadelyn away from us before we could deliver her to Tatius," he said. "After spending several days at a tavern so she could heal somewhat before we moved her, we rode north at a slow pace to Aysgarth so she could recuperate fully at her brother's home."

"That great norther bastion with a lord who refuses to declare his loyalties," William muttered as he turned to him. "Did Susanna tell you that?"

"She did, my lord."

"I have sent her home on occasion to see to her brother's activities, but it has never amounted to anything."

"It has now, my lord."

"Do tell."

Alexander complied. "When we arrived at Aysgarth, we immediately spied an army in a training ground that is located below the castle," he said. "I saw the men, as did Achilles, and we noticed their oddly-shaped shields. I did not see one man with a recognizable standard. In fact, they seemed rather rag-tag and disjointed."

"Explain."

"They were not a cohesive group, my lord. There were groups of men dressed quite differently from each other and seemingly segregated from each other. The language they spoke was something I'd heard in Thuringia and the shields they used were not English."

William was listening closely. "Who are they?"

Alexander lifted his shoulders. "If I had to guess, I would say they were mercenaries," he said. "There were at least a thousand, but strangely, de Tiegh mentioned that they do not belong to him."

William was puzzled. "He has a mercenary army that does not *belong* to him?"

"That is what he told us, my lord."

William stroked his chin thoughtfully as he pondered the information. "So he is holding a mercenary army for someone else," he muttered. "That is a bizarre statement."

"I thought so, too, but I did not press him for fear he would become suspicious of why I was so interested. I thought it best to return to London to tell you what we saw."

"Does he know who you serve?"

Alexander shook his head. "We were wearing the Pembroke standards but we told him that we ambushed two Pembroke knights and stole them," he said, grinning. "We told him that the Pembroke standard brought us an inordinate amount of free meals and lodgings, so we wore them in order to gain anything free they could provide for us. We made it clear that we did not actually serve you."

William had to shake his head at Alexander's rather clever, and mischievous, lie. "I wondered if he believed you."

"He seemed to. He knows my older brother, Estienne, so that seemed to cause him to instantly trust me. I did not feel at any time that he was suspicious."

William eyed him. "Lord Broxburn? Your brother is associating with de Tiegh?"

"They are evidently friends."

"Then you could always ask your brother what he knows."

"I have not spoken to my brother in almost fifteen years and I do not intend to start now, my lord."

William thought about pressing that but quickly decided against it. Alexander and his relationship with his unscrupulous older brother was a conversation for another time, so he let it slide.

"Aysgarth is near Richmond," he said. "That is a royal property but the garrison commander is loyal to me. Do you know Caius d'Avignon?"

Alexander's eyes widened. "Cai?" he repeated in surprised. "Of course I know him, my lord. He served Richard in The Levant in much the same capacity as the Unholy Trinity and I did, only Cai was far more… merciless, if such a thing is possible. The Muslims called him *Britania Faybr*."

"What does that mean?"

"The Britannia Viper."

That seemed to bring some mirth to William's eyes. "I have seen the ink he has on his arm in the image of a viper," he said. "Whoever tattooed the man did a remarkable job, for it is quite detailed."

Alexander nodded, warming to the conversation about a man he knew well and very much admired. "He received it in The Levant. All he had to do was show that image to the enemy and they would flee in fear. In fact, Cai and I served together on several occasions when that tattoo was used to our advantage. Once he showed it, he would strike. It was a harbinger of things to come."

William rather liked that kind of fear and the man who caused it. "Cai is indeed as unpredictable as he is deadly," he said. "But he returned home to serve me, at Richard's request, and he has been with me for several years. To be honest, I believe he is rather bored up in Richmond, but I need him there. England has many rogue barons in Yorkshire and I need Cai to keep watch of them. He might know why de Tiegh is building up a mercenary army that is not his own."

"Have you heard of de Meynell, my lord?"

William nodded immediately. "Whorlton Castle, which is not far from Aysgarth or Richmond. De Meynell is married to a Teutonic woman with ties to the Count of Gotha and he is very much opposed to our king. Why do you ask?"

Alexander glanced at Achilles. "Because we ran into a group of de Meynell knights when we were escorting Susanna home. Things got a bit… bloody, shall we say."

"How many knights?"

"Seven, my lord."

"Did you kill any of them?"

"I would say at least two or three, but they attacked us first. We had no choice. We were wearing Pembroke standards and they seemed to take that as an invitation for hostilities."

William grunted unhappily. "They would," he said. Then, he cocked his head as if he suddenly had a thought. "You say that you heard language spoken at Aysgarth that you recognized from Thuringia?"

"Aye, my lord."

"Gotha is in Thuringia."

The spark of realization flared. William looked at Christopher and the two of them shared a moment of shocking awareness.

"Whorlton is not far from Aysgarth," Christopher said. "As I recall, it is forty or fifty miles away. I have seen Whorlton, long time ago, and I recall that it is not a very big castle."

William was processing information, his mind working rapidly as it always did. "If de Tiegh and de Meynell plant a mercenary army in Yorkshire, that will be a threat to Richmond and any other lord loyal to John. Rebel barons could do a good deal of damage."

It was a concerning thought, but no one in that room was more concerned than Achilles. *I left Susanna in the middle of that*, he thought. He hadn't wanted to leave her for many reasons, but none more prevalent than leaving her with a brother who was clearly doing something subversive. It was true that she could take care of herself, but he didn't like the idea of having to. He should be there with her. But before he could say anything to that regard, however, William spoke up again.

"I must get this information to Cai," he said. "I want to know what he knows of this, and if he knows nothing, then he must find out what is going on between Whorlton and Aysgarth. Clearly, something is happening and we must know what it is. Sherry, can I trust you to lead another escort north to Richmond and tell him what you have seen at Aysgarth?"

Alexander nodded. "Aye, my lord."

"Then take de Lara with you because de Winter is demanding I return MacRohan to him," he said with feigned disgust. "Daveigh de Winter claims he cannot get along without his big Irish bull, so it is begrudgingly that I must let him return to Narborough Castle in Norfolk before Daveigh comes to London to personally retrieve him."

"Aye, my lord," Alexander said. "And Achilles?"

William turned to look at Achilles, still sitting in the same chair where he commanded the man to sit earlier.

"Take him," he said, but his next words were directed at Achilles. "You will go to Richmond first, do you understand? You and Sherry will tell Cai what you told me and wait for direction from him. I do not want you to go charging back to Aysgarth and risk both you and Susanna. Her brother does not suspect that she serves me and I do not need you ruining anything in your haste. Is that clear?"

Achilles nodded. "It is, my lord."

William's gaze lingered on Achilles as if he didn't quite believe the knight, but he let it go. He had only worked with Achilles for the past few several months, so the trust they had been building was fragile. He trusted him on his oath alone, not because he had experience with him. Achilles, and Maxton and Kress, had become changed men once they returned to England, so William was understandably wary. A woman could do strange things to a man's self-control.

After a moment, he turned to Christopher.

"Do you have anything to add?" he asked.

Christopher shook his head. "Nay."

"You do not mind that I am sending Kevin with them?"

Again, Christopher shook his head. "He will be a welcome addition," he said. "But I was thinking, William, Netherghyll Castle is south of Aysgarth by about a day. It is down near Bradford. They will pass near Netherghyll on their way north to Richmond. That's the seat of the House of de Royans, Constables of North Yorkshire and the Northern Dales. Bryton de Royans might also know what is going on at Aysgarth, or if he does not, he should be notified."

William nodded in agreement. "De Royans has a sizable army, too," he said. "If the worst comes with Aysgarth rebels, we can converge on him from both Netherghyll and Richmond. He and his mercenaries would be boxed in."

"Very true."

"Bryton's father, Juston de Royans, is further north at Bowes Castle. He's a little too far away to be directly involved in this, but if Aysgarth is involved in a rebellion, Bowes will eventually be a target, too."

Christopher crossed his big arms thoughtfully. "I would not think Juston is in any immediate danger. Besides, we do not want to work the old knight into a frenzy. Juston would not tolerate any foolery from Aysgarth and could very well take his big army down there just to beat up on them. My old master has been known to do such things."

They both chuckled at the thought of very old, but still very volatile, Juston de Royans charging Aysgarth. Juston had mentored Christopher and David, as well as the Unholy Trinity and many other knights in the days before they had gone to The Levant and earned their ferocious reputations. Even Achilles grinned because he knew that Juston would do precisely what Christopher had suggested. The man didn't tolerate foolery and he would have no hesitation in starting a ruckus about it.

"I adore Juston," William said fondly. "I miss the man. Another great knight who fell to the wiles of a woman."

Christopher simply grinned, shaking his head. "If you only did not see it that way. None of us do."

William waved them off, unwilling to admit that men had focus on something else other than their sworn duties. They could swear an oath, live by the sword, and fight a thousand battles, but a woman had the ability to change all of that. By this time, William should have accepted such a thing, but he didn't want to.

He was stubborn that way.

"I will send a missive for Bryton de Royans," he said to Alexander and Achilles, setting his empty wine cup on the nearest table. "You may sleep here tonight and then take it with you in the morning. Do not delay stopping at Netherghyll; simply find a messenger when you near Netherghyll and send it on. I will tell de Royans where you will be should he need to contact you."

The situation was clearly outlined and the meeting was coming to a close. They could all sense it. All things considered, Achilles thought the discussion had gone rather well. At least he had permission to return to Aysgarth and that was all he really cared about. In fact, he was eager to get started.

"Aye, my lord," he said as he rose from his chair. "We will seek you on the morrow."

William was already heading to a large table in his solar, cluttered with a great many things – maps, quills, empty ink wells. All of it in some kind of organized mess, the tools of a man who had been handling the reins of power in England for an abundance of years. He didn't reply to Achilles, so the man took it as a hint and headed to the door.

Departing the solar with Alexander, Bric, and Kevin, the next logical step should have been seeking a bed somewhere in The Marshal's vast house, but Achilles couldn't seem to do it. He wasn't tired. He would be returning to Aysgarth on the morrow and the excitement of seeing Susanna again, in spite of the circumstances surrounding Aysgarth, had him excited. He couldn't wait to hold her again, to kiss her, and to tell her that he loved her.

He never thought he would ever look forward to such a thing.

But first, there was the small matter of farewells to be made.

"Bric, we're going to miss your sword," Achilles said, extending his hand to the big Irish knight. "Safe travels back to Narborough for you."

With a grin, Bric accepted his hand. "It has been an adventure with you, lad," he said with a twinkle in his eye. "I hope everything works out well for you and Susanna. You are both always welcome at Narborough. Visit me sometime."

Achilles snorted. "I will," he said. "Sorry to have put you in the middle of our lover's quarrels, old man."

Bric laughed. "I would not have missed it," he said. "But I will say that you two flirt with the subtlety of garlic stew. Next time, leave me out of it."

That brought laughter from both Achilles and Alexander as Bric headed off, preparing to return to his liege and his usual duties for the House of de Winter. That left Kevin standing with Achilles and Alexander, scratching his head as he watched Bric go.

"Is that what I have to look forward to?" he asked. "You flirting with a woman who trained at Blackchurch?"

Achilles winked at him. "I'm much more adept at it these days. You'll see."

He said it with a good deal of confidence, even as he headed out of Farringdon House. Alexander watched him go, sighing heavily before following. It would not do well to leave Achilles on his own during a night in London. Because Alexander was following Achilles, Kevin did as well, and the three of them ended up back at The Pox.

Achilles wanted to eat and gamble, and he did, but after he'd had a bit too much to drink, he confessed that he'd come to The Pox one last time because he suspected his future wife would not approve of such things and the Blackchurch-trained knight could do a lot of damage if she did not approve of something. He didn't want a battle on his hands.

For once in his life, Achilles wasn't willing to tempt fate... and he didn't care a lick.

CHAPTER SEVEN

Aysgarth Castle

"STOP TUGGING, MY lady." The woman was trying not to scold. "If you pull at it, you will ruin the fabric."

Susanna dropped her hands from the neckline which, in her opinion, was far too plunging. She knew she had breasts. Of course, she knew she had them, but now *everybody* else in the world was going to know it, too. When she looked at herself, all she could see were what men joyfully called *paps*.

Big, white, round boobs.

"Are you certain that all the ladies are wearing this style?" she asked hesitantly. "It is quite beautiful, but it seems... well, it is rather low on the neck."

Standing in her chamber, Susanna was perched on a stool as a seamstress all the way from the larger village of Leyburn fitted three garments on her that she'd commissioned right after Achilles had departed. Susanna's goal was to have the dresses ready for him when he returned, but she wasn't so sure he would be happy to see that one of her new garments was rather lewd.

Even if it was spectacularly beautiful.

"That is the style, my lady," the seamstress assured her as the woman's assistant hemmed up the bottom of the garment to suit Susanna's height. "You are positively exquisite in it."

Susanna wasn't so sure. Looking down at herself, she ran her hand over the fabric, which was very expensive. She had paid a lot for it. It was a very fine woolen weave that was soft, and had a bit of give to it, so that it clung gracefully to her figure. It was a medium shade of green, quite lovely, and the seamstress had explained that it had been dyed with crushed chamomile and, not strangely, grass that had been boiled down.

The sleeves of the garment were long and snug, but then there was an extra layer of fabric over them that the seamstress called "angel's wings". They were big, drapey and, indeed, looked like wings. The entire dress was utterly beautiful and utterly impractical, but the shade had been chosen to show off her hair color and Susanna hoped that Achilles would be pleased even if it did show off a little too much flesh. But as much as she had been looking forward to dressing like a woman and learning to act like one, the reality of it was quite different.

It was going to take some getting used to.

There were two other garments that the seamstress had brought with her, a yellow brocade and a blue silk nearly the exact shade of Susanna's eyes. Both of them were of the latest fashion, or so Susanna was told, and they came with belts and hose and even shoes. When Susanna told the seamstress that she planned to wear her boots with her new dresses, the woman looked so stricken that Susanna decided to wear the matching dainty slippers so the woman wouldn't weep.

It had been a month since Achilles had left, time enough for the dresses to be commissioned and time enough for Susanna to wish with all her heart that Achilles would return to her very soon. Every day that passed saw her watching the gates, becoming excited every time a visitor came to Aysgarth and then disappointment set in when she realized it wasn't Achilles.

And then, there was Meggie.

Meggie Greenhow was her name and she was a friend of the seamstress, who went by the name of Mistress Bron. When Susanna had first found her way into Mistress Bron's seamstress stall in Leyburn, a very awkward conversation had ensued that had Susanna essentially telling the woman that she had no idea how to dress, or act, like a lady. It hadn't been in those exact words, but the message had been obvious, and Mistress Bron had immediately taken charge of the situation, especially when Susanna had pulled out her purse to pay for the dresses to be commissioned.

Sensing money to be made, Mistress Bron endeared herself to Susanna hugely.

After promising to sew her dresses, she sent for a friend, who happened to be Meggie. Meggie had been a lady's maid at Kendal Castle for the lord's daughter but when the daughters had married, Meggie's services were no longer required. Displaced, she'd returned to her birthplace of Leyburn to work in her father's tavern.

Meggie hated the tavern, however, and was more than happy to offer her services to Susanna, who really felt as if she had little choice but to accept. With Mistress Bron pushing on one side and Meggie begging on the other, Susanna accepted Meggie's service simply to shut them up. But it was also because she knew she needed their help, as difficult as it was for her to admit it. Susanna de Tiegh never needed help with anything, but she needed help now. Meggie had happily returned to Aysgarth Castle with Susanna to immediately begin her duties of tending her new mistress.

And that had been quite a process.

Everything Meggie did was modeled after the de Reimfrid daughter of Kendal Castle. Whatever Meggie had done for the young woman, she did for Susanna, and that included daily washings, constant hair brushing, hair dressing, face scrubbing, and most appallingly, removing unwanted hair from the eyebrows.

Susanna had been forced to endure Meggie plucking stray hairs from her eyebrows which, in the end, looked rather nicely groomed, but the entire process had been horrifically painful. Meggie had also suggested hair removal from her underarms and Venus Mound, as many fine women did such a thing, but Susanna had balked at that. She wasn't about to endure being plucked in private places.

The very idea made her shudder.

But her days with Meggie had been interesting and educational, nonetheless. Meggie was a little older than Susanna, rather plump and with a hooked nosed, but she had a bright smile and as Susanna got to know the woman, she could see that Meggie really only had her best interests at heart. She never sensed Meggie was out for money as she did with Mistress Bron, but that she simply had a desire to be of service. So, Susanna let her.

And then, there were the lessons.

Meggie had never fostered, so everything she'd learned had been from ladies who had. She knew how to play alquerque, a type of board game, and she knew how to play card games. Susanna knew how to roll dice and gamble, but Meggie frowned upon that, so Susanna was forced to learn more ladylike pursuits.

Meggie knew how to sew and she taught Susanna basic methods, which turned into horror pieces because Susanna had no aptitude for such things. Meggie knew a few songs so she tried to teach Susanna, but the woman had no voice, so the singing lessons were quickly stopped. Meggie also knew many romantic stories and she would tell Susanna of them on days when Susanna seemed particularly glum, not realizing that the stories of lovers were driving Susanna into an even deeper gloom.

Susanna had never mentioned Achilles to Meggie, so it wasn't as if the maid knew how the romantic tales hurt. In spite of everything, however, Susanna and Meggie had become friends and Susanna was learning to trust her. The only friends Susanna had ever known were her former charge, Cadelyn, and another young woman at Castle Rising named Lily-Elsie. But that was it; those were the only women she'd ever had frequent and personal contact with. She'd only been part of Lady Cadelyn's entourage but, now, she was building a little entourage of her own with Meggie.

Truthfully, she wasn't unhappy about it.

On this particular day, the weather was unseasonably warm as Susanna continued to stand on the stool as the assistant sewed her hem. Her thoughts drifted to Achilles as they so often did and she wondered if today would be the day that he would finally return for her. Mistress Bron was supervising the hemming while Meggie was in and out of the chamber because it was wash day and she had insisted that Susanna's bed linens be washed. Meggie was a bit of a tyrant that way. As Susanna stood on the stool with increasing impatience, Meggie swept into the chamber with a pile of linens in her arms. She came to a dead stop when she saw Susanna in her new green dress.

"How beautiful, my lady!" she gasped. "The green is perfect for you!"

Susanna smiled wanly. "You do not think that it shows... well, that the neck is too low?"

Meggie stood back, peering at the top of the dress. "You have perfect breasts, my lady," she said. "The dress shows this."

Susanna sighed faintly, looking the least bit perturbed. Meggie was becoming a bit adept at reading her mistress these days and could see that she wasn't pleased.

"If you do not like the way it fits, I am sure Mistress Bron can fix it," she said quickly, looking at Mistress Bron. "If my lady is not comfortable with the plunge of the neck, you can certainly fix it, can't you?"

Mistress Bron was a creator and didn't like to have her creations tampered with. Frowning, she went to take another look at the neckline as Meggie did the same. Together, they peered at Susanna's breasts, something that made her exceedingly uncomfortable. It was even worse when they started tugging and poking.

"I supposed I could put a piece of fabric that would make it so she is not so exposed," Mistress Bron finally said unhappily. "But it will ruin the lines of the dress. The bodice is perfect just the way it is."

Meggie was a friend of Mistress Bron, but she served Susanna, so that was where her loyalty lay. "But if the lady wishes it, you will do it?" she pressed.

Mistress Bron folded her arms stiffly. "If she wishes it."

Meggie smiled triumphantly, looking to Susanna. "Do you want her to put a piece of fabric to cover the swell of your bosom, my lady?"

Susanna did. But Mistress Bron was clearly unhappy with her and, given that the woman knew fashion, Susanna didn't want to look foolish. The garment really was beautiful and if adding a piece of fabric to it would ruin it, Susanna didn't want to do that. Reluctantly, she shook her head.

"I suppose not," she said. "If Mistress Bron believes it will look better this way, then I will trust her."

It was Mistress Bron's turn to smile triumphantly as she turned back to the hemming. Meggie simply shrugged and headed over to the big bed with its overly-stuffed mattress.

"You may as well keep the dress on, my lady, because your brother has visitors," she said as she put the linens on the bed. "I saw them coming through the gatehouse as I came in from the kitchen yard."

Susanna turned to look at her with surprise. "You are sure they are for my brother?"

Meggie nodded. "Already, he was being sent for. I could hear the men shouting."

Susanna's heart fell a little. "Who are they?"

Meggie shook out one of the freshly washed sheets. "I do not know," she said. "But I am sure you can wear that lovely garment to the great hall and find out for yourself."

Susanna looked down at herself, greeted by the tantalizing view of her white cleavage. She wanted to go into the hall to see who the visitors were, hoping beyond hope that it might be Achilles in spite of what Meggie said. But she was vastly uncomfortable venturing out of her chamber clad in what she considered a revealing dress. For a woman who had dressed in tunics and breeches for most of her life, dressing in feminine finery was going to be more difficult than she thought.

Still, she'd spent the money on the garments.

Better not to waste it.

"Is the hem nearly finished?" she asked Mistress Bron.

The woman peered down at the hem of the skirt, elaborately finished in tiny stitches. "It looks to be," she said, running an expert hand along it as her assistant cut the final thread with a sharp knife. "Aye, it looks just fine."

Susanna came down off the stool, looking at herself in a bronze mirror positioned near the hearth. The mirror used to belong to her mother and she'd had it brought down from a storage chamber. Now, with her new dress on, an entirely different person was staring back in the reflection.

Susanna turned from side to side, looking at the way the dress draped over her figure. It was rather pleasing, even if it was uncomfortably revealing. Meggie had dressed her hair that morning, so the usually untamed curls had been brushed and brushed again, oil applied to smooth them out, and then braided in a thick braid that draped over one shoulder while a smaller braid looped around her head. It was an elaborate style, but the more Susanna looked at herself with her groomed brows, groomed hair, and new gown, the more she began to see just how far she'd come from that rough Blackchurch warrior.

In fact, the plunging neckline didn't look so bad to her now.

"Well?" Mistress Bron came to stand next to her, also looking at the reflection. "What do you think of it?"

Susanna smiled faintly. "I think it is very pretty," she said. "And I think I need to have more clothing made, only make it clothing that is not so elaborate. Something simple that is durable and easily worn, and I do not have to fret if it becomes dirty."

Mistress Bron nodded in agreement, seeing more coinage in her coffers in that request. "I can make you two or three simple gowns from linen or a light wool," she said. "Tell me, my lady – is there any of your mother's old clothing left behind? Mayhap packed away in trunks somewhere?"

Susanna cocked her head thoughtfully. "I do not know," she said. "She died when I was so young. I do not know what has become of her clothing."

Mistress Bron smoothed at one of her sleeves. "If there is something left, mayhap I can look at it and see if it would be serviceable to you. If not, then mayhap you will sell it to me for other women to wear."

Susanna nodded. "I will see what I can discover about it," she said. "Meanwhile, return next week and bring me some samples of fabric for dresses that are more durable."

"I will, my lady."

With that, Mistress Bron went to pack up her things as her assistant brought Meggie the remaining two garments to be hung on a peg. Susanna spent a few more seconds watching her reflection in the mirror before turning for the door.

"Meggie, I will be down in the hall," she said as she lifted the latch. "And Mistress Bron, I thank you for your hard work. I am quite pleased with it."

Mistress Bron smiled humbly. "Thank you, Lady Susanna."

With that, Susanna left the women in her chamber and headed to the narrow steps that led to the floor below. She almost forgot to gather her skirts so she wouldn't trip, remembering at the last moment and taking the steps rather quickly. She was thinking that her brother was going to be quite surprised to see her in feminine attire for the first time, but as she headed out of the apartment block, she inevitably passed by the chamber where she and Achilles had made love.

In fact, she came to a halt because the door was open. The very bed that they had used was in front of her and she stared at it a moment, reliving those moments, feeling her chest swell with the lush memories of the man and his touch. A smile played on her lips at the lingering recollection until she finally pulled herself away, continuing from the apartments.

The courtyard outside was dusty and dry, and she quickly realized that the dust was gathering on the bottom of her skirt as she walked. Frustrated, she hiked her skirt up but then realized it was too high and she was showing most of her legs. Dropping the skirts, she tried not to kick up the dirt as she walked all the way to the hall. Being a lady in a fine dress was more difficult than she realized. By the time she reached the hall, she was literally tiptoeing and she stepped inside to immediately brush off the bottom of her skirt.

She heard a voice.

"Susanna?" Samuel was all the way over by the hearth, now coming towards her. "God's Bones, Susanna... is that you?"

Susanna stood straight, facing her brother with a somewhat shy smile on her face. "It is me," she said. "I told you I was having dresses commissioned. Did you not believe me?"

Samuel's expression told of his answer before he even spoke a word. "I confess, I did not," he said, looking her up and down. "I did not believe a word of it, but now... look at you. I have never seen you look like this. You are actually lovely."

Coming from Samuel, that was quite a compliment and Susanna blushed, both embarrassed and flattered.

"Thank you," she said, noticing a man over by the hearth. Realizing that it was not Achilles, she tried not to let her disappointment show. "I see that you have a visitor. I will not trouble you."

Samuel reached out and grasped her hand. "No trouble," he said. "Come with me. I should like to introduce my beautiful sister."

Susanna let him drag her across the floor, but as they neared the visitor, she tripped on the long hem of her gown. Chagrinned, she lifted up the skirt slightly, trying very hard to behave as if she knew what she was doing. The last thing she wanted to do was make an arse out of herself in front of her brother's guest.

"Witton," Samuel said. "I do not believe you have ever met my sister. Susanna, this is my dear and close friend, Witton de Meynell."

De Meynell. Susanna went into full warrior mode as she heard that name. Outwardly, she didn't react but, inwardly, she stiffened as if preparing for the battle to come. The same man whose knights had challenged her back at The Horse's Arse, the same knights she and Achilles and Alexander had summarily defeated. She began to wonder if one or more of the survivors had accompanied their liege to Aysgarth and she was well on her guard.

She had to force herself to be polite to the man.

"My lord," she greeted evenly. "It is an honor to meet you."

Witton de Meynell was a son of a very old family. Tall, with a crown of thinning red hair, his dark eyes raked Susanna in a way that made her skin crawl. She was looking right at the man as he focused on her exposed cleavage.

"My lady," he greeted in a voice that was dripping with filth. "I had no idea that Samuel even had a sister. God's Bones, Sam – where have you been hiding her?"

Samuel looked at Susanna as he fumbled for a reply. No man wanted to tell a friend that his sister was a fully-trained knight and had been off following manly pursuits. There was something quite shameful in that.

"She has been in Norfolk," he said simply. "But she has returned home and I am very happy to have her back. Do we look alike? She is my twin, you know."

Witton shook his head. "She is far more beautiful than you are," he said, reaching out to take Susanna by the elbow and direct her over to the feasting table. "Come, my lady. Sit and tell me of yourself. I want to know everything."

Susanna looked at Samuel with a bit of apprehension as she allowed de Meynell to lead her to the table. Samuel followed and the three of them sat, although Susanna was forced to sit bolt-upright because the bodice of her dress was rather tight and fitted. She felt as if she were in a vise, resisting the urge to tug at it.

"There is not much to tell, my lord," she said. "I have lived an uneventful life."

De Meynell waved her off. "I do not believe that," he said. "Tell me of your life in Norfolk. What did you do there? And surely you brought your husband back with you to Aysgarth?"

The man was probing her and she didn't like it. "I am not married, my lord," she said. "And my life at Norfolk was rather dull. It is a wild place, as you know. Nothing as exciting as London or even York. I lived at Castle Rising and served Lady Summerlin."

De Meynell seemed to be listening intently. "No husband? I find that shocking."

He was focused on one thing and one thing only. Susanna was trying very hard not to flush with shame. She wanted very much to blurt out that she would soon have a husband when Achilles returned, but she kept her mouth shut.

Now was not the time.

"Please," she said. "Let us not speak of me. I am much more interested in hearing of you and your family. I seemed to remember that, as a child, Whorlton Castle belonged to the de Meynell family. Samuel, do you remember that Father even took us there once?"

As Samuel nodded, de Meynell spoke up. "I was born at Whorlton, but I do not recall ever seeing you there as a child," he said. "I would have remembered you. It is possible that I was already fostering at the time."

"Where did you foster, my lord?"

"Gotha," he said. "My maternal grandmother was from Thuringia, so in my early years, I fostered at Wartburg Castle. Have you ever been to Thuringia, my lady?"

Susanna shook her head, but as he spoke, an idea occurred to her. All of those foreign soldiers in the training grounds below Aysgarth were Teutonic. In the weeks she'd spent at Aysgarth, she'd done a bit of reconnaissance of her own in the form of daily walks down to the field, pretending only to be mildly interested in where the men were from and being told by one of them, who spoke her language, that they were from Gotha. In that same conversation, she had asked the man why he was in England and he'd been coy in his response. He told her to ask her lord.

But she hadn't.

Susanna didn't want Samuel to know she'd been wandering, even though he surely must have known. She passed in and out of the gatehouse daily and the soldiers there had seen her. But she'd kept it all very casual, only making it to the field after she'd wandered into the trees and picked flowers. She had to make it seem as if she really wasn't interested in what was going on when the truth was that she was gathering as much information as she could for William Marshal.

Once a spy, always a spy.

But she hadn't sent the man any information as of yet. She truthfully felt as if she didn't have enough to send him, only enough to tell him what Achilles and Alexander had probably already told him – that there were foreign mercenaries at Aysgarth. She'd told Achilles that she believed her brother was part of something bigger, that the gathering of mercenaries wasn't something he had masterminded, and when de Meynell mentioned that he'd fostered in Gotha, the light of understanding gleamed in her mind.

They mercenaries were coming from de Meynell.

"I have never been beyond France, my lord," she replied belatedly to de Meynell's question. "Is it beautiful at Wartburg?"

If de Meynell sensed that her mind was elsewhere, he didn't give any indication. He simply smiled at her and moved closer.

"Quite beautiful," he said. "There are great mountains and great rivers. You would belong in a place like that because there is such wild beauty. The men there would appreciate you greatly."

Susanna was uncomfortable with the way he was looking at her, so she smiled weakly. "And your wife, my lord?" she asked pointedly to get him off her scent. "Is she from Gotha?"

That took some of the lascivious gleam out of de Meynell's eyes. "What makes you believe I am married?"

"Because you are a great lord from a great house. Surely you would be married."

"Samuel is not married."

She glanced at her brother. "He should be."

As Samuel cocked a disapproving eyebrow, de Meynell spoke up.

"In answer to your question, my wife is indeed from Wartburg," he said. "Her father is the Count of Gotha. A very powerful man who rules his people with a firm hand. He is not unlike a king, in fact."

"Is Wartburg a big castle?"

"The biggest," de Meynell said. "I was there for several years. I suppose it is in my blood, given that my grandmother is part of their family. But I returned to England and spent time at Nottingham and Lincoln before assuming command of Whorlton when my father died. And now you know everything about me and I no longer wish to speak of myself. I wish to speak of you."

Perhaps he did, but Susanna wasn't finished with him. She sought to play the naïve conversationalist, wondering if she could play it convincingly even though she fully intended to interrogate him.

"It is interesting that you mention Gotha," she said thoughtfully. "I have taken many walks since I have returned home and I have spoken to the soldiers in the training field. They told me they were from Gotha. Are they your soldiers, then?"

De Meynell didn't hesitate. "From my father-in-law," he said. "Whorlton is not big enough to house them all, so some have been moved here to Aysgarth."

"I have watched the men train and they seem to fight differently from English troops. They wear different clothing, I mean."

"A little."

"Are they here to help train my brother's English troops in different warfare methods, then?"

De Meynell lifted his shoulders noncommittally. "There are always little wars going about in England," he said. "That is what they are here for."

Susanna played the wide-eyed innocent. "*Are* there wars going on here? I had not heard that."

"Silly girl. We must always be prepared for a hostile neighbor. Or subdue a king who must be tamed. Has your brother not told you that?"

"I suppose that is true. *You* are not the hostile neighbor we must be prepared for, are you?"

She said it laughingly, as if teasing him, and he rose to it. "You never know," he said. "With the size of Gotha's army, I could be king of the north someday. But no more talk of business. Let us speak of pleasure. Tell me something about yourself that no one else knows, my lady. I wish to hear a secret."

With that, he put his hand on her leg, mid-thigh, but his long fingers were pointed towards her Venus Mound. In fact, they were quite close, and Susanna wasn't going to tolerate that kind of aggressiveness, not even from a friend of her brother's.

Especially not from de Meynell.

The mood of the light conversation between them plummeted and with a cold smile on her lips, Susanna leaned towards him as if to whisper. He eagerly leaned forward, as well. Her lips were near his ear when she murmured.

"If you do not remove your fingers, I have the skill to break every bone in your hand."

De Meynell's eyes widened as the hand was quickly removed. "What?" he demanded, incredulous. "Did you threaten me? Samuel, did you hear what she said?"

Susanna was finished with the conversation, disgusted by the company and by de Meynell's vulgar behavior. She stood up rapidly, practically shoving de Meynell aside as she did so. Samuel, who hadn't heard what she'd said, stood up as well.

"Susanna!" he said. "What did you say? Tell me immediately!"

She looked at her brother with absolutely no patience. "Is this how you allow a guest to treat your sister?" she fired back. "Tell him to keep his hands to himself or I am most capable of breaking them. Mayhap you had better tell him the truth about me, Brother, so he will not mistake me for an easy target in the future."

Samuel looked at de Meynell. "Did you touch her?"

De Meynell was outraged but he could see that he might not have Samuel's support in the matter. "An innocent touch, I assure you," he insisted. "But she threatened to break my hand."

Samuel sighed sharply. "I will not tolerate lewd behavior towards my sister," he said. "She will not tolerate it, either. And she is fully capable of breaking your hands and your neck, so you may wish to apologize for your forwardness, Witton."

De Meynell was looking between the pair with both great outrage and great curiosity. "Apologize? For a hand that slipped?"

It was clear that Samuel didn't believe him, which led Susanna to suspect that de Meynell may have had little self-control when it came to women. This kind of thing must have happened before and, certainly, he'd been quite solicitous of her from the moment they were introduced. But it was also clear that Samuel wasn't surprised that de Meynell was attempting to play the victim.

"Then be sure your hand, or anything else, does not slip again," Samuel said. "My sister is a Blackchurch-trained warrior. When I trained there, so did she. She is one of the most capable warriors you will ever meet, Witton, so do not take her for a weak woman. It would be a grave mistake."

As soon as Samuel told de Meynell of her true background, Susanna turned and headed out of the hall, picking up her skirts so she wouldn't trip this time. She didn't want to hear the ensuing conversation. Frankly, she didn't care.

Her point had been made.

She wasn't leaving simply because she was outraged at de Meynell's behavior. She was leaving because she was anxious to write a missive to The Marshal to tell him what she knew.

She finally had something to tell the man.

CHAPTER EIGHT

H E WAS STILL here.
It was nearing suppertime and the warm day had transitioned into a mild and clear night. Susanna was in her bower, where she'd been since leaving her brother and de Meynell in the hall a few hours earlier. One of the windows in her chamber faced the hall and she'd been keeping an eye on it to see if de Meynell ever left.

So far, she hadn't seen him.

But the truth was that she had been focused on something else so she hadn't spent all of her time staring out of the window. She had a lovely writing kit that she'd brought from Castle Rising, something she traveled with, and the kit had been opened to reveal several pieces of fine parchment, lying flat at the bottom of the box, and then a secured shelf in the box that contained ink phials, quill, sand, wax, and the stamp that used to belong to her mother. The entire kit, in fact, had belonged to her mother, the one thing she had of the woman.

It was her prized possession.

The stamp was a finely crafted item of an angel with a harp in his hand, with a big "B" in the harp for de Bowland. Her mother had been a de Bowland, a fine Cumberland family, and as Susanna used the quill and the precious parchment, scratching out a missive to Caius d'Avignon of Richmond Castle, begging him to deliver the enclosed information to William Marshal, she could feel her mother's strength behind her.

That wasn't something she often felt.

She'd chosen Richmond Castle for a reason – it was the largest royal bastion in the area, with direct ties to William Marshal, and she was certain d'Avignon would send her message along. Even if he was no longer there, surely the present commander would sense the urgency of the matter. Given that Richmond wasn't far from either Aysgarth or Whorlton, it would be critical news for them.

Far more critical than anyone realized.

Even as Susanna wrote the careful words, she felt apprehensive, something that was foreign to her. So much of her world had been covering up her feelings, pretending things didn't bother her because having trained in a world of men, she had been expected to have their callous attitude.

Especially at Blackchurch – she was proud to have trained there, but the truth was that it had been horrifically difficult. She had to endure things that would have crushed most women, but Susanna refused to let such things crush her. She was strong and resilient, and she liked to think she got that from her mother. Her father had been a rather weak man who liked his drink, but her mother... Isabail de Bowland had been a rock.

She'd inherited more from her mother than she knew.

It took nerves of steel to do what she was doing, sending a missive to William Marshal under the very nose of her brother, especially when she'd taken great pains to make it clear that she did not support the king in any way. In fact, the story she'd given Samuel about her wound was that she'd been in the knight's quarters at Castle Rising when one of the knights had spoken in support of the king.

Having had too much to drink, Susanna had challenged the man and demanded he speak of anything great John had ever done in his lifetime. One thing had led to another, and a fight had ensued. De Winter had released her from her oath because she had started the fight.

And that was the story she stuck to.

Samuel had believed her because he'd had no reason not to, and it was a trust she'd carefully cultivated. After what happened tonight, however, she was going to have to take advantage of that trust by sending a missive to The Marshal because clearly, de Meynell was up to something.

Mayhap a king who must be tamed.

That quietly-uttered sentence told her what the man's intentions were.

Sitting at a small table in her chamber, the same small table where she used to sit with her mother and eat her meals when her father didn't want his womenfolk down in the hall, Susanna carefully finished the missive as Meggie sat by the fire and tried to clean the dirt that had gathered on the skirt of her new green dress. Susanna sat in a heavy linen shift and a robe that belonged to her brother, too big for her, as she listened to the faint sounds of the crowded hall wafting over the bailey.

"You have been very busy writing, my lady," Meggie said. "Some of your poems must not have been successful."

Susanna looked up from the parchment in confusion. "Poems?"

Meggie pointed to the hearth where Susanna had already burned two half-finished missives because she didn't like the wording. Parchment was so precious, but she couldn't take the chance that the missive would fall into the wrong hands.

"Those," Meggie said. "It smells strange when it burns. The parchment, I mean. It smells like burning flesh."

Susanna didn't have much to say to that. She turned back to her missive. "I think this poem will be perfect," she said. Then, she paused, eyeing her enthusiastic new servant. "Meggie… I must ask you to do something for me."

"Anything, my lady."

"I must send this missive to the commander of Richmond Castle," she said, playing coy. "He is a special friend and this… this poem has been for him. I do not want my brother to know for fear he will become enraged with me. After all, it is unseemly for a lady to send a man a… poem. It would be a terrible thing for Samuel to know."

Meggie lit up with glee. "Is he your lover, my lady?" she gasped. "Why have you not told me about him before?"

Susanna pretended to be bashful. "Because I was afraid to," she said. "Meggie, this is very important. I want you to find someone to send this missive to him, right away. Do you know of anyone who could take this to him?"

Meggie nodded eagerly. "I have a younger brother who could take it to him," she said. "He is dependable."

"Good," Susanna said. "I will pay him a silver coin if he will do this swiftly. But, Meggie… you must keep this a secret. You must not let anyone know. I greatly fear that not only will my brother become angry with me, but he could very well become angry with Richmond. I do not want to cause a conflict."

Meggie shook her head sincerely. "Nay, my lady. I promise I will not tell a soul."

Susanna smiled. "Excellent," she said. "Tell your brother that he must deliver this missive to Richmond before my love marries another woman. Time is of the essence. He must read my… my poem if our romance is to flourish."

She made it sound both romantic and tragic at the same time, which fed Meggie's foolish heart. Susanna was clever in that she knew a romantic secret would be kept much better than something that didn't have an emotional pull.

Finishing the missive, she read over it carefully as Meggie chattered on about her brother and how the lad didn't want to work in their father's tavern, either. He wanted to be a soldier. She assured Susanna that she would leave at dawn and take the missive to Leyburn so her brother could be on his way before the day was out. If the weather remained good and all signs were favorable, he would be delivering it to Richmond by nightfall.

Susanna could only pray that everything went as planned.

The secure rule of a king might depend on it.

Once the missive was sanded and sealed, she tucked it into her bed and sent Meggie for some food. Dismissing the maid when the woman returned, Susanna ate alone in front of the fire, thinking on the missive, on Achilles, anxious to tell him what she'd discovered that day.

She was certain he would insist on marrying her immediately and taking her from Aysgarth, and she certainly wasn't opposed to that. She'd been daydreaming regularly about the life they would have together after they were married, wondering if they would end up at Blackwell Castle with his family or if she and Achilles would still continue to serve William Marshal. Perhaps they would even go to Scotland and find Kress and Cadelyn.

The future held endless possibilities and she was more than ready.

Susanna watched the fire crackle, seriously considering going to bed, when there was a soft knock at the door. Rising wearily, she padded across the floor to answer it herself.

Samuel was standing in the darkness outside.

"Sam?" she said curiously. "What is it?"

Samuel looked exhausted and he smelled heavily of alcohol. "You did not come to the hall to eat."

Susanna shook her head. "Nay," she said. "I assumed de Meynell was still there and I did not wish to eat with him. I am sure you can understand that."

Samuel sighed heavily and pushed his way into the chamber. Susanna stood back, watching him with some concern, before quietly shutting the door behind him.

"You do not understand, Susanna," Samuel said after a moment.

"What do I not understand?"

"De Meynell. We must treat him… carefully."

"Please, tell me why."

Samuel came to a stop at the little table where Susanna had written the missive earlier. At the moment, it contained the remains of her meal, including a pitcher of wine that was half-empty. Samuel poured some into her cup and took a long swallow.

"I have a confession," he said. "When Father died, he left us a tidy sum of money and I was not wise with it."

"What do you mean?"

"I mean that I was foolish. Stupid." He heaved a great sigh. "Do you know how I met de Meynell? In a gambling den in York. That should tell you how stupid I was with Father's money."

Susanna wasn't quite sure what he was driving at. "It is your money to do as you please," she said. "There is no judgement here."

He waved her off. "I know you would not," he said. "But it was more than the money. It was what it represented. When Father died, I found myself with responsibilities I did not want and I suppose I rebelled. I spent far too much time in that gambling den, Susanna. It was like a disease. The more money I lost, the more I gambled."

Susanna came away from the door, looking at her brother with great concern. "Samuel, what are you trying to tell me?"

Samuel sank into the nearest chair. "I am telling you that the money is gone," he muttered. "Worse still, I gambled away Aysgarth. To de Meynell. The castle and the Coverdale barony belong to him now and that is why you see his army in the fields below the castle. In fact, nearly all of the men at Aysgarth belong to him. I am here simply as his garrison commander."

Susanna was shocked. "Aysgarth is no longer yours?" she hissed. "Why did you not tell me this before?"

Samuel wouldn't look at her. "Because I am ashamed," he said. "Or mayhap I was too afraid. I did not want you to know, but after what happened today with de Meynell, I am forced to confess. He is our liege, Susanna, and you must be tolerant of him. I know that is a lot to ask but, for my sake, I beg you. Be tolerant."

Susanna could hardly believe what she was hearing. Stunned, she made her way over to the table and sat in the opposite chair.

"Oh... Samuel," she breathed. "I do not know what to say."

Samuel looked at her, then. "Mayhap it is best you say nothing," he said. "I know you are disappointed in me. I am disappointed in myself. Everything we had now belongs to de Meynell."

Susanna could see the abject shame in her brother's face. She'd told Achilles that Samuel was more of a follower than a leader, in spite being Blackchurch-trained, but even she didn't imagine the scope of his propensity to be a follower. He'd followed and gambled and ignored responsibility to the point of losing everything.

Susanna felt nothing but pity for him.

"This army from Gotha," she said. "Why is he keeping it here? What is he planning, Sammy?"

Sammy. She hadn't called him that in years but, at the moment, it seemed appropriate. It was a softly comforting nickname and he seemed very much in need of such comfort.

"Robert Fitzwalter is raising a rebellion against John," he said hoarsely. "You know who Fitzwalter is, don't you?"

Susanna nodded slowly. "He's a powerful man in London," she said. "He also controls a good deal of Essex. De Winter has spoken of his hatred of the king."

"It is worse than that," Samuel said. "He has allies in the north, including de Meynell. He also has ties to the Guy de Penthièvre, Duke of Brittany. You know that the dukes have periodically held Richmond Castle; sometimes it belongs to them, or sometimes the English king takes it back. That has been happening since the Duke of Normandy came to England's shores. Right now, it is a crown property, but not for long. Not only are Whorlton and Aysgarth staging grounds for a mercenary army from Thuringia, but the Duke of Brittany has promised French troops because he wants Richmond Castle back and he plans to take it by force. The French are expected in Middlesbrough by Christmas."

For the second time in as many minutes, Susanna was stunned. This was exactly the kind of information she had been looking for, now given so freely by her drunk and despondent brother. All she could think of was that missive she'd scribed to the commander of Richmond Castle, now tucked away safely in her bed. She had to make sure this information made it into that missive.

It was news of explosive proportions.

"Are you certain?" she finally asked. "Why would de Meynell involve himself in Brittany's issue?"

Samuel shrugged. "Because he has been promised French lands. That is simple enough, for he is a greedy bastard. He helps re-establish Brittany in Yorkshire and Fitzwalter has an ally when the barons rebel against John."

Susanna stared at him, overwhelmed. "Are you participating in all of this?"

Samuel kept his head down. "I am expected to lead men, aye," he said, looking up at her. "I do not want to be part of this, Susanna, but I have no choice. I serve de Meynell now."

"Over a gambling debt?" Susanna said, both outraged and incredulous. "I cannot believe this. How much do you owe him? What would it take to buy back Aysgarth?"

Samuel shook his head. "I have not asked him," he said. "I have not had the courage to. Mayhap I will ask him someday."

Susanna could see the defeat in her brother, but it wasn't just defeat – it was surrender. He had surrendered everything – his home, his pride – everything. And from what she could see, he had no intention of doing anything about it.

"Why not now?" she insisted. "Why would you not want to regain Aysgarth?"

Samuel brushed her off. "Because I am afraid that I will gamble it away again. If I could give it to you, Susanna, I would. You would have made an astonishing Baron Coverdale. A pity you were not born a man."

Susanna was feeling a good deal of frustration mingled with the sorrow she was feeling for him. The Samuel she had known her entire life had never been this complacent, willing to accept what life had dealt him. She always thought her brother had some fire in him; when he'd trained at Blackchurch, he'd had that fire. It had never been very strong, and he was one of the weaker men in training, but he was never a complete defeatist like he was now.

She didn't even recognize him now.

"I will think of something, Sammy," she finally said. "Give me time and I will think of something. I don't want you to worry."

Samuel shook his head. "When you are here, I never do," he said. "I am glad you have come home, Susu. Tell me you are home to stay."

Susu. Susanna hadn't heard that since she'd been a child. She smiled faintly. "I am home for as long as I can remain," she said. "Meanwhile, I want you to go to bed and sleep peacefully. Know that I will determine what needs to be done. I will help you, Sammy, I swear it."

"And you will be nice to de Meynell?"

Her smile faded. "I will not antagonize him, but if he puts his hands on me again, I cannot promise you that I will not fight back."

Samuel simply nodded in resignation, finally pushing himself off of the chair as Susanna looped her arm through his, walking him to the door. She kissed him on the cheek before letting him go, watching his slumped figure head off into the darkness.

A man with the weight of his lost legacy on his shoulders.

As soon as he disappeared from view, Susanna shut the door and quickly headed back to the missive she'd stowed in her bed. Pulling it forth, she rushed to collect her writing kit again, setting it back on the table and carefully breaking the seal on the missive.

There was some room at the bottom for her to include what her brother had told her, so she collected a quill and wrote a couple of sentences down by her signature. Careful not to smudge it, she sanded the ink and shook it off, blowing at it until it dried completely. Sealing the missive back up, she left her chamber and went on the hunt for Meggie.

The situation had changed.

Fortunately, Meggie wasn't far. There was an alcove near the stairs where the servants slept in order to be close to their lords and ladies, and she found Meggie curled on a pallet on the floor. The maid was groggy at first but then greatly concerned to see her lady. Susanna wouldn't tell her what the matter was until she pulled her back to her chamber and shut the door.

Then, it all came out.

Instead of waiting for morning, Susanna wanted Meggie to ride to Leyburn this very night. It was a clear night and the weather was good, so the short ride into the village should hardly take more than an hour at a clipped pace.

Susanna was desperate to get the missive to Richmond but Meggie, of course, believed it was a lover's emergency and she was more than willing to ride to Leyburn on a bright night. Susanna gave her a few silver coins as an incentive, to be split between her and her brother, and Meggie took them eagerly.

Wrapped up in a dark cloak, the maid followed Susanna from the apartments and down to the outer bailey, where Susanna passed another silver coin to one of the stable grooms to prepare a mount for Meggie and keep silent about it.

Considering what was happening, the sooner the message was out of the fortress, the better.

There was no time to waste.

Unfortunately, Susanna's movements from the keep had caught someone's attention.

A knight at the gatehouse that guarded the keep had been in the guard room when Susanna and Meggie had passed through. He thought he recognized Susanna, watching her movements as she headed down to the stables with another woman. She wasn't hard to miss with that rich, red hair, not even at night when the moon was full and the torches were burning brightly all around.

Surprised as well as stunned, he stood at the gatehouse, watching and waiting to see if she'd make another appearance and finally being rewarded when she emerged from the stables and headed back towards the keep.

As she drew near, the knight ducked back into the guard room so she wouldn't see him, coming out only when she passed by and headed back up to the keep.

Then, his suspicions were confirmed – he'd seen the woman in Skipton a couple of months ago with the two Pembroke knights. He'd been part of the group of Whorlton knights who had been in The Horse's Arse tavern, the same group that had antagonized the trio into bloody combat on the common room floor.

He'd been one of the lucky ones, however. His commander had been gored and had eventually died of an infection in his gut, two knights had been killed, while two other men were injured so badly that it was possible that they would never be able to return to duty. He had ended up on the floor, the victim of a devastating punch to the head, while only one of his companions had emerged unscathed.

It had been a harrowing evening.

But he'd returned with his injured companions to Whorlton, telling tales of the fifty men who had ambushed them. No one was willing to confess that two Pembroke knights and one woman bearing the colors of de Winter managed to triumph over them in that dingy little tavern. They were still trying to live down the shame, even if they were the only ones who really knew about it.

As luck would have it, he'd just found the de Winter woman at Aysgarth.

The knight, whose name was Henry Bellerby, had come to Aysgarth as part of the Witton de Meynell's escort. He'd mostly pushed that shameful event at Skipton out of his mind. But now… now, it all came back to him in a rush. He was the only one out of that seven-man group that had ridden escort with de Meynell, so there wasn't anyone else around who would have recognized her.

He didn't know who she was, but he was going to find out. When she passed him and headed back up to the keep, he headed straight for the stables.

He wanted to find the other woman she had been with.

She wasn't difficult to find. A small rider emerged from the stable, heading in his direction, and Bellerby recognized the cloak. The horse and rider had just come through the stable yard and were heading to the main gatehouse when he stepped in front of them, blocking their path.

"Halt," he said, grabbing the horse's reins. "Where are you going this time of night?"

The woman, plain-faced and with a hooked nose, seemed inordinately nervous. "I... I must leave," she said. "Why do you stop me?"

Bellerby didn't let go of the reins, but he stepped closer to the woman. "Because it is late at night," he said. "It is not safe for anyone to leave. *Where* are you going?"

The woman licked her lips. "My... my brother is ill," she stammered. "I am going to his aid."

"Now?"

"I just received word."

"No one has come in or out of the gatehouse in hours."

"I meant that I received it earlier today, but I have just been given permission to leave. May I go?"

Bellerby kept his grip on the reins. "That woman you were with," he said. "Who is she?"

That seemed to make the woman more nervous. "Why do you want to know?"

"Answer me or I will take you to Lord de Meynell this very moment."

She gasped, sounding terrified. "It is Lady Susanna," she said. "She is the sister of Baron Coverdale. She is very important here and you must let me pass."

His gaze lingered on her. "How long have you served her?"

"Long enough. Why are you asking me these questions?"

"Where is she residing? In the keep?"

"I am not going to tell you anything more!"

With that, Meggie tried to yank the reins away, causing the horse to start. That action almost brought her off of the animal, but she managed to keep her seat.

Unfortunately, the missive did not.

Tucked in her belt because it would not fit into her tunic, the jolting action of the horse shook the missive right out of her belt and it fell to the mud. The horse stepped on it and she yanked the animal away, diving from the horse and ending up on her knees in her haste to get to the missive.

Bellerby got to it first.

"What is this?" he asked, keeping it above her reach. "What don't you want me to see so badly?"

Meggie was in a state. "It is not for you!" she said angrily, jumping up and down. "Give it to me! It is not meant for you!"

Bellerby shoved her away by the head, hard enough to cause her to fall back and lose her balance. As she fell onto her buttocks, he flipped the missive over and noted that the horse's weight had broken the seal when the animal stepped on it.

Gleefully, he opened it up as Meggie picked herself out of the mud and threw herself at him again. She hit him hard, but it was barely enough to shake the man. He simply grabbed her by the hair to stop her from charging him again, holding fast as he began to read the missive.

"What do we have here?" he said, taunting her as he began to read. "A missive to d'Avignon? Surely this cannot be Richmond's d'Avignon?"

Meggie was struggling with him, horrified and panicked. "It is not for you!" she said. "I am going to tell the lady what you have done and you will be severely punished! Do you hear me? Stop this instant and give me back the missive!"

He was grinning, still clutching Meggie by the head. But as she struggled and he continued to read, the smile began to fade from his lips. All of the humor left his face. Once he finished reading it, he looked at Meggie with a taut expression.

"Who wrote this, Woman?" he growled.

Meggie was beating on the hand that held her by the hair. "I'll not tell you! Let me go!"

His response was to yank hard and she screamed in pain, but the action had the desired effect – she stopped moving. "Answer me," he hissed. "*Who* wrote this? Was it your lady?"

Meggie was starting to realize by the tone of his voice that something was amiss. "'Tis only a poem," she said, frowning in both anger and confusion. "You must not tell the lord."

Bellerby looked back at the missive. "Does he know about this?"

"About the poem? Of course not. She does not want anyone to know. Let me have it. I must take it to her lover at Richmond!"

Bellerby shook his head faintly, a gesture of disbelief. "So it *was* your lady."

There was no use in denying it. The next thing Meggie realized, she was being dragged across the bailey by the hair as Bellerby headed towards the keep where de Meynell was, still in the great hall. He knew his lord would be quite interested in the contents of the missive.

On behalf of himself and his colleagues, Bellerby knew precisely how to exact revenge for the beating in Skipton.

The de Winter woman was going to pay dearly.

CHAPTER NINE

Richmond Castle

"I'M SO CLOSE. *So close!*"

Achilles was having a difficult time focusing even though the massive bastion of Richmond Castle was right in front of him. It was a clear, dry morning and they'd already been traveling for hours, having departed the small village of Scotton before dawn to make their way north to Richmond.

But Achilles could only lament the fact that they were close to Aysgarth. About fifteen or sixteen miles, to be exact, and the previous night in Scotton had been equally difficult for him. He wanted to sneak away to Aysgarth simply to catch a glimpse of Susanna, but Alexander was firm with him. In fact, Alexander slept in the same room with him and every time Achilles moved, whether it was in his sleep or sitting up to use the chamber pot, Alexander was on his feet and running for the door to prevent Achilles from leaving.

It had been a restless night for all of them.

Kevin had actually remained awake the entire night, sitting in the common room in case Achilles made it past Alexander in his quest to see Susanna. He'd been fully informed of what the situation was between the two, even if he hadn't experienced it firsthand, so he knew what to expect.

And he was prepared.

Therefore, it was three exhausted men who made their way to Richmond Castle on a fine, bright morning. Richmond Castle was quite an impressive sight as they came in from the south. Emerging from a dense growth of forest that had covered the road for the past few miles, they were suddenly faced with the enormous castle on a rise overlooking the River Swale.

Honey-colored stone gleamed in the early morning light as Richmond Castle greeted the day in all her glory. England had her fair share of castles, but none so glorious as Richmond. It was one of the largest castles in the north, with twenty-foot walls spanning the perimeter. Vast didn't begin to encompass the size of the baileys; they were big enough, collectively, that a good-sized village could have fit within them. Richmond was very strategic and very important, and for good reason – she could hold a few thousand men in her bosom and no one would know anything about it until it was too late, as the Scots and early Norman enemies had discovered.

But Achilles wasn't paying any attention to the castle. He was unhappy, and longing for Susanna, and as the three of them crossed the river on a stone bridge and headed towards the main gatehouse, Achilles still wasn't having any luck at focusing on the task that lay ahead. He wasn't used to having feelings for anyone and therefore had no idea how to handle the distraction. He was feeling quite sorry for himself until Alexander slapped him right between the shoulder blades.

"Sit up and behave yourself," Alexander rumbled. "You'll not enter Richmond looking like a lovesick dog. We are about to face Cai d'Avignon and if he sees you like this, you'll never hear the end of it. Do you understand me?"

Achilles was sitting straight up in the saddle, rotating his shoulders because he could feel Alexander's handprint stinging on his back. "I understand you," he said. "You could have simply told me. You did not have to beat me."

"I have been trying to tell you for the entire ride north. You are not listening to me. I needed to get your attention."

Achilles didn't reply. He wasn't happy, unhappier still now that Alexander had taken to pummeling him. As they headed up the road that paralleled the gigantic walls of the castle, Kevin spoke with awe.

"I have never been to Richmond," he said. "What an incredible place this is. Outside of the White Tower, I've never seen a keep like that. It has to be one hundred feet tall."

Alexander looked up at the enormous keep. "It is quite large," he agreed. "It keeps watch over an equally large area."

"How many troops are held here?"

"I am not certain, but I heard once that there were two thousand, at least."

"It could easily hold that."

Coming around the walls, the entry came into view. There was a heavily-fortified barbican that one had to pass through before getting to the actual gatehouse. Once they passed through the guarded barbican, they came to the gatehouse, which was squat and thick, and built as an extension of the keep itself. It, too, was heavily-guarded but the three knights were admitted when Alexander identified himself and his purpose. Given that they were bearing Pembroke standards, they were admitted with little resistance into the immense, busy outer bailey. As a soldier went running into the keep for d'Avignon, they pulled their steeds to a halt and took a good look at their surroundings.

"God's Bones," Kevin muttered. "Heartily impressive."

Alexander nodded as he dismounted his steed. "Indeed, it is," he said. "I have not been here in quite some time, but the magnificence of this place never ceases to amaze me."

Achilles climbed off his horse, gazing off across the wide bailey and realizing he was looking south. He was probably looking straight at Aysgarth and the realization tugged at his brittle emotions. He knew Alexander was becoming irritated with him and even though Kevin had been neutral throughout the entire journey, he suspected Kevin had reached that point, as well. It wasn't that he was trying to be deliberately annoying.

His heart was simply hurting in ways he didn't understand.

"What are you looking at?"

Alexander had come up behind him, looking over his shoulder to see what Achilles was seeing. Not wanting to be lectured or worse, slapped again, Achilles thought of a plausible lie.

"The great hall," he said, pointing to the big building along the south wall. "I am thinking that I did not eat last night. Surely they will provide us with something."

Alexander nodded. "I am certain they will," he said. Then, he looked at Achilles with some remorse in his expression. "I am sorry I slapped you, but your mood needed to be dealt with. I would have slapped you in the face if I'd thought I could have gotten away with it."

Achilles managed a weak grin. "Considering I am not myself these days, you probably could have."

"Since when is Achilles de Dere not ready for a fight?"

Alexander patted him on the shoulder. "Be patient," he said quietly. "We will get to her, but we must be wise about it. You do not want to go rushing in there blindly, do you? When we return, we must have a plan, especially if de Tiegh is siding with the rebel barons. You do not know what has happened since we departed Aysgarth, so we must be updated on any and all conditions in this area before you return for her. Agreed?"

Achilles nodded reluctantly. "Agreed."

"Susanna can take care of herself, so it is not as if we are speaking of a weakling."

"God, no."

"Then stop fretting. We will get to her soon enough."

Achilles took a deep breath and nodded, forcing himself away from the sorrow and longing he'd been feeling. Or, at least he tried to. That was when he caught sight of men emerging from the keep, heading down the retractable wooden stairs quite rapidly. The smile on Achilles' face turned real.

"God's Bones," he muttered. "There he is. I would recognize that beast anywhere."

Alexander turned to see a group of men just coming off of the stairs, heading towards them at a swift pace. A very big man leading the group shouted at them.

"Sherry! Is it really you?"

Alexander laughed softly. "It is," he said. "There is no one else like me, though many have tried, including you. Kiss me, you fool."

The man who had shouted to him laughed joyfully. He was an enormous man, at least a head taller than everyone else around him, with hair and eyes as black as coal. His face was angular and strong, and the smile brilliant if not displaying charmingly crooked teeth. He opened his arms for Alexander, perhaps some of the biggest arms in all of England, and swallowed Alexander up in a powerful embrace. All the while, the two of them were giggling and grunting like fools.

"Sherry, you gorgeous creature." Caius d'Avignon didn't kiss Alexander, but he squeezed him hard enough. "How long has it been? Six, seven years? Far too long, my friend."

Alexander released the man from his fond embrace. "Nine, I believe," he said. "The last I saw of you was in Antioch. There was a matter of a house full of beautiful women and you were attempting to negotiate for every last one of them."

Caius threw his hands up in the air. "It worked, did it not?" he declared. "I had my own harem until their father came home and chased me around the house with a scimitar. But, God, it was worth it."

He snorted uncontrollably before catching sight of Achilles. Then, he shoved Alexander aside and rushed Achilles, picking him up off the ground in an enthusiastic embrace as Achilles grunted in pain.

"Achilles," he greeted happily. "My brother, my darling lad. I have missed you."

Achilles was grinning, rubbing his ribs when Caius finally let him go. "Good Christ, Cai," he said. "You nearly broke my spine."

"Really?" Caius said as if astonished. "The Achilles I knew nine years ago would have thrown a fist into my throat before saying that.

What has happened to you, lad? And where are Maxton and Kress?"

"Married," Achilles said, watching Caius' expression of shock. "Surprising, I know, but it is true. Take me inside and I shall tell you all this and more. We come bearing news from The Marshal, so someplace private, if you please."

Caius nodded, some of his happiness fading. Now, the seasoned and deadly commander was starting to take over. "Of course," he said. "It sounds serious."

"It is."

"Then follow me."

Not another word was spoken as they headed back into the keep, up the wooden steps and into a single chamber at the entry. The keep was very tall, but every floor had no more than two rooms. Caius took them up a flight of narrow stairs, built into the wall, and emerged on the floor above the entry where there was one enormous room, cluttered with a table and chairs, weapons, and a variety of other things, all of it relevant to the commander of Richmond Castle.

It was his seat of power.

One of d'Avignon's men had gone for food while a second man stood at the bottom of the steps leading up to the chamber, guarding it from unauthorized persons. Kevin, however, had followed Alexander and Achilles and although Caius didn't have any issue with his own men being part of a private meeting, he eyed Kevin dubiously as the man trickled in behind Achilles. Seeing where his attention was, Achilles made introductions.

"Cai, this is Kevin de Lara, another trusted Marshal knight," he said. "Kevin has spent time in Canterbury with David de Lohr, but he has come with us on this most important task because we may need his excellent sword. He is quite trustworthy, I assure you."

Caius' dark gaze lingered on Kevin. "De Lara," he repeated. "Are you related to Sean de Lara?"

Kevin nodded. "He is my brother, my lord."

Caius scratched his chin and turned away. "I see," he said. "I knew

Sean years ago when I first returned from The Levant. He was a good man, but that was before he decided to baptize himself in John's poison. What do they call him now? The Lord of the Shadows?"

Kevin kept his composure as they touched on the fragile subject of his brother. "All men must follow their own paths, my lord," he said evenly. "Sean has chosen his."

Caius pulled up a tall stool next to his table, which was cluttered with an array of maps, vellum, writing instruments, and more. "I am in no position to judge him, I suppose, given the sins of my past."

"The Britannia Viper," Kevin said. "I have heard."

Caius smiled without humor and looked to his table, shuffling through the maps in front of him. It was clear that his nickname, and his past, wasn't something he wanted to delve in to, so he changed the subject.

"Achilles," he said. "Tell me of Maxton and Kress. They are married, you say?"

"Indeed, they are," Achilles replied. "'Tis a long story, but they've both married well. Maxton is on the Welsh Marches with his wife and Kress is in Scotland with his. They seem to be quite happy."

Caius grunted. "They must be remarkable women to take those two," he said. "I never thought I would see the day when either of them took a bride."

"It is true, I assure you."

Caius simply lifted his eyebrows at the thought, astonishing as it was. But soon enough, his attention turned to Alexander. "Now," he said. "You said you had something important to speak of, Sherry. What is it?"

Alexander, standing near the table, pulled up a chair of his own. "We have come to you with information you should be mindful of," he said. "We were recently at Aysgarth Castle. Are you aware that there are about a thousand foreign troops there?"

Caius looked at him curiously. "Why were you at Aysgarth?"

Alexander cleared his throat softly, glancing at Achilles to see if the man wanted him to answer that question. Achilles, seeing that Alexander was uncertain about his reply, stepped forward.

"We were escorting Lady Susanna de Tiegh home," he said. "Susanna serves William Marshal. For the past ten years, she has been a bodyguard to a Marshal ward living at Castle Rising in Norfolk. Susanna is a Blackchurch-trained knight, a fearsome woman the likes of which you have never seen, and we were serving together in a recent mission where she was wounded. When she was able to travel, we escorted her home to recuperate and that is where we saw at least a thousand men, not from England. We believe they are mercenaries and we returned to tell The Marshal, who then sent us to you to ensure you knew about this."

Caius was listening carefully. After a moment he leaned forward on his table. "There is not much that happens in Yorkshire that I am not aware of," he said. "I have heard about this, but I've not had confirmation. In fact, this has been something we have been dealing with for the better part of a year."

"Dealing with what?" Achilles asked. "What is going on?"

Caius folded his enormous hands on the tabletop. "It all started a few years ago," he said. "We started hearing tale that Samuel de Tiegh was taxing his vassals heavily, which isn't too unusual with some of these local warlords. They do it to pay for their armies. But de Tiegh had very little army and even though he was taxing heavily, there was no clear reason why he would do such a thing other than the upkeep of Aysgarth. It's an impressive fortress, but given his taxation demands, it suggested something more."

"Upkeep of a fortress like that must be very expensive," Achilles said. "We were there for an evening and we ate like kings. But what about the mercenary army he seems to have? He told Alexander that it does not belong to him."

"I would believe that."

"Why?"

Caius unfolded his hands and pointed to his map. "Do you see this?" he said. "This is Yorkshire and Lancashire, from Middlesbrough to Lancaster. This is the area of England that is narrowest from sea to sea. Richmond sits more towards Middlesbrough while Aysgarth sits right in the middle, in Wensleydale, as the largest and only fortress in that vale. It's that vale that connects Yorkshire to Lancashire, making Aysgarth very strategic."

Achilles, Alexander, and Kevin were bent over the map. "You think de Tiegh is preparing to overtake that pass for some reason?" Achilles asked.

Caius shook his head. "Not de Tiegh," he said, moving his finger to the east until he came to rest just north of a large, dark area. "This is where Whorlton Castle sits, just north of the moors. The lord of Whorlton is a man named Witton de Meynell. I've met Witton on more than one occasion; the man has dreams of grandeur. Whorlton is a small castle belonging to an old family, and Witton is married to the daughter of the Count of Gotha. That is common knowledge in these parts. But my spies tell me that de Meynell is the one bringing over the Teutonic mercenaries."

Achilles was very interested. "De Meynell," he muttered, looking at Alexander. "The same knights we ran into at Skipton."

Alexander recognized the name as well. Shaking his head in mild disbelief, he looked at Caius. "We had an incident with seven de Meynell knights at a tavern in Skipton," he said. "We killed at least three of them and seriously disabled two or more. It was a bloody incident."

"How long ago?" Caius asked.

Alexander shrugged. "Well over a month ago."

Caius pondered that as he turned back to his map. "De Meynell is ambitious," he said. "That is no secret in Yorkshire. He's formed an alliance with de Tiegh and has sent some of the mercenary troops to Aysgarth. It's my belief that he intends to take control of Wensleydale. He has at least a thousand men at Whorlton and another thousand at Aysgarth. With two thousand men, he could easily hold that pass... and more."

"But why?"

Caius was staring at the map. "I believe it is the groundwork of what is to come," he said ominously. "Rumor has it that de Meynell's father-in-law is allied with the Duke of Brittany. In case you were unaware of the history of Richmond Castle, Brittany has held Richmond on occasion since the time of William the Bastard. Ownership has gone back and forth between Brittany and the crown several times and the crown only regained control of it about fifteen years ago. When Richard went on crusade and was allied with the King of France, Brittany held Richmond, but when Phillip was part of the abduction plot against Richard, William Marshal marched up here and tossed Brittany out. Now, I fear they want it back."

"And you think this troop build up has something to do with regaining Richmond?" Alexander asked.

Caius nodded faintly. "I think it is a distinct possibility," he said. "Being gutless and ambitious, I think that de Meynell is trying to be a very big player right now. If Gotha and Brittany are aligned, what better way to move on Richmond than to move mercenaries into Wensleydale and Yorkshire, building them up so there is a massive army to retake Richmond?"

"But what about taking control of Wensleydale?" Alexander wanted to know. "You mentioned controlling that vale."

Caius thumped on the map where the vale was. "Look at what is directly north of the vale," he said. "Bowes Castle. If Richmond is under siege, Bowes will send reinforcements. Controlling the vale means he can send men to intercept any help from Bowes. Juston de Royans would be unable to reach me."

Alexander grunted in understanding. It was shocking and quite logical, the perfect military strategy. He looked to Achilles for his reaction, who had been absorbing everything said. Achilles, however, was still staring at the map.

"You still have Skipton and Netherghyll to the south," Achilles said thoughtfully. "It would take tens of thousands of men to block those armies from coming to your aid. In fact, The Marshal sent a missive to Bryton de Royans about the situation with Aysgarth, so the man has been notified."

Caius sat back on his stool. "That is good," he said. "But Netherghyll is two days away should I need help. Bowes is less than a day. In any case, that is what I believe this build up is for. I do not think it has anything to do with rebelling barons. I think the target is Richmond Castle."

Achilles shook his head as he realized what the man was saying. "And you have not told The Marshal this?"

"Not yet," Caius said. "There is not much he can do at this point. I already have men coming up from Mount Holyoak Castle to the south to reinforce my ranks and also from Robert de Ros of Helmsley Castle, who is eager to get back into the king's good graces. He can easily do that by helping fend off a siege of Richmond. I am unconcerned that I will have the manpower to fend off a substantial siege, but any such action will keep me bottled up in Richmond. If the mercenary army decides to storm through Yorkshire, I will be helpless to defend the countryside and the smaller castles."

"Have you sent word to some of the smaller castles?"

Caius shook his head. "Not yet," he said, "but that day is coming very soon. I will hold a meeting here at Richmond next month to discuss it with them so they will know what we are facing. At that point, I will send word to The Marshal. He will need to know what is happening in Yorkshire and we may very well need the bigger armies from the south – de Lohr, de Winter, de Vaston, du Reims. My only concern is that if they all march north to chase the mercenaries from Yorkshire, that leaves London and the south without adequate defense, but that is something William will have to worry over. Not me. I have my own problems at the moment but I believe they are manageable."

It seemed as if Caius had things under control. This far north, men who served The Marshal had to think and act for themselves, which was exactly what Caius was doing. But now that the situation was outlined, that brought about the other reason they'd come to Richmond – the very woman without whose presence the mercenary army at Aysgarth would not have been discovered. Little did they know when they brought Susanna home that they were delivering her into a maelstrom of military turmoil.

Achilles cleared his throat softly.

"It seems that you have your finger on the pulse of what is happening around you," he said. "I would expect nothing less from The Britannia Viper. But there is something more to our presence here, Cai. To *my* presence here."

Caius folded his massive arms across his chest. "What is it?"

Achilles took a deep breath. This was going to be harder than he thought. "Remember I told you that Maxton and Kress have married?"

"Aye."

"I want to marry, too."

Caius eyebrows lifted with great interest. "Who?"

"Susanna de Tiegh. Samuel de Tiegh's sister."

That brought a smile of glee to Caius' lips. "The Blackchurch-trained women? The one you told me you had escorted home to Aysgarth?"

"The same."

Caius looked at him in confusion. "But I do not understand – if you want to marry her, why did you take her to Aysgarth and leave her there?"

Achilles scratched the back of his neck in a nervous gesture. "Well…" he said, paused, and started again. "I was not entirely sure I wanted to marry her until we were departing. I told her I would return and ask her brother for permission to marry her, but the situation is this – we had no idea of the chaos going at Aysgarth when we left her there. As far as Samuel de Tiegh knows, his sister served de Winter and has since left his service. He knows nothing about her serving William Marshal and we want to keep it that way. The Marshal has not denied me permission to return for her, but he feels that you would be better served to create a plan for her extraction since you know the situation with Aysgarth better than we do."

He was somewhat stumbling over his words at that point and Alexander put a hand on his shoulder. "The Marshal does not want Achilles to go charging into Aysgarth, revealing Susanna's true loyalties, and possibly getting them both killed in the process," he said. "We need ideas, Cai. We must extract Susanna from Aysgarth, but we need ideas on how to do it. It is an extremely delicate situation."

That was putting it mildly. Caius shook his head. "Christ, Achilles," he muttered. "You've got quite a situation on your hands."

Achilles nodded sheepishly. "I know," he said. "But one way or another, I shall return for her. It is a promise I will keep."

Caius scratched his head before standing up, clearly pondering the situation. "Samuel de Tiegh was a fairly innocuous lord until a couple of years ago when he and de Meynell became allies," he said. "I have met Samuel on several occasions and found him rather bland. He even came to Richmond a few years ago and we feasted. I forget why; it does not matter, I suppose. But it is important to note that he has also never officially professed his hatred for the king or William Marshal. He has never even officially lauded his alliance with de Meynell, either; I have received that information from my local spies. Samuel de Tiegh is a rare case of a lord who does not seem to have any particular loyalties."

"Except to de Meynell," Achilles said.

"Exactly," Caius said. Then, he drew in a deep breath, his expression thoughtful as he perused the map in front of him. "I suppose it would not be odd for me to travel to Aysgarth under the pretense of heading to Lancaster. I would simply be stopping for the night to seek shelter and perhaps a meal with de Tiegh. Everyone in Wensleydale knows that Aysgarth provides lavish feasts for their guests."

"And we could go with you," Achilles said, becoming increasingly excited. "Sherry and Kevin and I. But you would have to introduce us as newly-sworn knights to you, and insist that you do not know us well, because in order to distance ourselves from the Pembroke standards we were wearing when we escorted Susanna, we told de Tiegh that we had stolen them off of Pembroke knights."

Caius grinned. "You did *what?*"

He started to chuckle and Achilles continued. "Because we saw the mercenaries, we did not want him to think we were Pembroke knights who would report such information to The Marshal," he said. "I know it sounds foolish, but not knowing the situation, we were genuinely fearful he might not let us leave if he knew we served Pembroke. We concocted a great fabrication about stealing the Pembroke standards and heading north to pledge our fealty to the House of de Velt."

Caius lifted his hands. "I am clearly not the House of de Velt."

"Then we tell him that you made us an offer we could not refuse."

"Good enough."

Achilles stood up from his chair. "Cai, I am not going to ask for permission to marry Susanna at this point," he said. "If her brother believes I am a wandering knight, a fool with no past and no future, he may very well deny me. With the turmoil that seems to be engulfing Aysgarth, it is my intention to simply spirit her out of there."

"Steal her?"

"Aye."

"So my going along is simply to distract de Tiegh from your true purpose."

"Aye."

Surprisingly, Caius didn't take issue with that. He simply shrugged. "We did worse things in The Levant," he said. "It will be like old times again – stealing women and creating havoc. But I will tell you now that I am taking my army with me, especially if you are going to steal de Tiegh's sister. I will keep them out of sight, but they will be at the ready if we need them. I do not want to go into Aysgarth unprepared."

Achilles nodded. "Agreed," he said. "But know this – my intentions towards this woman are honorable. This is not a whim, Cai. This is… love."

Caius' eyes widened. "Love, is it?" he said. "God's bones, Achilles, I never thought I would hear that from you. This must be a spectacular woman."

"When you meet her, you will see."

"Then let us not waste any time. We can make Aysgarth by nightfall if we leave within the hour."

Achilles was more than ready. Food began to arrive at that point and the knights took their share, eating and talking, but mostly listening to Caius tell tall tales of The Levant and his adventures with the Executioner Knights. It seemed that there were three men officially dubbed the Executioner Knights, the Unholy Trinity by some, but there were more men that were part of that exclusive club, Alexander and Caius included. The adventures they had were wild adventures, indeed, but reliving them somehow fortified them and gave them strength. Stories and camaraderie that nourished souls, fed with the blood of fallen comrades and successful missions. Moments like these were what kept the Executioner Knights going, the thrill of duty of their chosen vocation.

This was who they were.

All except for Kevin. He was too young to have gone to The Levant, so he simply listened to the older knights speak of days gone by and wished that he had been there, too. He had been completely silent through the entire meeting and subsequent meal, but when Achilles and Alexander excused themselves to tend to their horses and collect their bags, he moved to follow them but Caius stopped him.

Kevin paused as the others left the chamber and headed down the stone steps. Hesitantly, he retraced his steps to Caius, who was sitting by one of the big lancet windows that faced over the barbican. A gentle summer breeze flowed into the chamber, mingling with the mustiness.

"My lord?" Kevin answered politely.

Caius had a cup of watered ale in his hand, looking out over the countryside. "Sometimes I spend hours staring from these windows," he muttered, finally turning to look at Kevin. "Do you know why?"

"I would not, my lord."

Caius' gaze drifted over the young knight. "Because I think about how far I have come from a past that is not so forgiving," he said. Then, he set the cup down and pulled up the sleeve on his left arm, revealing a massive tattoo of a viper with ferocious fangs. It was a spectacular work of art. "This reminds me of my past every single day, of the times when I did things that I am mayhap not so proud of but were necessary. That is what your brother is doing, you know. Things that he is not so proud of but are necessary."

When Kevin realized where the conversation was headed, he lowered his gaze and looked to his feet. "How would you know that, my lord?"

"Because I am well aware of Sean de Lara."

"Did you know my brother well, then?"

Caius nodded. "Very well," he said frankly. "Much better than I let on when we were introduced. You see, I love your brother dearly and I know of his task for The Marshal. Do you know how I know? Because when the opportunity arose to position a man close to King John, The Marshal spoke to Sean and me in private. Just the two of us. He presented the situation and asked which one of us wanted to assume the duty. Sean knew the sins of my past and because he knew of the terrible things I did, he spared me more sins and volunteered himself. Were it not for Sean, The Britannia Viper would now be the close bodyguard and advisor to King John. I would be burdening my soul with unconscionable things. Your brother made it so I did not have to and I will always love him for it."

It was a shocking admission. When Kevin's head finally came up, it was apparent that the news had thrown him off-balance. His emotions were on the surface as he looked at Caius with a mixture of distress and anger.

"*You?*" he said hoarsely. "You were there when all of this started?"

"I was."

Kevin wasn't sure how to respond to that, stunned with the realization. But the words, however painful, finally came forth. "Well, *I* do not love him for it," he said tightly. "Sean has become something I do not recognize. He is in bed with the devil and has taken the de Lara name with him. I have never in my life been ashamed of my name until the past few years because when men discover I am the Shadow Lord's brother, they look upon me with contempt. Sean did that to me. Do not tell me how great and self-sacrificing my brother is because I do not share your views."

Caius could see the tumult in his eyes and he felt for the young knight. "He is still your brother," he said quietly. "He has had to make a terrible choice, choosing to have people believe how evil he is over the love and respect of his family. Did you ever stop to think that your anger towards him is only making it worse?"

Kevin struggled for his composure. "Forgive me, my lord, but you are not in my position. I know what Sean is doing; I have been well informed. But it is something I cannot tell anyone. I must even keep it from my father, who weeps every time he speaks of his eldest son who is now a man known to kidnap women so the king can deflower them, or steal women away from their husbands so the king can have his way with them. John points a finger and Sean does his bidding, up to and including killing men in front of their wives and children. If the king wishes it, Sean does it. John has a knight of unfathomable power and intelligence at his disposal, a knight that everyone in England is terrified of. My brother has become Lucifer personified."

"And that is the price of Sean's service to his king and country," Caius pointed out. "William Marshal needs your brother there, at the king's right hand. The information Sean provides to The Marshal is invaluable for keeping this country stable. Do you not understand that?"

"I understand that."

"But you cannot forgive him."

"Nay," Kevin said flatly. "And now that I know you could have assumed that position, I cannot forgive you, either. You let Sean ruin himself."

Caius wasn't upset by the words because they were the truth. "If you think it does not eat at me every day of my life, you would be wrong," he whispered. "Sean has sacrificed himself in more ways than you can comprehend and it is a debt I can never repay. I am sorry to have disappointed you, Kevin."

"Will that be all, my lord?"

Clearly, Kevin had nothing more to say on the matter. Not that Caius blamed him; it was a great burden for an adoring younger brother to bear. Rather than force him, Caius simply nodded his head.

Their discussion, for the moment, was over.

He watched the young knight head back to the stairs, feeling a great deal of sorrow for a young, idealistic warrior in turmoil. Kevin saw the world only one way – righteous. He hadn't experienced what men like Caius and Sean and Achilles and Alexander had experienced. Living a brutal life where sometimes good and evil intertwine had a tendency to change a man. But Kevin didn't understand that. Caius didn't miss when the young knight wiped a hand over his face as he descended the stairs, wiping away the tears that had fallen.

It was like an arrow to the gut.

With a heavy heart, Caius went about preparing for his journey to Aysgarth.

CHAPTER TEN

IT HAD TAKEN twelve men to capture her and force her into Aysgarth's narrow vault. Twelve men with swords and clubs, but Susanna had put up a valiant fight. She'd burned down half of the apartments doing it, including her beloved writing kit and new clothing but, in the end, she had succumbed to overwhelming numbers.

Even then, she'd continued fighting.

They'd had to put her in chains.

Beaten, her clothing torn and stained with blood from her swollen mouth and nose, Susanna was chained to the wall of Aysgarth's vault. She had the ability to sit down and stand up, but that was where it stopped. A pile of straw was her bed but she hadn't slept, not one wink.

She sat against the wall, watching the door leading to the steps that led up to the main gatehouse, waiting.

Waiting for what, she wasn't sure. All she knew was that her true loyalties were now known and her life was more than likely forfeit.

Somehow, they'd gotten her missive to d'Avignon away from Meggie. Susanna didn't even know what happened to her servant and she was worried for the woman, but she couldn't spare too much concern. The truth was that she was in a good deal of trouble and she needed to save the concern for herself.

So far, no one had questioned her. With all the fighting going on, mostly from her, there hadn't been the opportunity, but she knew that was coming. Part of being a Blackchurch knight was being able to withstand various methods of torture, and she'd been through enough to know how much she could take. It was going to take quite a lot on their part to force her to say anything.

She was ready for them.

Being that she was in the vault of Aysgarth, with no windows, she had no way of knowing just how much time had passed since her capture. She assumed it was at least a night and a day, based on how hungry she was. As the minutes ticked away, she was becoming increasingly miserable, from her hunger pangs to her throbbing mouth and nose, to the fact that she'd had to piss over against the wall and was trying not to sit in it. She was coming to wish that someone would come and interrogate her just so they could get it over with.

But, so far, it has been a frustratingly long wait.

More time passed and out of sheer exhaustion, Susanna started to fall asleep. She wasn't sure how long she'd been asleep, sitting up, when she began to hear footsteps and voices. Instantly, her heart was racing and she forced herself to be alert, to be ready. She braced herself for what was to come.

And it was, indeed, coming.

Men with torches appeared. She couldn't make out any faces, but she didn't recognize their voices, which told her they were men she didn't know. De Meynell men and, perhaps, even the same men who had captured her and beaten her, including a knight she'd seen in the tavern in Skipton.

That had been a distinct shock.

One of the seven knights she and Achilles and Alexander had licked in the tavern in Skipton had been one of the men to capture her, and while she was throwing punches, she was fairly certain he was throwing them back. He was the one who hit her in the nose, or so she thought. She fully expected him to be part of this group approaching and wasn't disappointed to see that she was right.

He was front and center.

But so was Witton. The Lord of Whorlton kept his eyes on her as he had one of his men unlock her cell and even as he stepped into the large cell, which took up most of the vault, he kept away from her.

It was clear that he had a good deal of respect for her fighting abilities.

"My apologies for the delay, my lady," he said with strained politeness. "I will remove the chains if you promise not to disable my men. We have casualties from the fight last night and I should not like to see you injure any more of them."

Susanna's gaze lingered on him for a moment before turning away. She didn't give him an answer. Witton stepped closer.

"So you do not wish to talk," he said. "That is understandable but it is not wise. We have much to discuss."

"We have nothing to discuss," Susanna growled. "Whatever you are going to do, get on with it."

"I am not going to do anything, yet," he assured her. "But you and I must discuss the situation and come to a conclusion that suits us both, but I will not negotiate with an animal. If you promise to behave yourself, I will treat you accordingly. If you do not, then I will let you rot down here. Therefore, I will remove the chains if you promise to behave."

Susanna thought about ignoring him again, but she had been chained up for the better part of a day and a night, and the cuffs were chaffing her terribly. She was also losing feeing in her hands because she couldn't lower them. It would be much more comfortable for her to have the chains removed so that she could at least lower her arms.

"I will not strike anyone if you remove my chains," she finally said.

Witton motioned to the man standing next to him, which happened to be the very knight from the tavern in Skipton. He came at her with the key for the shackles, unfastening her legs before he unfastened her wrists. Susanna wouldn't look at him, but the moment he unfastened the last cuff, he slapped her across the face hard enough to snap her head sideways. Susanna responded in an instant by lashing out a foot and kicking the man right in the groin. As he went down, she pounced on him, going right for his face.

It was instant chaos in the cell as Witton screamed for his men to separate the combatants. Three men pulled Susanna off of the knight, but not before she'd managed to dig her thumbs into both eyes. He was howling with pain as she was hauled away and immediately put back where the chains were. The men were beginning to chain her up again but Witton stopped them.

"Nay!" he shouted. "Do not restrain her. Leave her!"

Susanna yanked away from the men trying to chain her up again, throwing herself in the opposite direction and ending up over in a corner of the cell. Witton was ordering his men to back off and they complied, though reluctantly.

"He hit me first," Susanna shouted angrily. "I will not allow him or anyone else to strike me again. I can and will defend myself."

Witton held up both hands to try to ease the situation. "Easy, my lady," he said. "You have understandably drawn their ire. Men will react in kind."

"And I will react in kind if they try to strike me again!"

"Calm yourself," Witton ordered quietly. "You and I have a good deal to discuss and I will not have a shouting match with you. Is that clear?"

Susanna was edgy, like a caged animal, backed up against the wall as her eyes darted to de Meynell's angry men behind him. She didn't answer him but rather stood there, twitching with rage. Realizing he wasn't going to get an answer, Witton simply continued.

"Now," he said. "You and I must discuss the missive you were attempting to send to Richmond Castle. I can only assume you got your information from your brother."

Susanna had no idea where Samuel was and she wasn't going to cast any blame on him. At the cell door, the knight from the tavern in Skipton was just being helped to his feet as he grunted and groaned, giving her an idea.

"If you want to know where I received my information, ask the bastard who slapped me," she said. "I saw him in Skipton several weeks ago where he and his comrades had too much to drink and willingly told me everything. Thanks to your men, I am not the only one who knows this information."

She was trying to deflect blame, something that had been wholly endorsed by Blackchurch. It was one of their techniques in a situation such as this to create confusion and doubt. It had the desired effect. Witton's eyes widened and he whirled to the knight as he was just finding his way out of the cell.

"Bellerby!" he boomed. "Is this true?"

The man could barely see and one eye refused to open at all. He paused at the cell entry. "Is what true, my lord?"

"Did you speak on our plans for Richmond Castle?"

Bellerby looked at his lord in shock. "I did not, my lord, I swear it!"

"He is lying," Susanna snarled. "Of course he told me. How else would I know?"

Bellerby couldn't see very well, but he could certainly see the woman who was accusing him of treasonous behavior. "She's mad!" he cried. "She is lying!"

Susanna went on the attack. "He and his comrades were very drunk at The Horse's Arse," she insisted. "If you do not believe me, send someone to the tavern to ask. They bragged on how Richmond Castle would soon belong to the French again. Who knows who else they have told!"

Bellerby tried to charge her again, held back by his fellow men, and Witton had the unhappy position of standing between him and the lady he wanted to throttle. Witton believed Bellerby for the most part, but there was something in the back of his mind that told him such things were possible. He'd seen his men drink before, too many times to count, and silence was not one of their virtues. The leader of the contingent from The Horse's Arse, the man who had died of an infection to the gut, was a man named Gael le Sommes and he was not a man known for keeping his mouth shut. He had been brash and aggressive.

Still, Witton had little doubt that the lady was lying. His men weren't the ones who had sent a detailed missive to the commander of Richmond Castle warning him of future plans.

The lady was alone in that action.

"My lady, allow me to make things clear," he said, struggling to gain control of the situation. "Your actions were your own. No one told you to write that missive. I suppose it does not matter where you received the information. What matters is what you did with it. Why were you trying to warn Caius d'Avignon. What is he to you?"

"I have never met the man."

"Yet you were sending him a message."

Susanna looked away, calming now that her rumble with Bellerby had subsided. "You know that I will not speak to the accusations," she said. "And they are only accusations. You cannot prove anything."

"Your maid said you wrote it."

"She is lying."

"She swore it was the truth before we slit her throat."

Susanna didn't react outwardly but, inwardly, she was feeling sick on Meggie's behalf. He could be simply trying to get a reaction out of her, but she couldn't be sure. She kept her composure.

"That is unfortunate," she said.

"Have you nothing more to say?"

"I have nothing to say at all."

Witton sighed sharply. He eyed her a moment before turning to his men, still clustered back by the cell door, and waved his arm at them, silently ordering them out. All but one man; he remained by the door, holding the torch, while the others complied, including Bellerby. He was rubbing his eyes furiously as he quit the vault. When it was just Witton and Susanna facing one another, and Witton's man standing back by the open cell door, Witton spoke quietly.

"I want you to understand something, Lady Susanna," he said. "I am fairly certain that you received your information from your brother, the weak bastard that he is. It does not take a great intellect to deduce that. But he swears he knows nothing of your loyalty to Richmond Castle. He could be lying. I will bring him down here and ask him again, and if he tells me he has no knowledge of your loyalties again, I will cut his tongue out right in front of you for lying to me yet again. Do you understand that I am capable of that?"

Susanna could take abuse and torture. She knew she could and she was unafraid to face it. But this was the type of threat she'd been dreading; using her own brother against her. She couldn't, and wouldn't, stand by and watch them torture Samuel and she suspected there was some part of Witton who knew that. It was one thing to threaten her, but it was another thing entirely to threaten a beloved sibling.

She couldn't let it happen.

"I understand," she said, turning to look at him. "What do you want from me?"

"The truth."

"About what?"

"Why you were sending the missive to Richmond?"

"I told you. It is merely an accusation that you cannot prove."

Witton was becoming impatient. "Then I will bring Samuel down here and ask him what he knows," he said. "Mayhap you would be more willing to tell me the truth if Samuel was here."

Susanna really didn't want Samuel in the cell with her, especially if they were going to use the man to make her talk. She wasn't going to let her brother take the brunt of abuse for her actions, but that was clearly the implication. Therefore, the only thing she could do was negotiate her way out of this.

She had to try.

"Do not bother," she said. "If you want to talk, then let us talk. Let us come to an understanding, shall we? You want answers to questions, answers I cannot provide to you. Therefore, let us move past the questions to the crux of the situation – let us theorize that if I were to tell you what you wanted to know, I must have to have certain assurances in order to do so."

"What did you have in mind?"

Susanna was walking the careful line between admitting she knew something and plausibly denying everything, as she'd been doing. But she could see where this conversation was going and she was trying to be preemptive about the situation – striking while she could, negotiating before she was desperate.

Trying to take control of something she had no control over.

"My brother would be held harmless," she said. "And I would simply leave and never return. You would never see me again and I would never again cause you trouble. This, I vow."

Witton eyed her, mulling over what she was offering. After several long moments, his eyes narrowed.

"That would not do," he said. "You see, my lady, I have all of the evidence against you that I need. You truly need not tell me anything because I already know. I simply wanted to see if you would be smart enough to confess everything to me, but I see that you would rather blame others to save yourself. Hardly honorable behavior."

Susanna didn't appreciate being called a liar, even if she had used that tactic to deflect suspicion away from herself. Unwilling to respond because she wasn't sure what Witton's intentions were, she simply looked away. Witton kept his gaze fixed on her.

"No witty reply?" he said. "No more offers? Let me tell you how I know this, my lady. You see, Bellerby saw you and two Pembroke knights at The Horse's Arse, the very same knights who robbed me of three of my best men. You injured the other four to varying degrees, but they will heal. You tried to deflect your activities and loyalties by blaming Bellerby, as we just saw. But in the end, I trust my men over you. Given the fact that you served de Winter, which is established, and traveled with Pembroke knights, I would say that your loyalties are to the king or to William Marshal, or both. That is why you were sending the missive to Richmond – to warn them. The garrison belongs to William Marshal and you were simply doing your duty."

That was the situation, exactly, but Susanna didn't show any emotion one way or the other. She didn't respond, either, which perhaps made her look more guilty than anything thus far. Witton, knowing he had the upper hand, went in for the kill.

"This is what is going to happen, Lady Susanna," he said. "If you do not comply with my command in any way, I will take your brother apart before your very eyes, piece by piece. Do you understand so far?"

Susanna was starting to feel a great deal of apprehension and struggling not to show it. She refused to admit that she'd lost control of the situation when the truth was that she never really had control to begin with.

It was a bitter realization.

"Speak your mind and be done with it, de Meynell."

Witton lifted a hand because he was going to grab her by the chin and force her to look at him, but he thought better of it. She might lash out at him and, as he'd seen, she had a powerful strike.

"You are going to accompany me back to Whorlton Castle," he said, "but not as a knight. You will return as a lady, and a beautiful lady, and when my wife's father finishes sending me the rest of the troops he has promised me, I shall send you to Wartburg Castle as a gift to him. Any resistance and I will kill your brother. If he is dead and you continue to resist, then I shall make you wish you had never been born. You will become a concubine for my soldiers and I will allow every dirty, filthy knave to touch you in ways that will make you wish you were dead. They will bed you and bed you again, as many men a day as want to bed you, and any bastards you bear will be sold into servitude. From this day forward, you belong to me and I will do with you as I please or your brother, and you, will pay the price. Is this in any way unclear?"

Susanna knew he meant every word of it and given that she was at his mercy, she had no choice but to comply. As she tried not to think about his very real threat, visions of Achilles filled her mind.

Terror surged.

Since the moment she'd been captured, the most predominant thing on her mind was the fact that Achilles would be returning for her any day, returning to ask Samuel for her hand. As soon as he entered Aysgarth's gates, he would be a target for de Meynell and the very thought made her ill. He had no idea what he would be walking in to and she was frantic to get word to him, but such a thing was surely impossible.

She had to warn Achilles off somehow.

... but how?

As she fought down her panic for Achilles, she realized that Witton was waiting for an answer.

"It is clear," she said hoarsely. "But I want to see my brother. Will you take him to me?"

"Will you swear to me that you will not resist any longer? No more fighting my men?"

"I will no longer resist your men, but if they strike me, I will strike back. Make sure they know that."

"I will ensure they treat you fairly. If you behave yourself, I will move you back to the apartments, into an unburned chamber, and you will remain there for the time being under guard. A woman of your beauty should not be kept in this moldering vault."

There was a lascivious hint to his tone and Susanna could see that she was going to have to deal with his advances now. That was obvious. He saw her as a caged bird, one he intended to toy with. The very thought made her want to vomit.

At this point, however, she had little choice but to comply.

"Aye, my lord."

His gaze lingered on her, on her bruised mouth and swollen nose. He leaned forward, lowering his voice.

"If you swear to me that you will comply with my wishes, I will believe you," he muttered. "But know that I will only believe you one time. If you break your vow, just once, everything terrible I have described to you will come to pass. There will be no second chance. Do you understand?"

"I do, my lord."

"Then I will bring your brother to you."

Reaching up, he dared to stoke her cheek with a dirty finger and Susanna closed her eyes against the disgust it provoked, but to her credit, she didn't fight back. But all the while, she was slowly dying inside.

Is this what is waiting for me?

God, she couldn't even stomach it.

When Witton finally left the cell and locked it behind him, Susanna allowed herself the luxury of a few hot tears.

CHAPTER ELEVEN

THEY WERE RIDING to battle.

At least, that was what it felt like.

Caius had summoned nearly eight hundred men from the fifteen hundred he had stationed at Richmond and, by mid-afternoon, the entire army was mobilized. Caius had quartermasters who were geniuses at their tasks, and senior knights who were at the top of their career. One of the men was a nephew to the Earl of Wolverhampton, a young and dynamic knight named Morgan de Wolfe. He was big and dark, with hazel eyes, and he had a strong sense of command about him. He had the army mobilized and ready in very little time.

Caius had planned this all out very carefully. He'd made it clear that they were not going to Aysgarth to simply retrieve Susanna, but also to see for himself what was going on there. He'd known of the mercenaries at Aysgarth, and his network of spies throughout Yorkshire was keeping an eye on them, but with the information from Alexander and Achilles, he decided that it was time to pay a visit to de Tiegh.

If Aysgarth was going to be that big of a threat, then he needed to scope it out for his own information because he would, ultimately, be the one making the decision to break down Aysgarth and scatter the mercenaries or leave it alone as a mild risk.

But he had to see it for himself first.

A few hours before sunset, the army from Richmond set out, much to the delight of the village surrounding it. People turned out in droves, watching the army depart, handing them fresh loaves of bread to take with them or even a flower. They had no idea where the army was going, but the villagers of Richmond loved their troops and their castle. They were well protected and well treated, and when Caius passed through, they did everything but throw money and women at him.

And that's how Caius liked it.

As they passed through town and Caius waved to the townsfolk like a conquering Caesar, Alexander eyed the man with disbelief. When Caius caught a glimpse of Alexander's expression, he broke down laughing, as did Alexander. Caius was arrogant and full of himself, and had every reason to be because he was a truly great knight, but as Alexander had told him, the last time he saw the man was when he was trying to negotiate for a houseful of women. Caius liked his hero-worship, wherever he could get it – from villagers or a houseful of daughters desperate for the touch of a handsome man.

Caius was a complicated and proud man.

It definitely felt like old times to Achilles, riding behind Caius and Alexander, watching the two of them smirk and laugh at one another. Under normal circumstances, he would have been part of that group, but his overwhelming concern for Susanna prevented him from enjoying his time with his comrades.

All he cared about was getting to Aysgarth and locating her.

It was true that he agreed with Caius and even The Marshal on not being reckless, but the greater truth was that he was going to do as he pleased, anyway. He was coming to understand Kress de Rhydian's mentality when he was determined to take Lady Cadelyn and flee with her, no matter what the consequences. At the time, Achilles really didn't understand that kind of passion and longing, becoming so strong that it turned into reckless determination.

But now, he did.

He understood it completely.

Therefore, he was working on a plan. As the army headed out of the village and to the road leading south, the very road that Achilles and Alexander and Kevin had taken into town, Achilles was planning his future with Susanna. He'd told The Marshal that they would continue to serve him even after they were married, and they would, when the turmoil of the situation died down. Stealing Susanna away without her brother's permission was going to cause some turmoil, so it was best that they go far away and stay out of sight until the uproar died down.

Or perhaps he simply wanted to go away with her for a while.

No William Marshal, no spy rings.

Nothing but just the two of them.

Aye, that was his true goal, if he was honest with himself. He wanted to get her alone and have her all to himself, if only for a short while, because when they returned to the service of The Marshal, the course of their lives and their time together would be uncertain.

Achilles thought back to the last carefree days he could remember, those of his youth, and one of his fondest memories was when his parents would take him and his siblings to the shore at Maryport when the weather was fine in the summer. He had recollection of wandering the rocky shore with his mother and older brother, Tobias, finding shells that they would collect by the dozens. The gulls would scream overhead and the waves would crash onto shore as a damp breeze blew in from the sea. That was the last time he remembered ever being carefree and happy, the innocence of youth.

That shore had a special meaning for him.

Perhaps he would take Susanna there and they would hide out from the storm surrounding their departure. He wanted to walk on the shore with her and collect shells, far away from the politics of England and mercenaries from across the sea. Just for a few stolen moments, he wanted to be with Susanna and come to know her better than he'd ever known anyone in his life. That strong, courageous, and beautiful woman would become his world.

In truth, she already was.

His desperation to reach her grew.

Spurring his horse forward, he pulled up beside Caius as the man was speaking to Alexander about some kind of cheese made in Wensleydale that caused his guts to explode in all directions. He liked it so much that he ate it nonetheless, suffering the consequences afterwards, wondering aloud if he was eating himself into an early grave by punishing his insides with that rich, white cheese. As Achilles rode up, Caius turned to him.

"So you intend to join us, do you?" he said. "I thought we had offended you somehow. We were speaking of the white cheese that is made in these parts with sheep's milk. I like the cheese but it does not like me."

Achilles smiled weakly. "Mayhap it is poisoned," he said. "It is the Duke of Brittany out to kill you with cheese so they may have their castle returned to them without a battle."

Caius looked at him as if awed by the very suggestion. "That would be very clever of them," he said. "But, alas, cheese has never been kind to me, not in my entire life. I did much better on the food in The Levant, the lamb and rice and vegetables that constituted the diet. I yearn for those days."

"Only the food?" Achilles said. "Not for the adventure?"

Caius shook his head. "Those were days of living like an animal at times," he said. "I do not miss *those* days. But I came straight home to England when it was over and you did not. I heard that you and Maxton and Kress ended up at the Lateran Palace for a time."

Achilles nodded. "For quite some time," he concurred. "We were treated like kings as the pope tried to convince us to assassinate our own king. When we refused, he imprisoned us and then sold us to the Lords of Baux. Had it not been for William Marshal believing that we were the only hope to stop the assassins that the pope eventually sent to England to eliminate John, we would probably still be in that vault in France, slowly wasting away."

Caius was listening to him seriously. "I had not heard that," he said. "I'd heard of the attempt against John, of course, at St. Blitha's Church, no less, but I'd not heard your roles in it. Astonishing, Achilles."

Achilles nodded as he remembered a rather turbulent time only a few short months ago. "More than you know," he said. "The assassins were the nuns at St. Blitha. We only came to realize that when a postulate told us of the pervasive wickedness within the convent. In fact, Maxton married that postulate."

Caius shook his head, astounded by the entire situation. "And the nuns?"

"Killed by the postulate herself, with poison meant for the king."

"That took great bravery."

"That was why Maxton married her."

Caius grinned as he looked off to the green Yorkshire landscape. "I still cannot believe he and Kress fell victim to feminine wiles," he said. "And now you. It looks as if Sherry and I are the only ones with our manhoods intact."

Achilles laughed softly. "You have no idea what you are missing," he said. "A good woman will change your stars."

"I do not want to change my stars."

"Should you ever marry, I shall make sure to tell your wife that."

"There will be no wife. A harem, aye, but never a wife. In fact, I have been thinking of having my own harem here in England."

"I think they call it a brothel."

That brought a guffaw from Alexander and Achilles joined him in his laughter at Caius' expense. But Caius stood his ground, shaking his head at the two of them.

"And what does that make you, Achilles?" he asked. "You are to steal a woman away from her home so you do not risk her brother denying you. Why are you so set on having her?"

"Because she belongs to me."

A gleam came to Caius' eyes. "Do I detect a man who has bedded a woman before marriage?"

Alexander looked at Achilles, quite interested in the answer. In fact, he started shaking his head. "If that has occurred, I would be astonished," he said. "Cai, you cannot know how those two have battled each other since the beginning of their association, and I do mean battle. Susanna is not afraid of him and she made that very clear. At one point, we had to let them fight it out because the tension was unbearable. It was a damn good fight, too."

Caius looked at Achilles, amused. "Who won?"

Alexander answered. "We had to pull them apart, but I would say that the lady was getting the upper hand," he said. "It was a battle with those two from the very first day and it was exhausting. The fact that he thinks himself in love with her is bewildering, but mayhap not so bewildering considering she stood up to him at every turn. He must like a woman who fights back."

"I like a woman who is strong and brave," Achilles said, oddly subdued. "Do not speak of her as if she is something reckless and wild. She is not, you know. She is courageous beyond measure, wise beyond reason, and brilliant beyond imagining. I do not simply think myself in love with her – I *know* I am. And, yes, I bedded her, if you must know. Make no mistake – the woman is marked upon my heart as surely as the stars are marked upon the sky. In fact, I told her that my skies were starless without her. I know I can be aggressive and emotional at times, but do not diminish my feelings for Susanna. In a way, she has helped me to realize the man I want to be. I understand what it means to feel something for a woman you cannot live without."

By the time he was finished, Caius and Alexander were looking at him quite seriously. It was Alexander who finally spoke.

"I am sorry if you thought I was diminishing you," he said. "That was not my intention. Incredulity was. If you say you love her, then I do not dispute you. I find it as surprising as I do marvelous. It is a rare thing, Achilles, to love a woman you were so intent on beating."

Achilles smiled weakly. "She has made me see otherwise."

Alexander simply nodded, still astounded that the fighting knights he'd known had fallen in love with another. As he said, it was truly surprising. He didn't reply to Achilles, instead looking to Caius, who seemed to be baffled by it all. But one thing was certain – it gave the journey to Aysgarth a much more critical feel. This wasn't simply a folly for Achilles to steal away a woman he was obsessed with.

This was Achilles retrieving the woman he loved.

Much more critical, indeed.

Richmond wasn't too terribly far from Aysgarth as far as distance went. It was precisely sixteen miles and they were making excellent time. About five miles out, however, Caius called a halt and gathered the knights around him.

He had some decisions to make.

"I am stopping the army here because I do not want Aysgarth catching sight of them," he said. "They could very well think I am rushing to lay siege and that is not my intent, but I do not want the army far from me or from Aysgarth once I enter."

Alexander spoke quietly. "Remember that there are about a thousand mercenaries in a field to the west, Cai," he reminded him. "If there is trouble, there are those reinforcements for Aysgarth, so you will want to position your army out of sight from them."

Cai nodded. "Indeed," he said. "My thoughts are this – we shall enter Aysgarth and determine where the lady is and I will see for myself the strength of Aysgarth in terms of manpower and command. Aysgarth has always been a sleepy fortress and not much of a threat, but that may have changed. If they are, indeed, allied with de Meynell, and I walk in there as a representative of William Marshal and Richmond Castle, I may be putting myself in grave danger. I understand that. And that is why I have brought my army – I may need them if de Tiegh decides I am the enemy."

"My lord," Morgan de Wolfe spoke in a deep, rich voice. "If we are here to retrieve the lady, as you say, then why do you need to enter in order to assess Aysgarth's strengths? Surely that can be done by reconnaissance. You can stay out of sight."

Caius shook his head. "I need to see de Tiegh," he said. "The man has remained ambiguous in his loyalties long enough and I want to see the interior of Aysgarth and assess the situation for myself."

"And if there is trouble and de Tiegh decides you are the enemy?" Morgan pressed.

Caius glanced up at the sky, the dwindling day. "It will be nightfall soon," he said. "I will stay for the evening meal and for all de Tiegh will know, I am simply a visitor. But if you do not see me by dawn – if you do not see any of us by dawn – assume we are being held against our wills."

"And how do we proceed, my lord?"

Caius looked to Morgan and Kevin. "I want you two to remain with the army," he said. "If you do not see us before dawn, then you will have to get into the castle somehow. But if you do, know that the mercenaries will probably be alerted and you must prevent them from getting to the castle."

Morgan nodded, but it was Kevin who spoke. "We can send a contingent into the castle while the rest of the army holds off the mercenaries."

"There are a thousand mercenaries, Kevin," Achilles spoke. "We have seen them, gathering in a field to the southwest. They are fully armed."

Kevin understood. "Mayhap we should have brought more men with us, then."

But Caius shook his head. "I do not want to deplete Richmond," he said. "You'll be able to hold the mercenary charge with fewer men if you plan accordingly. But if you do not see us by dawn, come in and get us."

"Aye, my lord," Kevin replied.

Caius pointed at Morgan, but he spoke to Kevin. "Morgan knows my army and this area, so listen to him," he said. "But I will trust you with the tactics since you are a Marshal knight. That means you must be clever. And you are a de Lara, which means you are better than most men."

Kevin wasn't particularly happy that he wasn't going into Aysgarth with Alexander and Achilles, but he understood the need for strong command for the army. After a moment, he simply nodded his head and Caius turned around, facing west, towards Aysgarth. They were on a rise, looking down into the green and fertile Wensleydale vale, with Aysgarth in the distance.

"That is the River Ure down in the vale," he said, pointing to the heavy line of trees that meandered down in the valley. "Take the army down to the river and follow it. It is heavily-forested all the way to Aysgarth, which sits right next to the river. You can use the trees as cover and get as close as you can to the castle. Make sure you can see both the gatehouse and the mercenary army. Hide there until you receive word from one of us. Is that clear?"

Both Kevin and Morgan nodded. "Aye, my lord," they replied in unison.

"Be gone with you."

With that, the knights began to move back through the ranks, shouting out commands, and the army began to move off the road and down the sloping fields, heading for the trees that marked the river below. Achilles, Alexander, and Caius watched them go, waiting until they were all shielded within the trees before turning for Aysgarth in the distance.

"Remove your standards," Caius told them. "We do not want to announce who we are any sooner than we have to."

They peeled off their tunics, Achilles and Alexander with the Pembroke colors and Caius with the Richmond colors of blue and red. They stuffed them into their saddlebags, tucking them away and simply leaving the mail coats and heavy under armor. They began to move down the road, discussing their plans once more.

Now, it was time to carry them out.

CHAPTER TWELVE

"**S**USANNA."

It was dark in the vault and Susanna, pushed beyond her limits of exhaustion, had fallen asleep on the musty straw. But a soft voice pierced her veil of slumber and she sat up instantly, before she was even fully awake, only to find herself staring at her brother.

Samuel was in her cell, holding a torch. He was standing over by the cell door, which had been opened by one of de Meynell's men. Clearly, they weren't going to allow the brother and sister to speak privately. When Susanna saw who it was, she rubbed at her eyes, struggling to wake up.

"Samuel," she muttered, trying to get a look at him in the darkness. "Are you well? Have they hurt you?"

Samuel was looking at his sister with the greatest of sorrow. "Nay," he murmured, very conscious of the de Meynell man standing by the cell door. He came closer so they could not be overheard. "I am unharmed. But they seem to have beaten you from head to toe."

Susanna blinked at the bright light of his torch, lowering her head and running a hand over her mouth. "I must look terrible."

"Is anything broken?"

"Not that I can tell. Surprisingly, no loose teeth."

"That is good."

There was a lull in the conversation until Samuel crouched down in front of her so he could see her better. Moreover, their conversation would be less likely to be overheard.

"Why, Susanna?" he breathed. "Why did you do it?"

Susanna was moving her sore jaw around gingerly. "Is this the brother asking or the ally of de Meynell?"

"The brother."

"You know that de Meynell was down here trying to interrogate me. I did not tell him anything."

Samuel sighed faintly. "He is watching me like a hawk sighting prey," he murmured. "I think he is waiting for me to try to send word out as well."

"I am surprised that you are not down here in chains alongside me."

Samuel sat back on his heels. "To tell you the truth, so am I," he said. "I may be, yet. But for now, I have a reasonable amount of freedom because you did not tell him that I was the one who gave you the information. I suppose I should have been smarter about it, but I did not think you would do what you did. You still serve de Winter, don't you?"

Susanna didn't reply for a moment. "You can stop asking questions, Samuel," she said. "I will not tell you anything that you can, in turn, tell de Meynell."

Samuel grunted unhappily. "You are my sister," he said. "I will not tell him anything you tell me in confidence, I swear it. You did not tell de Meynell that I told you about Richmond, so I swear upon my life that I will not repeat anything to him that you tell me. Please, Susanna, tell me what is going through your mind. Why did you try to send that information to Richmond?"

Susanna thought long and hard about her reply, but the truth was that she didn't trust her brother with a confession. She believed he would not voluntarily tell de Meynell, but he might very well crack under pressure. She didn't want to put him in that position.

Besides... there was something more important on her mind.

"Sammy," she said quietly. "Will you do something for me?"

"Anything."

"I need your help."

"Other than the obvious, what do you need?"

Susanna looked up at him, her eyes glimmering with emotion. "The two knights that escorted me to Aysgarth," she said. "Achilles and Alexander. You remember them, of course."

"Of course."

"Achilles is going to return for me."

Samuel frowned. "But why?"

"Because he wants to marry me."

Samuel's eyes widened. "He *does*?"

"Aye. But you must send word to him not to come. He must not return."

Samuel held up a hand. "A moment, please," he begged. "Susanna, you have a knight who wishes to *marry* you? I find that incredible. Do you want to marry him?"

She nodded, struggling not to tear up at the thought of Achilles. "Aye," she said hoarsely. "Very much. Sammy, I love him. He must not come back here for me. There is no knowing what de Meynell will do to him if he believes he is in league with me."

She had a point and Samuel frowned. "But what can I do?" he asked. "They are watching me closely. If they catch me trying to send a missive out of Aysgarth, I will be in the same predicament as you."

Susanna knew that. She didn't want to jeopardize Samuel, but she didn't want Achilles to walk into a dangerous situation, either. It was a horrendous choice that she had to make and perhaps even an unrealistic expectation that Samuel should jeopardize himself so for her.

But she had to ask.

"Then you must watch the gatehouse for his return," she said. "Are there any soldiers that are loyal to you?"

Samuel nodded. "A few."

"Have them watch the gatehouse when you cannot. Tell them to watch for Achilles and when they see him, they must hide him from de Meynell. You must tell him that he must leave."

Samuel shook his head. "He will want to know why," he said. "If the man wants to marry you, surely he will not leave you in this situation."

Susanna was trying not to become agitated. "Then tell him I have left," she said. "Tell him I have gone somewhere – anywhere – and that I am expecting him to join me. Tell him anything so he will leave, Sammy. *Please.*"

Samuel could see the great emotion in her eyes, unusual for his normally-stoic sister. That told him that this situation, and Achilles, meant a great deal to her. Frankly, he was stunned. But he was also intensely curious.

"I think you need to tell me everything, Susanna," he said quietly. "Who is Achilles? Who does he serve? And how did you meet him?"

Susanna didn't want to tell him, but she supposed she owed him that much. She was asking him to do a great deal based on faith. Therefore, she was inclined to tell him as much as she dared.

"He is part of a group of elite warriors called the Executioner Knights," she said quietly. "He serves William Marshal."

Samuel's eyebrows lifted. "Then he *is* a Pembroke knight," he said. "That story he gave me was a lie."

"It was."

"And de Sherrington? He lied, too?"

"He did. But they did it because of the mercenary army attached to Aysgarth. They were afraid that you would not let them leave, fearful that they would report what they saw to William Marshal."

Samuel was rather annoyed that he'd been lied to. "I had no intention of not allowing them to leave," he said. "It is not as if I can hide a mercenary army, so it would do not good to throw them in the vault. I am sure word has already reached William Marshal one way or another."

"And mayhap it has already reached Richmond, too."

"Then why did you send that missive?"

"Because Richmond must know that the Duke of Brittany is coming. They must prepare." She looked at her brother, feeling great frustration. "Samuel, how in the world could you become allied with Witton de Meynell? The man is ambitious and rash. He is going to get you killed with his dreams of great alliances and delusions of power."

"I told you how. I gambled away everything."

Susanna knew that but she simply couldn't believe it. She was a fighter and always had been; she didn't understand the complacency her brother was showing. It made her angry.

"Then it is time for you to do something about it," she said. "You are a Blackchurch knight, which means you are one of the best in the world, yet you follow de Meynell around like a puppy and blame it all on the fact that you gambled away everything to him. Samuel, I am in a good deal of trouble. If you do not help me, de Meynell is going to send me to his wife's father as a concubine. He told me if I show any measure of resistance, then he is going to let his soldiers have their way with me. Is that what you wish for me? Your only sister?"

Samuel's jaw was ticking as he listened to her, disgusted by what she was telling him. "Of course I do not wish that for you," he said. "But you got yourself into this by sending that missive. That was your choice, Susanna. No one forced you to."

"That is because I am a warrior of honor. Unlike you, I keep my vows."

Samuel's eyes narrowed. "If you want me to help you, insulting me is not helping your case."

"You are free because I did not tell them where I got my information. Do not make me regret that decision."

"Then what do you want me to do?"

"Help me escape."

He looked at her, incredulous. "From the vault?"

She shook her head, eyeing the soldier at the cell entry. "De Meynell said he would move me into the apartments," she said. "I want you to help me escape from there."

"How?"

"We will have to think of something. If we do not, then my dreams of marrying Achilles are at an end and I become another man's whore."

Samuel eyed her unhappily, but he was obliged to help her. He knew he could never live with himself if he did not. Susanna was far too great to end up as the concubine to a Thuringian count. Between the two of them, she had always been the greater sibling and Samuel had always admired her because of it. He knew, for a fact, that if he were in trouble, she would risk everything to help him.

It was time for him to show a fraction of his sister's courage.

"That will not happen if I can help it," he said. "For now, I will tell my men to watch for Achilles and once you are moved into the apartments, we will do what needs to be done."

For the first time since being tossed into the vault, Susanna was starting to feel some hope. "Thank you, Sammy," she whispered. "I knew you would not abandon me."

Samuel simply nodded in response, standing up from the damp straw and making his way out of the cell, past the de Meynell man who locked it back up when he was gone. With him, he took the torch, and the vault was once again pitch dark.

But to Susanna, it didn't matter. She had hope now and she was going to cling to it with every bit of strength she had. She knew Samuel was frightened, fearful of betraying the man he gambled away his legacy to, but she knew that, deep down, he had the resolve and determination to do what was right. She'd seen that side of him, long ago, so she knew it was in him, somewhere.

Now, he was going to have to dig deep to find it again.

CHAPTER THIRTEEN

THE FLIMSY GATEHOUSE of Aysgarth was open.

Achilles, Alexander, and Caius entered through the open gates without any resistance at all. They were barely even questioned. But Caius was the first to notice that a few of the men at the gatehouse were wearing a distinctive red tunic with a thin white cross on it. He'd see that before.

It was the House of de Meynell.

Immediately, he was on his guard.

The three knights reined their horses to a halt in the outer ward and as Caius announced himself to one of the soldiers and declared he'd come for a visit with Baron Coverdale, Achilles and Alexander noticed that the blacksmiths were still working at full capacity and the smell of hot steel was heavy in the air. Nothing seemed to have changed from the last time they were there.

It was Achilles who finally took their horses over to the stables as Alexander remained with Caius, waiting to be greeted by Samuel. But Achilles had no intention of stabling the horses because he intended to find Susanna and leave immediately, so he had the grooms put the horses in the small corral and feed them. He didn't even want their saddles removed.

When he fled, it was going to be quickly.

He wanted to be ready.

God, he was nervous. His stomach was in knots. He wasn't sure where to start looking for Susanna, or if she would find him, so he remained with the horses, watching Alexander and Caius in the distance as they spoke to a couple of soldiers. He was taking his time in gathering up his saddlebags when he noticed that one of the soldiers that Alexander had been speaking to was now heading in his direction. He didn't think much about it until the man walked right up to him.

"My lord?" the soldier said. "You are Sir Achilles?"

Achilles eyed the man warily. "I am."

"Coverdale wants to speak to you. Will you wait here?"

Achilles nodded, wondering why in the world Samuel would want to speak to him. But then, it hit him – Susanna must have spoken to her brother, so clearly, Samuel had something to say to him.

Nerves turned to excitement. Maybe he wouldn't have to steal Susanna away after all. Perhaps, Samuel wanted to speak to him and agree to the marriage. Susanna was past marriageable age, after all, so why wouldn't Samuel be thrilled that someone wanted to marry his spinster sister? Of course, Achilles would never say that to Susanna for fear of being on the receiving end of a blackened eye, but it was the truth.

Perhaps Samuel even wanted to thank him.

All of these thoughts rolled through his head, but the wait for Samuel to make an appearance was excruciating. Achilles had told the soldier that he'd wait, but he was coming to wish that he hadn't. He wanted to run into the keep and find the man, and then he planned to marry Susanna before the day was out. He wasn't going to delay it. He'd waited his entire life for a woman who made him spark and he'd finally found her.

Sparks.

He couldn't keep the smile off of his face.

More time passed. Alexander and Caius eventually left the outer ward, heading towards the keep, but Achilles remained. He was coming to think that Samuel might never come when he finally saw the man emerging from a door in the two-level gatehouse. The soldier was with him, the one who had asked Achilles to wait, and he saw the soldier point in Achilles' direction.

Samuel was heading towards him and Achilles, unable to remain still, went to greet him.

They came together somewhere midway in the bailey. Before Achilles could say a word, Samuel spoke.

"She said you would come back."

Achilles was a bit stumped by the blunt statement, but he nodded. "Did she tell you why?"

"She did."

There was no indication whether or not Samuel was happy about that. Samuel simply looked at him for the longest time, long enough so that Achilles became a little uncomfortable. Perhaps no thanks would be forthcoming; perhaps there was even reservation on Samuel's part. Achilles began to feel some trepidation as he realized this may not be a smooth path, after all.

"She told me that she loves you," Samuel finally said. "Since you have returned for her, I will assume you feel the same."

Achilles didn't hesitate. "I do," he said. "I came back to marry her. I would like to have your permission. May I?"

He added on the last part purely as a courtesy, even though he didn't mean it. But Samuel didn't have to know that he'd planned on marrying her with or without approval. But Samuel didn't say anything right away, instead, turning to look around the outer ward casually before returning his attention to Achilles.

"Are you certain that you want to?"

"I am."

"Then I give my permission. But before you can marry her, we have something of an issue on our hands."

"What is that?"

"Since you love my sister, and I love my sister, I am going to be perfectly truthful with you," Samuel said. "Susanna did not want me to be. She wanted me to lie to you, but I am not going to do that. I need your help."

Achilles' brow furrowed. "What kind of help?"

For the first time, Samuel looked him dead in the eye. "I want you to listen to me very carefully," he said. "You must not react to anything I am going to say. If you do, it could go very badly for both of us. Do you understand?"

Achilles' trepidation grew. He didn't like the way Samuel was looking at him. "Aye," he said. "What do you need help with? And where is Susanna?"

"She is in the vault," Samuel said. "I have just come from her because she is in a good deal of trouble. You see, Witton de Meynell is here. He is in the keep, and that mercenary army you asked about when you first came to Aysgarth belongs to him. I fear I do not have a good deal of time to tell you everything that has happened, so I shall try to be succinct. De Meynell is gathering a mercenary army on behalf of the Duke of Brittany. His wife's father is allied with Brittany and has sent the manpower. More troops, French troops, will be arriving by Christmas. Their target is Richmond Castle. If you know anything about the history of the castle, it has changed ownership between Brittany and the English crown many times. Now, Brittany wants it back and they intend to take it by force. I told Susanna this and she was caught trying to send a message to the commander of Richmond. De Meynell threw her in the vault."

Achilles was trying very hard not to react. He had promised he wouldn't, but the struggle was real. He found himself focusing on his breathing because anything less would see him responding in a way that wouldn't be good for any of them. He was an emotional man, never more so than at this very moment.

It was everything Caius had told him.

Caius!

"The commander of Richmond Castle is here," he said through clenched teeth. "I just rode in with him. Even now, Caius d'Avignon is heading for the great hall and he is looking for you. *Where* is de

Meynell?"

Samuel tried not to look too stricken. "Probably in the hall," he said. "Why in the hell is Caius here?"

"A variety of reasons. Is de Meynell going to arrest him? Hold him?"

Samuel was starting to feel sick. "He may think that all of his problem are solved if he holds Richmond's commander," he said. "I do not know for certain. Listen to me, Achilles. While de Meynell is distracted with d'Avignon, you must get my sister out of here. My man will take you down to see her and you must get her out of the vault. Remove her now or her life is forfeit."

Achilles was being torn into pieces. The shock of the information was coming too fast, too hard, and he was trying desperately to sort it out and do what he needed to do. He wanted to remove Susanna in the worst way. But if he did, he was leaving Caius and Alexander to suffer at the hands of de Meynell. It was the worst choice he'd ever had to make and it was one he was going to have to make instantly.

No thought, no reflection. Simply gut.

It was wrenching.

"God," he finally groaned. "I will remove her, but I am coming back. Do you hear me? I will remove her from the vault, but I am coming back with an army to remove Caius and Sherry. They have unknowingly walked into the belly of the beast."

Samuel grabbed him by the arm. "You can do nothing for them now," he said. "Get my sister out of here. That is your priority."

Achilles let the man drag him towards the gatehouse. "I cannot leave my friends behind."

"It is Susanna's life or theirs."

"It does not have to be!"

Samuel would not let him go. "Get into that vault and get her out of there," he said. "Do it now while de Meynell is distracted. I will do what I can for your friends, but you must remove Susanna."

Achilles was feeling angst enough to hurt. His entire body hurt with the choice he was being faced with. But in truth, as much as he loved Caius and Alexander, there was really only one choice. He knew his friends would understand.

He had to get Susanna out of Aysgarth.

"Then go," he said, yanking his arm away from Samuel. "I will remove Susanna. You go and help Cai and Sherry. Hurry!"

Samuel looked strained and frightened, but he nodded. Over by the gatehouse, his man was waiting, and the soldier stepped forward as soon as he saw Samuel rush off towards the keep. Achilles charged towards the gatehouse, nearly running the soldier down.

"Come with me, my lord," the man said quickly.

Achilles did.

THE GREAT HALL of Aysgarth Castle smelled of something spicy. Both Caius and Alexander could smell it as they approached a big hall set within the circular curtain wall with a small courtyard in the center. Alexander pointed to the apartments on the east side.

"Look, there," he said. "It looks as if they have suffered a fire."

Caius looked to see what he was talking about, immediately seeing the blackened windows on the north side of the apartments. "I can smell the smoke," he said. "It must have been recent."

"That was not there when we were here only a month ago."

The scorched stone had each man's attention, but not for long. The entrance to the hall loomed before them and they stepped through, lured by the smells of something delicious.

Once through the door, they were hit by the cloying warmth of the chamber. A blue haze gathered up near the ceiling and they could see a few men sitting over by the hearth, which was burping sparks and smoke into the room. They progressed into the chamber, looking upon the men at the table with some interest, until Caius abruptly came to a halt.

"Christ," he hissed.

Alexander looked at him with concern. "What is it?"

"Back out," Caius whispered tightly. "Just… back out."

Alexander did as he was told. He turned around, pulling his gloves back on, and Caius did the same. He had no idea why, but Caius seemed oddly nervous. But a voice from the table called out to them just as they made their way to the door.

"Come in," a man said. "Do not leave. Join us."

The two knights came to a halt. Alexander looked at Caius without really turning his head. "Who *is* that?" he muttered.

Caius sighed faintly. "Witton de Meynell."

Alexander struggled not to react in shock. "Are you certain?"

"I have seen the man before."

"Does he know you on sight?"

"As famous as I am in Yorkshire? He would be a fool not to."

A both truthful and arrogant statement. But Alexander was thinking quickly. "He does not know me," he said. "Let me see if I can distract him. You head for the door."

He broke off before Caius could reply. As Alexander made his way to the table where de Meynell was with several other men, he was fully prepared to lie about who he was, who Caius was, and make haste back to Achilles when the knight standing next to de Meynell suddenly hissed.

"It's *you*," he blurted. "It's the bastard that killed le Sommes!"

Alexander looked at the knight, suddenly realizing he'd seen the man before. It was one of the knights he'd faced off against at The Horse's Arse in Skipton those weeks ago and it was a distinct shock to see him. It was also as confusing as hell. He'd expected to see de Tiegh in the Aysgarth hall. But looking at the men around the table, de Tiegh was nowhere to be found.

These were all men he didn't recognize – except for one.

Very quickly, Alexander assessed the situation. There were at least six men, no more, from what he could see, but turning and running from the hall wouldn't help the situation. It would only make it worse. Shockingly, he and Caius had walked into something unexpected and he was going to have to talk his way out if they had any hope of surviving.

Immediately, he went on the defensive.

"And you are part of the gang of knights that attacked me and my colleagues without any provocation whatsoever," he said steadily. "I told you I did not want to fight. I told you that we were minding our own business. But your commander ignored our declaration of peace and deliberately provoked us. We had a right to defend ourselves."

The knight's face turned red as the man seated at the table stood up, his intense gaze on Alexander.

"Who are you, Knight?" he asked.

"My name is Alexander," he said. "And you?"

"Witton de Meynell."

Alexander took a good look at the man, the very de Meynell whose named he'd been hearing since that run-in with the man's knights in Skipton. He hoped things weren't about to go from bad to worse.

"My lord," he greeted politely in spite of the fact that the man's knights were going for their weapons. "I have come in peace. We have come to seek Coverdale. I am sorry if we have disturbed you."

De Meynell came away from the table, heading in his direction, with his men following. Alexander immediately put his hand on the hilt of his sword and he could feel a body come alongside him, turning to see that Caius was doing the exact same thing. With a man the size of Caius, he made a very big target but he was also extremely formidable in battle. Alexander had faced many of them with Caius and there was no one better or stronger in a fight.

He hoped that wasn't what they were about to face.

De Meynell must have thought the same thing with all of the men around him going for their weapons, so he threw up his hands.

"Stop," he commanded. "No weapons. I do not want any blood-shed, at least not at the moment. But I am very interested to know why you are here. I was told the men who attacked my knights in Skipton were Pembroke."

Alexander wondered how long he could hold out with the story he'd told de Tiegh, the one about stealing the Pembroke standards. "We stole the tunics," he said, laying the foundation. "We were causing no one any harm when we were attacked by your men."

De Meynell looked him over. "How many men did you have with you?"

"There were three of us my lord, including a woman."

De Meynell immediately turned to his knight. "You told me there were at least fifty."

The knight's face turned a deep shade of red. "He's lying," he snarled. "There were many more than three."

Alexander quickly realized that de Meynell had been lied to about the fight. "There were only three, my lord, I assure you," he said. "If you do not believe me, I would encourage you to go to Skipton and ask the tavern keeper of The Horse's Arse. He will tell you the truth. You will also see for yourself that the tavern is not big enough to hold fifty men."

De Meynell's knight was so embarrassed that he unsheathed his sword. De Meynell had to throw out another hand to prevent the man from moving against Alexander, who was ready to unsheathe his own weapon. It was an extraordinarily tense situation, but de Meynell seemed strangely calm in the midst of men who were ready to go to battle. In fact, his gaze moved to Caius.

"I know you," he said.

Now, the focus switched to Caius. He was hoping that wouldn't be the case but, clearly, he was recognized. The question was – did de Meynell know *who* he was?

He wondered. In any case, he wasn't going to give the man any help.

"Mayhap, my lord." It was all he would say.

But de Meynell was becoming intensely curious, much more focused on Caius than on his posturing knights. "I know I have seen you," he said. "Do you recognize me?"

"Should I, my lord?"

De Meynell couldn't seem to take his eyes from him. "I can almost place you," he said. "I know I have seen you more than once, but we have never spoken to one another. Where do you serve?"

Caius wasn't sure how far he could get with a lie, so he didn't really try. "Richmond, my lord."

"Pembroke," the knight from the fight in Skipton interrupted. "He's Pembroke, my lord, and so is the other one. Somehow, the lady's message must have gotten through to Richmond. Can you not see that? They are here to spy on you!"

De Meynell was still fixed on Caius. "Is that true? That you have come to spy."

"It is not, my lord," Caius said.

But the knight, the one who had endured the humiliation of being defeated by a blow to the head at The Horse's Arse, would not let the situation die so easily.

"There was another knight with him," he insisted. "There were two of them. This big bastard is a different one from the knight I saw at the tavern in Skipton, but it seemed to me that they traveled in pairs. They traveled with that woman, who is de Tiegh's sister. He's here for her!"

De Meynell's eyes narrowed. "Is that true?" he asked Alexander. "You were traveling with Lady Susanna?"

Alexander nodded. "I was, my lord."

"Then mayhap she can tell me who you are. And where is the companion my knight is speaking of? Did he come here with you?"

"He is with the horses, my lord."

"Then Lady Susanna would know who he is, too," de Meynell said. "I was going to release her from the vault, anyway. I shall bring her here to clear up the mystery of just who you two are."

"He is Estienne de Sherrington's brother."

The announcement came from the hall entry and everyone turned to see Samuel entering. His gaze was on de Meynell.

"You know Estienne," he said. "Alexander is his brother and we must show him all due respect."

De Meynell peered at Alexander with great curiosity. "I see the resemblance now," he said. "How interesting. Does your brother know you serve Pembroke?"

"My brother and I have not spoken in fifteen years, my lord."

That brought de Meynell a moment of pause. But suddenly, he turned to Samuel as he pointed to Caius.

"Quickly," he snapped. "Who is this man?"

Caught off guard, Samuel looked to Caius, whom he had known for years. They had feasted together once, years ago, but he hadn't seen Caius since. Having no idea why de Meynell was asking such a question, and afraid to give the wrong answer with a lie, the only thing he could do was answer truthfully.

"That is Caius d'Avignon."

De Meynell's eyes widened. "The commander of Richmond Castle," he said incredulously. "The Britannia Viper in the flesh? God's Bones, I *knew* I recognized him. I simply could not place him."

Samuel realized he'd just done a very bad thing. He'd just given away Caius' identity. He'd promised Achilles that he would protect Caius and Alexander, and all he'd done was bury them deeper. Knowing he had to do something to cover his gaff, and quickly, he gestured towards the feasting table.

"He is here as my guest," he said. "Come, let us sit and enjoy the fine hospitality that Aysgarth has to offer. From the smell of things, I would say the cook is making her famous oat cakes. They are not to be missed, good men. I shall bring forth some very fine wine that comes all the way from Genoa."

He was acting casually, as if this were just any other normal visit from a neighbor, but de Meynell wasn't moving and neither were his men. In fact, de Meynell was looking at Samuel somewhat suspiciously.

"There is a third knight with them, I am told," he said. "Where *is* the man?"

Samuel struggled to remain casual in his manner. "I saw him with the horses, I believe."

"Another Pembroke knight?"

"He is not wearing the standard."

Evidently, that wasn't what de Meynell wanted to hear. He looked at the knight standing next to him, the one who had been in Skipton, and nodded his head. That brought forth both a wicked grin and a sword from the knight, pointed directly at Samuel.

In fact, the rest of the knights unsheathed their swords, heading for Alexander and Caius, who reacted in kind. Their swords came out and, very quickly, the situation was about to turn deadly. De Meynell moved out of the range of the coming fight, but his attention remained on Caius and Alexander.

"Something very strange is going on here," he said thoughtfully. "First, the lady is caught trying to send information to Richmond Castle, very sensitive information, and now I have the commander of Richmond in my midst. Stranger still, my knight swears that Estienne's brother is Pembroke, and so is the third knight in question. These are the same men who traveled with the lady and the third knight is not here. That begs the question – *where* is he?"

Samuel, who wasn't armed, was eyeing the swords around him with a good deal of trepidation. "I told you," he said. "He was out with the horses. These swords are not necessary, Witton. Tell your men to stand down."

But de Meynell shook his head. "I do not think so," he said. "In fact, we are all going to go down to the bailey and locate that third knight. I wonder if he is really with the horses."

"Where else would he be?"

De Meynell cocked an eyebrow. "He could be looking for the fourth Pembroke warrior, which happens to be your sister. Mayhap they have returned to save the spy they planted in your midst?"

Samuel stiffened. "My sister is not a spy."

De Meynell didn't waste any time. Snatching the sword from the nearest knight, he walked up to Samuel and put the tip of the sword right in the man's face.

"We are going to find out," he hissed. Then, he eyed Alexander and Caius, who were braced for battle. "If you do not drop your swords, I will drive this blade through Samuel's foolish head. And when he is dead, I will go straight to the lady and do the same thing to her. You will have your spy returned to you, but she will be in pieces. Is this in any way unclear?"

Alexander dropped his sword without hesitation, with Caius a split second behind him. As de Meynell's men rushed them and took away all of their weapons, shoving them around in the process, de Meynell kept his sword leveled on Samuel. When both Alexander and Caius were stripped of anything sharp and deadly, de Meynell looked at Samuel.

"Come along, Samuel," he said, almost pleasantly. "Let us find the third knight. What is his name?"

Samuel was sick to his stomach. God help him, the situation had deteriorated rapidly thanks to him. He felt like such a fool; a worthless fool.

"Achilles," he said quietly.

De Meynell smiled humorlessly. "Then let us find Sir Achilles."

With a heavy sigh, Samuel turned for the hall entry, praying with every ounce of strength that Achilles had managed to remove Susanna from the vault. He would simply have to deal with the consequences of a vanished knight and a missing prisoner, but he would deal with it when the time came.

If the time came.

He'd never prayed so fervently in his entire life.

CHAPTER FOURTEEN

S USANNA THOUGHT SHE was dreaming.

Crumpled up on the musty, damp straw, she was sleeping heavily when the sound of the clanging cell door opened again. Suddenly, someone was lifting her up and, half-asleep, she swung her fists in a panic, making contact with some part of a head and listening to a man grunt in pain.

"Sparks! Stop fighting! 'Tis me!"

Sparks. Opening her eyes in shock, Susanna sincerely thought she was dreaming when she found herself face to face with Achilles. With a gasp, she threw herself at him, arms around his neck, squeezing the life from him. But just as quickly, she let him go, looking at him with horror.

"What are you doing here?" she hissed. "You are not supposed to be here!"

Achilles had his hands on her, feeling her trembling in his grip. But he wasn't hearing her words as much as he was looking at her face – it was bruised and cut. That beautiful face had taken a beating and his heart sank. Reaching up, he stroked a soft, if not swollen, cheek.

"Oh… Sparks," he sighed heavily. "What did they do to you?"

Susanna put her hand up, covering his hand as it touched her face. "They got it worse than I did," she said, trying to smile. "It took twelve of them to capture me."

Achilles, in spite of feeling so terrible, started to laugh. He couldn't help himself because he had a mental image of exactly what it took to capture a woman who would not be captured. He would have expected nothing less. Gently cupping her face in his two big hands, he kissed her tenderly.

"I believe you," he said. "But you're in a bit of trouble now."

She nodded, her smile fading. "Did you see Samuel? Is that why you are here?"

He nodded. "He found me in the bailey," he said. "He has asked me to help you escape."

Susanna didn't look pleased. "I told him to tell you to run away," she said. "I do not want you caught up in this."

"I am already caught up in this."

Susanna put her hands on his stubbled face, gazing at him imploringly. "De Meynell is accumulating an army of mercenaries from his wife's father," she said softly, quickly. "The Duke of Brittany is involved and French mercenaries are expected by Christmas. The target is Richmond Castle, Achilles. The Duke of Brittany wants it. I was trying to get that message to Richmond but de Meynell's men intercepted my missive. It might not have been so bad except for the fact that one of the de Meynell knights we battled in Skipton, at The Horse's Arse tavern, is here with de Meynell. He identified me as having been seen with you and Alexander – Pembroke knights. That is another reason you must leave quickly – he will identify you, too."

Achilles had heard most of that from Samuel. But he hadn't heard the last part, about the knight who had been at The Horse's Arse.

"Did you recognize him as one of the knights?" he asked.

She shook her head. "He saw me first and recognized me," she said. "Unfortunately, he was the one who had intercepted my missive from my maid."

"Your maid? I did not realize you had one."

Susanna nodded, running her hand down his cheek because he was just so beautiful to her. "I had a maid and three fine dresses made," she said proudly, a glimmer of mirth in her eyes. "They were quite fine dresses and I was eager to show them to you."

He smiled, the thought of seeing her in a lovely garment already pleasing him. "I am eager to see them."

"You cannot. I burned my entire chamber out when de Meynell's men came to capture me. Somewhere between throwing burning clumps of wood at them and hurling a bank of candles at someone's head, I ended up burning about half of the apartments."

Achilles chuckled quietly, more imagery of her fighting off twelve men filling his mind. He chuckled because she was so fearless and so bold. He chuckled because he was proud of those traits, traits that had greatly annoyed him in the past.

But those days were long gone.

"I can have more garments commissioned for you," he said. "I may be old and gray by the time I see you in them, but I am determined to see you in fine clothing at some point in my life. You will not deny me that joy."

He meant it as a jest, something to lighten the mood, but it was a moment short lived. Susanna's smile quickly faded.

"I will ask you again to go, Achilles," she said softly. "I do not want de Meynell's venom turned on you."

He looked deeply into her eyes before reaching up to stroke her matted curls. "Would you leave me if the situation were reversed?"

She hesitated even though she knew what her answer would be. "I would not."

"And I will not leave you, either. Your trouble is my trouble, do you understand?"

She nodded, a smile of infinite sorrow coming to her lips. "Unfortunately, I do."

His eyes glimmered with warmth. "I know you do," he said. "There is no more time for talk. I must figure out how to get you out of here without being noticed, for you are very noticeable."

He was indicating her hair and her hand instinctively flew to it. "My clothing, too," she said. "If you only had a cloak so that I could cover myself."

He turned to look back at Samuel's man, still standing back by the cell door. The man was wearing a simple tunic, draping down to his knees, and Achilles pointed to him.

"You," he snapped quietly. "Give me your tunic for the lady. We must disguise her somehow to get her out of here so the gate guards will not notice."

The man rushed forward, pulling his tunic off and handing it over to Achilles. "Hurry, my lord," he hissed. "We must hurry."

Achilles knew that. He handed the tunic over to Susanna, who took it but didn't put it on. She simply looked at it. "This will not do any good," she said. "As soon as they see this head of hair, they will know it is me. Do you have a dagger with you?"

Achilles nodded, unsheathing a razor-sharp blade he had at his waist. "What do you want with it?"

Susanna took it from him. Before he could stop her, she held out a clump of her thick, curly hair and cut it right of, down by the scalp. Achilles' eyes widened.

"What are you doing?" he hissed.

Susanna took another clump and sliced that one off, too. She kept going, grabbing at her hair and slicing it off near her scalp. Pieces of red hair began to fall.

"I must get rid of this," she said, watching big chunks of her hair collapse into the straw. "You said it yourself; they will recognize me in an instant with all of this hair. But if I get rid of it, we may have more of a chance to escape unnoticed."

It was actually quite logical and quite reasonable, but Achilles was heartbroken as he watched her slice of chunks of hair. He couldn't even stop her because it was the smart thing to do. That beautiful, curly, untamed hair, copper-colored and glorious, was being unceremoniously hacked off.

He'd never seen anything so brave.

In stunned silence, Achilles watched her until she came to the back of her head and she couldn't quite get to it. With a heavy heart, he silently took the dagger from her, cutting off the rest of her hair and watching the beautiful curls fall to the musty straw. Because he shaved his own head regularly, he was rather skilled with the sharp blade and ended up cutting what he could close to her scalp so it didn't look so choppy. In the end, he sliced her hair as short as he could get it without actually shaving her head.

But it was a painful thing to have to do to so beautiful a woman, if only to save her life. He realized as he finished shaping it up that he was close to tears. When Susanna caught a glimpse of him, her expression was wrought with uncertainty.

"I am sorry to look so terrible," she said. "I would never shame you if I can help it, but I feel this is necessary. My hair is too recognizable. It will grow back. I promise."

He shook his head. "Is that what you think?" he said, incredulous. "That was not what I was thinking at all. I was thinking that I have never seen you look so beautiful."

Tears came to her eyes, knowing he was lying but loving him all the more for saying such a thing. She smiled timidly and he grinned, running his hand over her stubbly head, kissing her sweetly because she was tearing up. As she wiped at her eyes, de Tiegh's soldier waved his hands at them.

"We must go, my lord," he said. "We cannot delay any longer."

Achilles was on his feet, pulling Susanna up next to him as she quickly pulled the long tunic over her head. She kept touching her hair, or lack thereof, trying not to look at the pile of it on the ground. Achilles moved to the cell door, looking to the steps that led up to the ground level above.

"I want you to go to the doorway and ensure there is nothing between us and the stables," he said. "We will be making haste for the horses. You must be at the gatehouse when we ride through so they do not try and stop us. Do you understand?"

The soldier nodded quickly. "Aye, my lord."

"I do not even know your name."

"Byron, my lord."

"You have been most helpful, Byron. I shall not forget it."

Byron ran on ahead as Achilles held out a hand to Susanna, who took it and squeezed it strongly. He kissed her hand, smiling encouragingly at her. He watched Byron step outside, cautiously.

He never came back.

Concerned, Achilles let go of Susanna's hand and hesitantly made his way towards the stairs to see if he could hear, or see, anything happening above. It was still and silent from what he could see; no movement. He was about to take the first step, heading up to see what he could see, when he heard a voice.

"You had better come out now." It was an unfamiliar voice. "I know you are down there with her, Sir Achilles. You had better come out."

Achilles had no idea who it was until he turned to look at Susanna, who was a few steps behind him. He would never forget the expression of sheer terror on her face.

"De Meynell," she whispered tightly. "It is de Meynell."

They'd been found.

CHAPTER FIFTEEN

A CHILLES CAME THROUGH the vault entrance first, but Susanna was close behind him. They were holding hands as they emerged into the worst scene they could have possibly imagined.

Byron was on the ground, several feet away, where he'd been dumped by de Meynell knights who had captured him as he'd emerged from the vault. He had a gash on his head from having been struck, sitting upright with his hand on his head. But it wasn't Byron who had Achilles' attention.

It was Alexander and Caius.

They were stripped of their weapons, standing several feet away and surrounded by heavily-armed men. Their expressions were emotionless for the most part, but standing just a few feet from them and directly in front of Achilles was Samuel and another man he didn't recognize.

Samuel appeared pale and drawn, but the man next to him appeared curious, almost pleasant, until he got a good look at Susanna. Then, his face darkened.

"God's Bones," he spat. "What happened to your hair?"

Susanna put her hand on her head, an instinctive reaction. "I cut it off," she said steadily. "I no longer have any use for it."

De Meynell stared at her. Then, he started to move towards her, as if they were the only two people standing in that bailey. He came closer and closer, his features taut with rage. But before he could get to her,

Achilles stepped into his path.

De Meynell came to an abrupt halt.

"What are you doing?" he demanded, looking at Achilles, who was a head taller than he was. "Get out of my way."

Achilles shook his head. "If you have anything to say to her, say it to me."

De Meynell's features screwed up with confusion. "I will deal with you in a moment," he said. "Get out of my way or this will not go well for either of you."

Achilles held his ground, at least for the next few moments. But then, gentle hands were on him, pushing him aside as Susanna stepped forward to defuse the confrontation.

"Please, Achilles," she said softly. "It is all right. I will speak with him."

Achilles did not like it, but he complied, moving aside as his eyes were shooting daggers at de Meynell. It was an extraordinarily threatening move, one that could have gone very badly in Achilles favor, but Susanna was there, taking de Meynell's focus off of Achilles.

"Well?" she said. "What is it you wish?"

De Meynell was glaring at her. Coming from a man who normally kept his temper well, it was an unusual state.

"Your hair," he growled. "What did you do?"

She lifted a well-shaped brow. "That should be obvious."

He grunted in frustration. "I can see that you cut it," he said. "*Why* did you do it? It makes you look like a man!"

Susanna didn't respond to his anger or his insult. "I like it better this way."

De Meynell's eyes widened. "You did it deliberately," he said, as if the idea had just occurred to him. "You did it so you would look less attractive, didn't you? I told you what your fate would be and you did this to deliberately make yourself undesirable!"

Susanna lifted her shoulders. "I do not care what you think. It is done."

De Meynell was furious. All of that gorgeous red hair that made her something worth looking at, a prize of amazing stature, was gone. In its place was an uneven cut, close to the scalp.

He could hardly believe it.

"It will not work," he said. "Whatever you think you have done to make yourself unattractive will not work. Your fate is the same regardless. You have breasts and a womb, and that is all you need to please men."

Achilles flinched but Susanna held out a hand to him, stopping him from charging. "Insult me all you wish. It does not change things."

De Meynell clenched his teeth. "Mayhap it does not, but you should remember what I told you if you tried to resist. I was not jesting."

"What we discussed had nothing to do with my hair."

She was being defiant, which was rebellious as far as de Meynell was concerned. She had been warned. He was wildly angry that his plans for her had been thwarted, by her own hand no less.

He wasn't going to let her get away with it.

In a fit of rage, he marched over to one of his knights and unsheathed a dagger from the man's belt. Then, he stormed over to Samuel, who was simply standing there quietly. Raising the dagger, he plunged it right into Samuel's shoulder.

Samuel let out a mournful cry and grabbed his shoulder, sinking to his knees. Susanna, acting on instinct, rushed to help her brother, but Achilles was there, throwing his arm out and catching her around the torso as she bolted past him. He held on fast, pulling her back and away, but it was like trying to wrestle a wild horse.

"Stop," he hissed in her ear. "This is what he wants. He wants an excuse to cut you down. *Stop!*"

Through her haze of rage and fear, Susanna heard him. As she struggled to calm down, de Meynell turned his venom on her.

"I told you what would happen if you resisted," he said, holding up the dagger stained with Samuel's blood. "You did not believe me and I was forced to prove my intentions. Continue resisting and I will poke your brother full of holes until all of the blood drains from him. One infraction, one wound. That is the price."

Susanna was so angry that she was trembling. Achilles could feel her in his grip but he held her tightly, afraid of what would happen should he let go. With Samuel on his knees on the ground, bloodied hand over his left shoulder, Achilles could see that the situation was going from bad to worse. He caught a glimpse of Caius and Alexander, who had their eyes trained on de Meynell. Like the good knights they were, their eyes were on the threat to see what he was going to do next.

Achilles was afraid that the next target would be Susanna. He, too, was watching de Meynell very closely. All he knew was that he would defend Susanna to the death which, in this instance, might very well be the case. Coiled up, he watched.

He waited.

"Let us return to business," de Meynell said, still gripping the bloodied dagger. "Lady Susanna, do we understand one another now?"

Susanna didn't respond at first but a squeeze from Achilles had her nodding. "Aye."

De Meynell nodded. "Good," he said. "Now, then. I believe I have finally figured you out. It would seem that you are part of a ring of spies, spies that you brought to Aysgarth. Now your fellow brethren have come to free you."

Susanna shook her head. "That is not true," she insisted. "I am the only one at fault here. They are innocent. Let them go and I will confess everything to you."

De Meynell stopped his pacing. He looked at Susanna in surprise, as did nearly everyone else, Caius and Alexander included. Achilles was holding her tightly but she was pulling away. The harder he held on to her, the more she pulled until she finally peeled his hands off of her and escaped his grip.

"You have wanted a confession," she said to de Meynell. "I will give you one. But you will let these men go."

De Meynell cocked his head thoughtfully. "My lady, I need no confession," he said. "The appearance of your comrades proves that you are a spy. You were sending word to d'Avignon of Richmond Castle and the man miraculously appeared, which means you must have been sending him information prior to the missive we intercepted. He brought colleagues with him, *your* colleagues, men who you evidently travel with and are Pembroke knights. They are all part of William Marshal's dirty deeds and political compost. Everything about them, and you, reeks of your underhandedness. Now they have come to help you escape my custody. What else is there to confess?"

Susanna could see how utterly confident he was and she was sickened by it. From the moment she and Achilles had emerged from the vault until this very second, de Meynell acted like a man who had supreme control, which he did.

He had their lives in his hands.

Behind de Meynell, Samuel was regaining his feet. He was trembling and pale, and the wound was bloody, but he was standing again. Susanna looked at him, seeing her beloved brother so very beaten by this man who had taken everything from him – his legacy, his pride – everything. It was true that Samuel was to blame for the vast majority of his misfortune, but de Meynell gloated over the situation. Now, he had taken to abusing Samuel when Susanna didn't behave the way he wanted her to behave.

It was only going to get worse.

Her gaze flickered over to Alexander and the enormous knight standing next to him. It was Caius d'Avignon from what de Meynell had said. She'd never seen the man in her life and she seriously wondered why he had come because his presence made it seem as if, indeed, she'd been passing him information and he'd come to see for himself. It was all too strangely coincidental.

She didn't blame de Meynell for being suspicious.

But she did blame him for this situation. She didn't want to provoke him, but they simply couldn't stand out here in the bailey for the rest of their lives. She had to do something.

Even if she paid the price for that action.

"I have never had contact with Caius d'Avignon," she finally said. "This is the first I have ever seen of the man even though he has been commander of Richmond Castle for many years. And Alexander and Achilles did not return because we are all part of some great spy ring. We are not, you know. They came back because Achilles wanted to ask my brother for my hand in marriage. It is as simple as that."

De Meynell looked at Achilles, standing a foot or so behind Susanna. His expression was incredulous. "Marry her?" he repeated. "You want to marry this... this woman?"

Achilles didn't hesitate. "I do, my lord," he said. "That was the only reason we returned. It has nothing to do with whatever you seem to think. So you have a big mercenary army here; that is no secret. It is not as if you are trying to hide it, as the entire countryside can see it. Therefore, there is nothing secretive for anyone to discover if it is spies you are looking for."

De Meynell eyed him. "But d'Avignon is here."

"I am here because I was traveling to Lancashire and stopped at Aysgarth for the night," Caius said, sticking to the pretense they'd made back at Richmond. "Aysgarth always sets a fine table and that is the only reason I am here. It is you who have overstepped yourself by stripping me of my weapons and assuming I am here to do you harm."

"I told you he was here as my guest," Samuel said, his features strained with pain. "I've not lied to you, Witton, not ever. Your paranoia is controlling your common sense."

De Meynell looked at Samuel, his expression rippling with uncertainty. Suddenly, he wasn't so much in control. His gaze lingered on Samuel for a long moment before returning his attention to Achilles.

"The fact remains that you took her from the vault," he said. "You were helping her escape."

"Because I want to marry her and for no other reason than that."

It was logical. All of it, logical. But de Meynell wasn't feeling reasonable or logical at the moment. He had Pembroke knights and the commander of Richmond Castle in his grasp. They were extraordinarily valuable hostages, but they were also dangerous hostages. Especially d'Avignon; his garrison was at the center of everything de Meynell was doing and if the man didn't know that before, he knew it now. If he let d'Avignon go, he would return and tell everyone what was coming from the Duke of Brittany and there would be no surprise when the mercenary armies moved on Richmond.

But if he kept him, surely Richmond would figure out where he was, and who was holding him, and even with his two thousand mercenaries, de Meynell knew he couldn't withstand an attack from Richmond and her allies in the north.

It would be a bloodbath.

De Meynell was ambitious, but he wasn't stupid. D'Avignon aside, he had a real issue with the remaining three Pembroke knights.

"Be that as it may, *she* is my prisoner," he answered Achilles belatedly. "She was caught trying to send secretive information to Richmond, so she will remain in the vault until I decide what is to be done with her. You cannot change that."

Before Achilles could reply, the knight who had been at the inn in Skipton stepped forward. There was an expression of rage on his face.

"She's not only a spy, but a killer, my lord," he seethed. "I watched her and those other two Pembroke knights slay three of your men. They killed le Sommes and I saw it with my own eyes. They must be punished!"

De Meynell's focus was shifted over to the fight at The Horse's Arse, which more or less started this entire situation. It seemed to be the incendiary point for everything. "Bellerby is right," he said to Achilles. "I was deprived of a fine captain. You did that."

"He attacked us first," Achilles reiterated. "We were eating peacefully when he and his men attacked us first."

"That is a lie!" Bellerby shouted.

Achilles was a man who never backed down from a fight. He crooked a finger at Bellerby. "You know it is not," he said. "If you are so concerned with us being punished, then come here and do it yourself. I challenge you."

Bellerby had seen the big, bald knight in the fight and he wasn't about to tangle with him, but he'd just been issued an invitation that, to refuse, would make him look like a coward. Desperate to deflect the attention away from him, he turned to de Meynell.

"They are liars and spies, my lord," he said. "Do you know what the woman told me? That her colleagues were called Executioner Knights. She said they were legendary in The Levant."

De Meynell was interested. "Is that so? Then it would make sense for them to be at home in a fight and execute my men."

Bellerby had his lord's attention and he pressed hard. "Since they like to go around challenging men to fights, why not make a sport of this," he said. "Let the Executioner Knights fight each other to the death. I will face the winner in vengeance for the colleagues they struck down. *I* was there, my lord; I saw what happened. Do not permit them to deny what they did. Do not deny me the chance to seek vengeance for my friends who were so cruelly cut down."

De Meynell rather liked that idea. "You have a point," he said. "Le Sommes had been with me for a very long time. He did not deserve to die the way he did."

"He did not, my lord. Make these men pay."

"Men?" de Meynell looked at him with surprise before returning his attention to those he held prisoner. Specifically, he was looking to Achilles. "Since you killed my captain and two of my finest knights, punishment is not out of order. And since you like to fight so much, you can fight the woman you profess to love. As a spy, it is my right to execute her, so let her death be at the hands of an Executioner Knight. Fitting, wouldn't you say? I am sure you will be much more merciful with her than you were with my own men."

Achilles' eyes widened. "Fight her?" he repeated, aghast. "I have no intention of fighting her and I will kill the first man who makes a move against her."

De Meynell was prompt in his reply. He lifted the bloodied dagger, that was still in his hand, and moved straight for Samuel as Susanna and Achilles and even Alexander begged the man to stop. They could see what was coming and Samuel put up his hands, backing away as he prepared to defend himself. But the message was clear.

Continue resisting and I will poke your brother full of holes.

He'd meant it.

"He will fight me!" Susanna finally screamed. "Please... leave Samuel alone. I will fight him, I swear it!"

De Meynell lowered his dagger, but Achilles was beside himself. He looked at Caius, at Alexander, with an expression of pain that they never seen before.

Caius noticed it first.

The commander of Richmond Castle had remained quiet through de Meynell's raging, mostly because he wanted to get a sense of the situation as a whole. Was de Meynell mad? Was his control over the situation firm? The answer to both questions seemed to be in the affirmative, but stripped of his weapons, Caius could do nothing at the moment.

But he had an army waiting out of sight that could.

All they had to do was make it until morning when Kevin and Morgan would bring the tide of Richmond men to the rescue. The main thing would be to make sure he personally was not put in the vault because someone would have to get to the gatehouse to ensure his army made it into the fortress. De Meynell's rage didn't seem to be directed at him, which was good. It gave Caius room to maneuver. But he couldn't let Achilles fight the woman he so clearly, and desperately, loved. It was pure madness.

Therefore, he had to do what he could.

He deflected attention.

"I have little stake in this," he said as everyone looked in his direction. With his booming voice, it was difficult not to. "I came to Aysgarth to feast and that is what I shall do tonight. I have no desire to see a fight, which can just as easily wait until morning. Throw those two in the vault if you must, but I am going back to the hall and I am taking Coverdale with me so his wound can be tended."

He started to move but swords were pointing in his way. "You will remain until I tell you to move," de Meynell said. "This is not your command, d'Avignon. I am in charge."

Caius smiled as if amused. "Do you really think to hold, me, de Meynell?" he asked as if the man was a fool. "Let me tell you what will happen if I do not return to Richmond soon – my men know I have stopped at Aysgarth. When I do not make it to Lancashire, they will retrace my steps and discover that the last place I was seen was, in fact, Aysgarth. I have almost two thousand men at my disposal plus thousands more from neighboring allies who will raze this place. When they are finished with Aysgarth, they will go to Whorlton and raze that, too. Do not toy with me, de Meynell, for you will lose."

It was a threat and nothing he said was untrue. De Meynell knew it; he'd known it from the start. Everyone else knew it, too. Frustrated that Caius was essentially emasculating him in front of his men, de Meynell struggled to regain control that seemed to continually want to slip from his grasp.

"I could kill you," he said. "It would be my right to execute a spy."

Caius rolled his eyes. "I am not a spy," he said. "I am a knight of the highest order, sworn to William Marshal, and a seasoned veteran of Richard's holy quest to The Levant. The Britannia Viper does not slink around in shadows, waiting for crumbs of information that will change destinies. What I do, I do face to face. Now, what you do with the three knights you seem to have issue with is your problem. I am not part of that and I resent that you have included me. So, I will say again – whatever punishment you have planned for them can wait until tomorrow. Let us eat and drink and forget about the politics of England for a night. Frankly, I'm exhausted by it all."

With that, he kept moving, taking Samuel by his good arm, and pulling him towards the keep. He was such a big man with such a commanding presence that everyone seemed to instinctively obey, including de Meynell's men. Even though they had their swords drawn, and pointed at him, no one made a move to stop him. Caius and Samuel headed up to the keep, leaving de Meynell and his men standing there with Alexander, Achilles, and Susanna.

In fact, de Meynell was rattled. He was losing control of the situation and grossly unhappy because of it. D'Avignon was taking it all away from him and he was embarrassed. With a frown, he gestured to Achilles and Susanna.

"Lock them in the vault," he commanded.

Bellerby nodded with satisfaction at the command, but he pointed to Alexander. "And him, my lord?"

De Meynell grunted. "Him, also," he snapped. "But come the morning, we will let them battle it out to the death and be done with this. That bitch is no longer useful to me with her hair cut off and I have no desire to look at her. Get her out of my sight."

As de Meynell turned for the keep, his knights and soldiers swarmed on Achilles, Susanna, and Alexander. The first man that went for Susanna received a blow to the face that smashed out all of his front teeth and from that point on, the fight was on.

Achilles wasn't going to let them touch Susanna and neither was Alexander. He jumped into the fray, throwing punches and wrestling a sword away from a man he sent to the ground with a devastating blow. But once he had the sword in his hand, the soldiers panicked and all blades focused on him.

The fight was about to turn deadly.

The odds were too much, even for Alexander. He was armed now and that made him a target, and men would cut him down and say it was justified because he held a weapon. Knowing that, Susanna broke away from Achilles and ran to put herself in front of Alexander.

"You'll not kill him!" she shouted. Then, she turned her head to Alexander and spoke quickly. "If you value our lives, you'll drop the sword. They'll kill us, Sherry."

Alexander knew that, in theory. There were at least four knights and more than twenty soldiers, plus more on the walls and at the gatehouse who were starting to migrate in their direction to see what the trouble was. But Alexander was a knight above all, so battling great odds was something he was born to do. He was a fighter. But being a seasoned warrior also meant that he knew when to drop the weapon so he could live to fight another day.

This was one of those times.

The sword fell to the dirt of the bailey and the soldiers began to swarm, grabbing Alexander and Susanna, completely enveloping Achilles because he was still throwing punches. It took more than a dozen to finally subdue him and only by sheer number did they manage to do it, dragging him down into the vault as Susanna, over the chaos, begged Achilles to stop fighting.

Down to the vault they returned.

It was a horrific ending to a horrific day.

CHAPTER SIXTEEN

"WHAT'S WRONG?"

The question came from Morgan de Wolfe. Kevin was standing at the edge of the tree line to the south, facing Aysgarth. He'd been standing there since arriving earlier in the day and he'd even sent out men to scout around Aysgarth and the village, discreetly, simply to keep abreast of what was going on. The men had come back to tell him everything seemed quiet, but something in Kevin's gut wouldn't rest.

He was sensing trouble.

"I am not sure," he finally replied, watching the sentries on the walls as they went about their rounds, torches in hand. "I feel as if something is amiss."

"But what?"

Kevin shook his head. "I do not know," he said. "I feel a sense of uneasiness that I cannot seem to shake."

Morgan came to stand beside him, his attention on Aysgarth, lit up with fire against the night sky. "What is it?" he asked. "The men we sent out came back to tell us everything seemed quiet."

"But not all of them are back yet."

"That is true, but those who have returned have told us there is nothing amiss that they can see."

Kevin knew that. But he still shook his head. "No one has been inside the fortress," he said. "So much could be happening in there that we would not even know of."

"And you believe that is the case?"

Kevin could only shrug. "I never thought it was a good idea for d'Avignon to go to Aysgarth, especially if he believes it is a staging ground for an attack against Richmond. Who knows what is going on in Coverdale's mind?"

"We have until morning to find out."

Kevin sighed faintly. "Then it is going to be a long night."

That was the truth.

Lodged in the woods directly across the river from Aysgarth, they were mostly clustered near the shallowest part of the river, an easy crossing to the other side through the icy waters. They'd been watching the road in and out of the castle, plus the roads in and out of the village that surrounded the castle. They were even watching the training grounds where the mercenaries were settled down for the night. What Morgan said was true – it had been very quiet.

But Kevin wasn't willing to let his guard down.

Something felt off.

The evening progressed. The sounds of night were all around them, the night birds singing and the chirping of various bugs. Kevin could hear his men slapping at themselves as the night wore on, slapping at the bugs who wanted a taste of their flesh. He, too, had been forced to slap away a bug or two. But the entire time, his focus was on the castle in the distance, as if waiting for something to happen.

It was a fragile and permeable silence.

The night deepened. It was very late now and some of the soldiers were sleeping in the darkness. Kevin could hear them snoring, but he wouldn't join them. He wasn't tired. He kept his gaze on the fortress as if expecting something to happen at any moment.

Then, he saw movement in the darkness.

Ducking down behind the foliage, he watched someone dash from a copse of trees near the fortress and across the road into a heavy growth of forest. As he continued to watch, that same figure plunged into the river, wading through in a section that was hidden from the view of the castle. Kevin realized that it was one of his men and both he and

Morgan went to intercept him.

It was a young soldier, skinny and freezing from his dip in the water, but skilled enough not to be seen. Kevin and Morgan heaved the lad out of the river and pulled him into the trees.

"Well?" Kevin hissed. "Where have you been?"

The young man's teeth were chattering. "There's a postern gate on the north side of the castle, by the kitchens," he said. "I was watching the gate."

"And?"

"And a maid came through because there's a brook where they do their washing, outside of the castle," he said, turning to point north. "You cannot see it from here, but it's there. She came to wash and I spoke with her."

Kevin was confused. "This late at night she came out to wash?"

The young man shook his head. "She came out at sunset," he said. "She wanted to know what I was doing and I told her I was a shepherd looking for a lost sheep. I think she believed me because she didn't run. We became friendly and I asked her about Baron Coverdale."

Kevin grunted. "God," he said. "You didn't, did you? If she tells anyone that a shepherd has been asking about Coverdale, they might get suspicious."

But the young man shook his head again. "I do not believe so, my lord," he said. "She didn't seem suspicious of me at all. I told her I'd never been inside such a great castle and she told me all about it, including a few interesting things."

"Like what?"

"Like Coverdale has a visitor he's entertaining and there was to be a great feast tonight."

"She meant d'Avignon?"

"Surprisingly, no. She told me that it is Witton de Meynell."

Kevin's eyes widened. "De Meynell is inside the castle?"

"That was what she told me, my lord."

Kevin looked at Morgan. "*That* is what I meant by an uneasy feeling," he growled. "The very man who has been plotting against d'Avignon is in there, waiting for him. Damnation, he walked right into it."

He was agitated now and for good reason. Even Morgan's features were stiff with concern. He looked over to the castle in the distance.

"Caius said if he does not emerge by dawn, then we must assume something is wrong," he muttered. "If de Meynell is in there…"

"Then d'Avignon may not emerge at all."

Morgan nodded in resignation. He was thinking that he should have listened to Kevin's gut.

"What do you want to do, Kevin?" he asked.

Kevin looked at the fortress in the darkness. "I want to get in there," he said. "The guards on the wall will be there all night, but they should change shifts before dawn."

"And?"

"And it's my intention to make it onto those walls at that time." Kevin returned his attention to Morgan. "You know your men better than I do. Select fifty of them to go with me, fifty of your best. Our objective will be to get to the gatehouse and ensure the gate is open for the bulk of the army to come through. I would suggest you and this fine young soldier go back to the postern gate and enter from that access point once I reach the top of the walls."

Morgan agreed with the formulated plan. "It shall be done," he said. "But what if the situation is normal? How do we explain breaching the walls and the gatehouse?"

Kevin lifted his big shoulders. "I am following d'Avignon's orders," he said. "Let him explain why we breached the fortress. But I would rather do it and be wrong than not do it and wish I had."

That was the truth, for all of them. With that, they took the wet and freezing soldier back to the bulk of the army, gave him something to eat, and spread the word among the men that soon enough, they would be moving out. Their great lord was in need of them and the men were eager to help.

When the first hints of pink began to appear on the eastern horizon, they were ready.

CHAPTER SEVENTEEN

"COVERDALE, WAKE UP."

A voice in the darkness shook Samuel. At first, he thought he was dreaming. But when someone reached out and shook him, he startled himself awake and sat up, throwing himself away from the body in his chamber. As he struggled to become coherent, a weak light in the darkness showed the face of Caius d'Avignon.

Samuel hissed with relief when he realized who it was.

"Bloody Christ," he breathed. "What in the hell do you want, d'Avignon? You nearly scared me to death."

The hour was late in Samuel's sparse bower, a vast chamber with a bed, a table, and little else. Everything else had been sold or traded to fund his gambling habit, so there was very little left in the chamber, and the entire apartment block, that Samuel hadn't already done away with.

But Caius didn't care about a smelly bower with a bed that was in disrepair. As Samuel cowered against the wall, wiping his hands over his face, Caius loomed over him.

"I have just spent the past half-hour dodging de Meynell's men to get to you," he growled. "You and I must speak, Coverdale. We have a situation on our hands."

Samuel's hand immediately went to the wound on his shoulder. It was a deep wound but the surgeon said nothing vital had been clipped. Still, it was very painful, making Samuel willing to listen. D'Avignon was right – they had something terrible on their hands and Samuel was integrally involved in it.

They all were.

"Aye," he said after a moment. "We certainly do."

"Do you want to live?"

"Of course I want to live."

"You heard de Meynell tonight at the feast," he said. "You heard him speak to his men about the coming battle between Achilles and Susanna and how to make it more interesting. My God, the man wants to turn it into something greatly entertaining."

"I know."

"Then you also know that we must have a plan of attack come the dawn, because I will not see your sister and Achilles battle to the death. I assume you do not wish to see that, either."

Samuel sighed heavily. "Of course not," he said. "But if she resists, I become a target for de Meynell's blade."

"If you do not do something to help your sister, you will not live to see your next day of birth because if de Meynell does not kill you, I will. Is that plain enough?"

Samuel didn't like being threatened, even if d'Avignon was justified to a certain extent. "What do you want from me?" he demanded. "What can I do?"

Caius set down the taper he was holding. Reaching around to his back, he appeared to be fumbling with the backside of his breeches. Suddenly, there was a blade glittering in the weak light of the chamber as he extended it to Samuel.

It was a dagger.

Samuel's eyes widened.

"A weapon?" he hissed in shock. "But I saw them strip you. Where did you get this?"

"It does not matter," Caius said. "Just don't smell it."

Because he'd told the man not to smell it, Samuel immediately lifted it to his nostrils. It must have smelled atrociously, because he quickly held it away from his face.

"God," he groaned. "It smells like…"

"I know."

"Are you telling me that you just pulled a dagger out of your arse?"

"I told you not to smell it."

Samuel looked at the dagger with a good deal of distaste, finding the entire idea of hiding a dagger in one's arse crack wholly distasteful but, in the same breath, it was ingenious. No wonder de Meynell's men hadn't found it. He set it down on the bed beside him, wiping it off with his linens so he wouldn't have a man's arse-smell on his hands.

"Why are you giving it to me?" he asked.

"Because you are going to use it."

Samuel stopped wiping, looking at him in shock. "I *am*?"

Caius rested his enormous hands on his hips. "On de Meynell," he said. "You have become his whipping post, Coverdale. The barons of Coverdale had a reputation for strength and fairness until you came around. Now, all anyone knows of Baron Coverdale is that he sets a fine table and taxes his people heavily. Does it not even concern you that your sister will be fighting for her very life come the morrow?"

Samuel found that he couldn't look Caius in the eye. "Of course it concerns me."

"And yet, you have no plan to help her? You are sleeping the night away even though your sister may face her death on the morrow? What a pathetic excuse for a brother you are."

Samuel couldn't very well dispute him. "More than you know, d'Avignon," he muttered. "More than you know."

"Then do something about it," Caius hissed. "If I could use that dagger on de Meynell tomorrow, I would, but they will be watching me. I will be heavily guarded. You, however, will not be."

"How do you know?"

"You were not watched today, were you? No one was looking at you because they know you're a weakling. Therefore, you are the logical choice to sink that dagger into de Meynell's chest. If you do not, he will sink his into yours. Is that what you want?"

Samuel sighed again, thinking on his sister and on the situation in general, wondering where he had gone so wrong. Over the years, he'd sunk into gambling debt and depression, and now he found himself living in his ancestral home when it no longer belonged to him.

He'd done that.

And Susanna... strong, noble Susanna... was locked in the vault, arrested by de Meynell for spying. She'd spared her brother an arrest by not revealing he was the one who had given her the information about Richmond. He was free because of her.

And how had he repaid her for that?

He hadn't.

Samuel couldn't even remember when he became such a worthless wretch of a man. It was as if he woke up one morning and suddenly lost every bit of character he'd ever possessed. He'd known that for a while now, but it was never so obvious as it was now. He'd grown lazy and complacent about it, but if he didn't do something soon, his sister was going to pay the price.

They were all going to pay the price.

"Very well," he said, eyeing the smelly dagger. "I will do what I can."

A big hand shot out, grabbing the front of his tunic, and Samuel found himself looking into angry black eyes.

"Listen to me and listen well," Caius said. "Whatever fear you have, put it aside. Whatever reluctance you feel, kill it. Too many lives depend on you, Coverdale. You will not simply do what you can – you will do *all* you can and do it with the bravery your sister has shown before a man who wants to execute her for being a spy, because I swear before our Lord that if you do not, I will end you. If de Meynell does not kill you, I will."

Samuel knew simply by looking into his eyes that he was serious. Everything screamed sincerity. Samuel should have felt anger at the very least but all he could manage to feel was submission. He knew that

Caius was trying to save Susanna; he was trying to save them all. But now the man had put that determination into Samuel's hands and he wasn't entirely sure he could carry it out.

But he had little choice.

"I will not fail," he said hoarsely.

Caius immediately released him. "See that you do not. Coverdale… I want to be proud of you. I want to say that I saw you do something courageous. Do not disappoint me."

With that, he turned and left the chamber, leaving his burning taper behind and his smelly dagger. But even after he was gone, Samuel could feel the man's lingering presence. Caius had a way about him that filled a room and then some.

The Britannia Viper was all that and more.

Samuel turned to look at the dagger once more, knowing he had to dig deep to find that Blackchurch knight he'd lost somewhere along the way.

He hoped that knight wasn't gone for good.

CHAPTER EIGHTEEN

T HEY ENDED UP in two different cells.

De Meynell's guards had placed Susanna back in her cell, managing to attach one of her shackles to her left ankle, but they were unable to secure the other three limbs and left her as she was. They didn't even try to restrain Achilles or Alexander because it was all they could do to get the men into the cell and slam the door. Even then, Achilles managed to grab one of them through the bars and choke the man until he was rendered unconscious. The only reason Achilles let him go was because someone had used a dagger and stabbed him in his left forearm. The shock of it had caused Achilles to loosen his grip just enough so they were able to get their man out.

It had been a chaotic and bloody battle down to the last moment.

But that had been hours ago. When the fight was finished and the de Meynell soldiers fled, Susanna, Achilles, and Alexander were plunged into darkness. A few words were spoken between them, mostly to make sure everyone was uninjured, and then silence as the reality of it settled.

It was the shock of what was to come.

Susanna felt guilt. So incredibly guilty. She felt as if all of this were her fault and her doing. Had it not been for her, none of this would have happened. Achilles and Alexander would be safe somewhere. Or, perhaps not – she always knew they would return for her, so it wasn't as if she could have prevented it.

Still…

So, she'd sat in silence, wallowing in guilt that was consuming her. She wasn't even afraid about fighting Achilles. It was simply the guilt that they were all in this predicament, together. The remorse was almost more than she could bear.

"Sparks?"

It was Achilles voice in the darkness. Susanna had been sitting up against the wall, dozing, and her eyes slowly opened to the pitch blackness around her.

"Aye?"

"Are you disappointed with me?"

"For what?"

She heard him sigh. "For not getting you out of Aysgarth when I had the chance."

She lifted her head to look at him even though she couldn't see him. "You never had the chance," she said. "There was never a chance, Achilles. That's the saddest part of all. I was just thinking on the fact that I got you both into this mess and I am sorry for it."

She could hear him shifting around in the next cell. "We have been in worse, haven't we, Sherry?"

Alexander, who had clearly been dozing, grunted sleepily. "Much."

"This is not the first time I've been in a vault, isolated away from the world," Achilles continued. "When I was with Maxton and Kress in the vault at Les Baux-de-Provence, it was full of men. Men who had been there for years, dying men, men who cried day and night… it was a very noisy place."

He didn't sound upset or frightened. He didn't even sound angry. He sounded as if this was just one more adventure in a long line of them but, to Susanna, that wasn't the case. She took this very seriously.

"I have never been in a vault," she said. "I have spent the last ten years in the wilds of Norfolk, shadowing a fiery young woman. Life was easy and it was kind. There was not one time, in all of those years, that I even had to draw a sword in defense of Cadelyn."

"But you trained, did you not?" Achilles asked.

"Aye," she replied. "I trained with the knights constantly, with the garrison commander. Before I was assigned to Cadelyn, I was assigned to the House of de Russe, at their townhome of Braidwood in London. I saw a good deal of action there, in fact. The House of de Russe is a warring house."

Achilles grunted. "I would say so," he said. "The family has been around since the days of William the Bastard. If there is a war, they are in the forefront of it. Did you actually go to battle with them?"

Susanna sighed faintly. "Nay," she said. "I was left behind to protect the women. Always to protect the women. I have confession to make."

"What is that?"

"Other than small skirmishes, I have never fought in a major battle."

"Why not?"

"No one would let me. I am a woman, after all."

"But you are Blackchurch-trained."

"It does not matter to most."

Achilles fell silent for a moment. "You are as skilled as any man I have ever seen, Sparks. I promise that I will let you fight in any battles that I am in command of."

"Would you?"

"I said I would."

"I have never wished so hard for a future battle in all my life."

Achilles laughed softly. "Unfortunately, I am not usually in charge of battles, but Alexander is. He is a natural leader, much as Maxton of Loxbeare is."

"I have never met Maxton. What is he like?"

"He is the meanest man you will ever meet," Alexander said groggily, unable to sleep any longer because of the talking going on. "But he is also one of the fairest commanders you will ever know. He is the unofficial leader of the Executioner Knights, a man known for the strength of his sins as well as the strength of his accomplishments."

"You will meet him someday soon," Achilles said. "Maxton and Kress and I could never stay apart for very long, so there will be a time soon when we reunite."

"And Sherry, too?"

"Sherry, too."

Alexander shifted around in the darkness. "As much as I would love to be part of this joyful reunion, there will not be one if we do not figure a way out of the situation we are in," he said. "I can only imagine it is another hour or so until dawn, so we must speak on such things and do it quickly. We must have a plan of action."

It had been the subject Susanna and Achilles had been trying to avoid speaking of, as foolish as that was. It was the axe hanging over their heads, the storm that was looming on the horizon. They knew it was coming.

They couldn't ignore it.

"I know," Achilles finally said. "In truth, I have been thinking about it all night. Cai bought us some time by demanding that the battle take place at dawn. That took de Meynell's focus away from us, however briefly."

"He told Kevin to bring the men at dawn," Alexander said quietly. "He is waiting for that moment so, until then, we must do all we can to delay anything serious."

"There is no question," Achilles said staunchly. "I will simply refuse to fight her."

"If you do, then he may pick someone else to do it. He will probably select me."

"And?"

"And if I refuse to fight her, he may start stabbing Coverdale again. He is not beyond such motivation."

"I do not want to see my brother injured," Susanna spoke up, moving over to the edge of the cell, a cage that shared a common wall with the cell that Achilles and Alexander were in. "One of you must fight me.

If you do not, then de Meynell might even pit me against one of his men who, I am sure, would follow his orders to fight me to the death."

Achilles had heard her chain rattle and now, her voice was very close. He felt his way over towards her cell in the darkness, coming to the slats of the iron cage and reaching through. He found her arm and she instantly latched on to him with both hands. That warmth, that connection, was electric. It fed and fortified him like nothing else he had ever known.

"I will do it," he said softly. "Have no fear, Sparks. It will be me and I will drag it out until Kevin and Morgan come charging in to save us."

"But we will have to make sure that it looks as if we are giving effort," she said. "I do not want him to think we are making light of the whole thing."

Achilles scoffed. "You and I have been fighting without hurting one another since the day we met," he said. "Remember the tavern in Heckington? We spent the better part of an hour rolling around on the floor, making it look as if we were hurting one another."

"I *was* hurting you."

"You were not. In any case, that is what we shall do again – drop the swords and charge one another. We can make a fist fight last much longer and it is far more entertaining."

He couldn't see her smiling in the darkness. "Are you sure you want to engage in close quarter brawling with me again? I nearly ripped your ears off the last time."

"I was screaming in pain to feed your pride. It did not really hurt."

She started to laugh, as did he. On the other side of Achilles, Alexander groaned. "Christ, you two are sickening," he said. "Achilles, you know damned well she was hurting you and Susanna, if he'd wanted to disable you, he could have at any time. He was holding back because you are a woman, so do not get any foolish notions of superiority. You were winning because he was letting you and I have seen the man in battle enough to know that. But I will tell you this – it was convincing, all of it, so if you can repeat that battle for de Meynell, do it. Do it long enough for the Richmond army to make an appearance."

The laughter faded at the reality and truth of Alexander's words. Achilles squeezed Susanna's hands as she placed her cheek on the back of is big mitt. All jesting aside, the situation was critically real and they all knew it.

"We will do what needs to be done," Achilles muttered. "We can only pray that Kevin is able to get in or Cai is able to stop this madness. I will not consider the alternative."

Although Alexander wanted to discuss that possibility, he refrained. There was no point. If it came to that, all would be at an end and there would be no recovery, so he let the conversation die. They knew the situation and they knew the stakes. All they had to do was hold out until the Richmond army arrived.

If it arrived.

Surprisingly, it was Susanna who brought up what Alexander could not. Or perhaps not so surprising, considering she had the most to lose.

"But what do we do if the worst comes?" Susanna asked quietly. "If d'Avignon cannot stop what is about to happen and his army cannot come to our aid, what do we do?"

Achilles squeezed her hand again. Usually, he was the emotional one, the aggressive one who made decisions based on impulse. That had been his problem his entire life. But in this case, there was time to think about the situation and consider all scenarios. He didn't want to think about a scenario where the Richmond army was delayed, or worse, prevented from coming to their aid, but Susanna had asked a question about something he didn't want to consider. He had no choice and his guts were starting to churn with apprehension.

"Whatever we do will not be to the death," he said firmly. "Sherry will help us, as will Cai. It will not come to that. Somehow, we will escape. But, Susanna... you must consider that we may not be able to take Samuel with us. I know you are worried for your brother and it does not make any of us happy that de Meynell tries to control you by threatening Samuel, but you may have to face the fact that he will have to remain behind. Are you willing to do that?"

Susanna was in a bind. Of course, she didn't want to leave her brother behind. But on the other hand, she wanted very much to leave with Achilles, to become the man's wife and live a long and healthy life with him if the opportunity presented itself. But that might entail leaving her brother behind. As she thought on it, she knew she could only come up with one answer –

She couldn't.

In her heart, she knew she couldn't.

"Sammy is my brother," she said, feeling tears sting her eyes. "We shared a womb together. It has always been the two of us, even when years separated us. I cannot leave him behind knowing what de Meynell would do to him, Achilles. I am sorry if that is not the answer you were seeking, but it is an honest one. Much as I would not leave you behind, I will not leave Samuel behind, either. Would you leave one of your brothers behind?"

Achilles shook his head, though she could not see it. "Nay," he said. "I could not. But if it comes down to it and we are able to get free and he is not, would you not take that chance? Remaining behind with him does not ensure his survival. Quite the contrary if de Meynell is willing to use Samuel to control you."

"Your brother would want you to go," Alexander said in support of Achilles. "Much as you would want him to go if he had the chance to be free. You must think on it that way; remaining will not help him and he will suffer the guilt of knowing you remained because of him. This is a situation with no winners, Susanna. But in the end, you must do what is best for you. No one will fault you for it."

The tears were starting to flow. "I simply do not know if I can leave him."

Achilles was still holding her hand. "I hope it does not come to that," he whispered. "But know this; no matter what you decide, know that I love you. That will never change, Sparks. From the beginning of time until the end of all things, I will love you just as I do now. Nothing can destroy that."

That only made her tears fall faster. She opened her mouth to reply but a noise from the vault entry stopped her. Someone had opened the door and the faint glow of light could be seen. Footfalls were heard, the sound of many boots, and with the light behind them, Susanna and Achilles and Alexander were able to make out several figures entering the vault. The fact that there was light streaming through the doorway told them everything they needed to know.

Dawn had arrived.

The time had come.

CHAPTER NINETEEN

T HE SOUNDS OF water rushing was quite loud, drowning out any
noise from their movements, which was fortunate. They didn't
want to be heard. As Kevin and fifty Richmond men moved across the
river upstream from the falls, everything about their movements were
masked by the flowing waters of the River Ure.

Kevin and his men had been ready to move the moment a ribbon of
pink on the eastern horizon signaled the approach of dawn. As soon as
they saw it, they made haste into that freezing river, using the rocks to
cross as much as they could, before disappearing into the trees on the
other side.

Luckily for them, no one had cut back the trees from the Aysgarth
Castle for more than twenty years. There were stumps all around where
the trees had been cut down in years past, but those were old markings
of what had once been maintained land surrounding the castle.

As it was, the current Baron Coverdale had allowed trees to grow
again and, being so close to the river, those trees had an endless supply
of water and grew up strong and tall very quickly. Kevin had been
scoping out his path for most of the night, at least from what he could
see in the darkness, and he wasn't surprised to see that the trees ran
right up to the moat. In fact, there were trees growing in the moat itself,
which was a swampy mess. At one point, the moat had drawn water
from the river, but over the years, dams of debris had built up and there

was no longer water flowing in the moat.

That was to be Aysgarth's mistake.

As Kevin maintained his position in the trees, determining the best way to get to the walls, Morgan took his contingent of fifty men to the postern gate along with the young, skinny soldier who had scoped it out so ably. The plan was that as soon as the sun began to appear on the horizon, they would make their move on the castle. For those at the postern gate, it depended on someone actually opening it, like a servant or a cook, but for those planning to mount the walls, it would take a little more doing.

But they were prepared.

A grappling hook was a staple of any attacking army and Richmond had brought several. They had ropes attached to them, quite long, and the ropes were knotted so the men climbing them would have something to grip as the ascended. Kevin and his men had been watching the walls carefully, waiting for a break when the men changed shifts, and that came, as predicted, just as the sun peeked over the horizon.

Once Kevin saw that, he and his men moved.

It was Kevin's intention to scale the wall first and get an idea of what was on the other side before sending his men in. Given that the walls of the shorter but wider motte weren't very high at all, he was able to make his way across the swampy moat and up the other side, throwing the grappling hook and scaling the wall quite ably. He was young and strong, and he made his way up the wall with very little effort. Once he was at the top, he could see nearly everything.

And what he saw struck him with fear.

Shocked, he watched a scene in the outer bailey that was both puzzling and terrifying. He could see several men standing around in a big circle, including Alexander, who seemed to be surrounded by heavily-armed men. Kevin moved his gaze around the bailey and saw Caius being escorted away from the fight by a contingent of men with their swords pointed at his back. Kevin didn't know where they were taking him. But before he could ponder that, his attention was drawn back to the big circle of men. And what he saw in the middle of that circle was what had attracted his attention –

There was a battle going on.

As Kevin watched in horror, he could see Achilles and a much smaller warrior doing battle. They were fighting with their fists, throwing punches and rolling around in the dirt. Clearly, something horrific was going on and Kevin's attention moved to the gatehouse, which was heavily-manned as the shifts of sentries changed. That meant it would be well guarded if his men breached the walls and tried to attack it.

But he had to do something and do it fast.

Kevin slid down from the wall, removing the grappling hook when he hit the bottom. Rushing over to his men, waiting in the trees, he found himself surrounded by a host of concerned and eager faces.

"My lord?" an older soldier asked what they were all thinking. "What has happened? What did you see?"

Kevin was thinking quickly and logically, or at least, trying to. "It seems to me that d'Avignon is a prisoner," he said. "I only caught a glimpse, but he was unarmed and being marched somewhere by heavily-armed soldiers. I know not where they were taking him, but we'll have to find him quickly. He was headed towards the gatehouse. I saw Sherry, too. However, there is a fight going on that many men are watching involving Achilles and someone I did not recognize. I have no idea what is going on, but it cannot be good."

"But the gatehouse?" the old soldier pressed. "Can we get to it?"

Kevin looked at the anxious faces around him. "They are changing shifts and it is heavily-guarded at this moment," he said. "We can get over the walls but I fear getting through the gatehouse would be very difficult. By the time we were able to get it open, the mercenary army on the west side could be summoned and we do not want to deal with those men."

"What do we do?"

Kevin expression was serious, controlled. He was a de Lara, a knight in a long line of knights dating back to William the Bastard. A de Lara did not fail, in any case. Smart and resourceful, he came up with a plan.

"We need a distraction," he said. "We have to draw the soldiers, inside of Aysgarth, out and we have to prevent the mercenaries from getting to the castle to repel our invasion."

"What kind of distraction, my lord?"

Kevin gestured in the direction of the mercenary encampment. "We are going to set that mercenary encampment on fire. While everyone is fighting that fire, we extract d'Avignon and the others." There was a young soldier next to him and he grabbed the lad by the arm. "Run back to the bulk of our army and take twenty men with you. Get over to that mercenary encampment as quickly as you can and start setting it ablaze. Stay undercover and do your best, but everything depends upon you igniting their tents and possessions. Move like the wind, lad. There is no time to waste."

The lad fled, sailing through the woods and disappearing. When he was gone, Kevin turned to the closest man.

"You," he said. "Run to the postern gate and tell Morgan to hold. Tell him what we are doing. He is to wait to enter the compound. When he sees the smoke from the mercenary encampment, that will be his signal to move. That is when the gates of Aysgarth will be opening."

The second man fled to the north, following the trail that Morgan and his men took. With everything in motion, the old soldier turned to Kevin once more.

"What do we do now, my lord?" he asked.

Kevin turned his attention to the gatehouse, of which they had an angled view. "Move the army so that we are watching the gatehouse," he said. "When those gates open and men start pouring out to fight the fire, the army pours in. But for the rest of us – we'll be mounting the walls. We'll be entering Aysgarth from all sides."

Men were on the move. Something was going on inside of Aysgarth Castle and their commander was in danger. Until all of the pieces of their plan fell into position and that mercenary encampment began to burn, all they could do was wait.

CHAPTER TWENTY

"I HOPE YOU slept well last night," de Meynell said in tone some-where between a threat and cheerfulness. "It is going to be an eventful morning."

The sun wasn't quite up yet as Achilles, Susanna, and Alexander faced de Meynell and about fifty of his men beneath clear morning skies. All of de Meynell's men had their weapons drawn and there were even a few archers, which concerned Achilles a great deal. He had no idea why archers were even summoned, wondering if they'd been brought to take aim at Samuel. Instead of stabbing the man if Susanna showed defiance, perhaps they were going to shoot arrows at him instead.

It was a horrifying thought.

He didn't dare look at Susanna, afraid he would see that she had the same concern. That would only enrage him and, at this point, it was too early for him to lose his temper. He didn't reply to de Meynell's statement, which only made the man more solicitous.

"What?" he said. "No witty reply? No demands? Surely you are concerned with what is to happen today?"

"Would it matter?" Achilles asked. His gaze moved to Caius and Alexander, who were grouped together this morning once again. "I see that you are still holding Richmond's commander hostage. This will go very badly for you once Richmond discovers what you have done, not to mention once William Marshal discovers what you have done. Have you considered that he will bring the whole of his armies to Yorkshire and destroy you and your allies? The Duke of Brittany will not stand a chance against William Marshal. Enjoy your power while you have it, de Meynell. It will not last."

Some of de Meynell's cheeriness left him. "So you have a sharp and logical tongue, Achilles," he said. "In fact, I do not even know your full name."

"Achilles de Dere."

He lifted his eyebrows. "I do not know the family."

"Do you know de Velt?"

That drew a reaction. "Everyone knows de Velt."

"My mother is a de Velt. Congratulations. You will also have the de Velt army down around you, too."

That drew almost more of a reaction from him than the threat of William Marshal. The House of de Velt, forty years ago, had been the most ruthless and barbaric house in England. In fact, the king at the time, Henry, had paid the head of the House of de Velt, Ajax de Velt, to stay away from his properties. De Velt had a way of capturing castles and then putting entire armies on poles, sticking them through the bodies of living men, and then posting the poles for all to see. Henry wanted no part of that, so he paid the man to stay away.

The horrific and ruthless reputation of the House of de Velt was still intact even though they'd become more civilized as the years passed. But no one wanted to tempt fate.

Except, perhaps, an arrogant Yorkshire lord.

"Then if you have de Velt blood in you, you must be a formidable warrior, indeed," de Meynell taunted. "But the fact remains that you are a spy. The lady is a spy. It is my right to do as I please with spies and no man will dispute my rights. Therefore, I will tell you how our battle will happen this morning – you and the lady shall face one another and fight until one of you cannot fight any longer. Wounded or exhausted, it does not matter to me, but the loser will die. By his or her opponent's hand or by my archers. One way or the other, one of you will not live to see the sunset."

Achilles was trying very hard to control himself. "And the winner?"

De Meynell pointed to Alexander. "The winner will face de Sherrington," he said. "The winner of that bout will live. I would not disappoint such a warrior. But he, or she, will spend the rest of their lives in the vaults of Aysgarth."

"Nay," Caius spoke up. "They will not. The winner comes with me. He, or she, will have earned their freedom."

De Meynell was genuinely intimidated by the big, black-haired knight. In truth, he was intimidated by all of them, hiding behind the strength of the soldiers he had with him. Otherwise, he would have never stood up to them.

And that was the truth.

"I have not yet decided what to do with you, d'Avignon," de Meynell said. "Surely you do not expect me to release you after you have witnessed all of this."

"If you do not release me, everything Achilles said will happen and more. You will not survive."

"But if I release you, you will simply run back to Richmond and bring your army to destroy me."

"If you want to be a big player in the politics of England, you must expect bigger players to quash you. That is the price you pay, de Meynell. But keeping me captive will most certainly only make the situation worse."

De Meynell knew that, in theory, but he didn't like hearing it as it came from Caius. He was coming to think that he should simply let him go and perhaps Caius would take that into consideration when thinking of mounting his army against him. He hadn't harmed Caius in any way, but if things continued, that might change.

De Meynell was starting to feel some doubt.

Perhaps Caius was too much of a liability to hold any further.

"Then I shall show mercy," he said abruptly, motioning quickly to his men. "Escort him to the gates. Leave, d'Avignon, but do not make me regret being merciful to you."

It was an extraordinarily unexpected move, one that caught Caius off guard. He'd expected much more of a fight about it. Perhaps the threat of tens of thousands of men descending on Wensleydale and Whorlton had worked.

"I want my weapons," he said. "And my horse."

"Leave now, as you are, or you will not leave at all."

With that in mind, Caius didn't hesitate. With a lingering look to Samuel, silently reminding the man that the fate of his sister rested with him and that clandestine smelly dagger, he headed towards the gatehouse, followed by a contingent of de Meynell's men. They had their swords drawn, pointed at the man's back, and everyone watched as the flimsy gates of Aysgarth's gatehouse swung open and expelled him.

When the man was gone, Achilles and Alexander breathed a sigh of relief. At least Caius was safe from whatever madness de Meynell had planned. But they were not safe at all; once Caius departed, de Meynell's attention was back on them with the added layer of irritation now for having made the decision to release the commander of Richmond Castle.

Any semblance of pleasantness was gone from his face.

"Think not that this changes your fate," he said to the three accused spies. "It has no bearing. Susanna, since you are a weaker female, you shall choose the weapons used in this battle. Take care and do not choose something Achilles will excel at more than you."

It was a dig at the fact that she was a woman and as de Meynell grinned, the men around him tittered. All but Samuel, that is. He simply stood there, looking at his sister with an expression of great sorrow.

There was no laughter on his face.

But Susanna wasn't looking at her brother. She'd stopped looking at him, not wanting de Meynell to think she was emotional about Samuel and use that to his advantage as he'd done yesterday. Instead, she was ignoring her brother outright as she stood next to Achilles, her head held high. She hadn't come from the vault holding his hand as she had yesterday, but rather came out beside him, strongly prepared for what was to come.

She wasn't going to give de Meynell the satisfaction of knowing how frightened she was. In fact, she looked him in the eye when she chose her weapon.

"I choose fists."

De Meynell's eyes widened with shock. "*Fists?*" he repeated. Then, he started to laugh, joined by the men around him. They were having a great time at Susanna's expense. "Are you daft? He will kill you much sooner than I would hope."

"Then that is my problem, is it not? I choose fists. If you will cease to cackle like a flock of hens, let us get on with this."

The laughter stopped unnaturally fast at the insult. "It will be a pleasure to watch you and your unruly tongue meet justice this morning," de Meynell said. Then, he shook his head sadly. "You were so beautiful. You could have had a life of pleasure, but I see now that you cannot make a silk purse from a sow's ear. That is all you are, Woman – a sow's ear. Now, make your move."

Susanna turned to Achilles, noting the strong lines of his face in the early morning sun. In the light, she could see that his hair was starting to grow in because he hadn't had the opportunity to shave it. He'd told her once that he had a full head of hair but he'd gotten in the habit of shaving it to keep the vermin away.

As the sun rose, she could see his hairline, well defined, as light brown stubble grew in. She'd never seen him like that before and she smiled faintly, a sweet moment of discovery amidst hell. But the moment was short lived. Her pause was only temporary before she charged Achilles, ducking low when he braced himself, and took him out by the legs.

The fight was on.

Achilles ended up on his face because of the way she'd hit him and, suddenly, she was on his back. She had him by the ears and pulled enough so that he roared in pain. He reared up on his knees and fell over backwards, on top of her. Hearing her grunt, he knew he'd knocked the wind out of her, but before he could flip himself over and attack her, she brought up a handful of dirt from the bailey and smashed it into his nose and eyes.

It was vicious from the start.

Reeling from dirt in his face, Achilles already had enough. He knew she was trying to put on a good show, but he had to put one on, too, and try not to hurt her in the process. That was virtually impossible, but he had to do his best. Getting hold of her hands as they rubbed dirt in his eyes, he managed to climb to his feet, twisting her the entire way. She was fighting him fiercely, but he was stronger. He managed to lift her up and toss her several feet away, wincing when she grunted painfully as she landed on her back.

Not giving Susanna time to breathe, Achilles pounced.

The brawl got nasty after that, but Susanna didn't give up. She even rammed her foot into his privates, although it was more of his bottom than his manhood, but it was enough so that Achilles reacted by shoving her away from him, as hard as he could, trying desperately not to actually strike her. She ended up falling onto her face and he was right behind her, putting his foot on her neck as she struggled to rise. He wasn't trying to strangle her, merely pin her down, and Susanna struggled appropriately. She had a little room to breathe, but not much. She was sucking in plenty of dirt.

Unfortunately, from the way she was pinned, there wasn't much she could do and it looked to those observing that the fight had already ended. Susanna was on her face, slowly suffocating because Achilles had his boot on her neck. De Meynell, standing over with his men, shook his head with disapproval.

"I knew this would not be a fair match," he said unhappily. "He is simply too strong for her."

His men agreed, including Samuel, who was quickly approaching a panicked state. He had the dagger Caius had given him, tucked into the sleeve of his tunic. He hadn't quite made the final decision to use it, although he was hoping to. In his wildest dreams, he'd never planned to use it on Achilles, but as he watched his sister's slow death, he began to rethink that strategy. Fearful, he turned to de Meynell.

"Order him to step away from her," Samuel said, struggling not to sound as if he were terrified. "Tell him to step away and let her recover. They can fight when she has caught her breath."

De Meynell eyed Samuel before returning his focus to the fight at hand. Achilles was still standing there and Susanna was still struggling. He shook his head.

"They will only end up like this again. We must make the fight more balanced in your sister's favor." With that, he signaled to the archer who had been standing with his men. He pointed to Achilles. "Disable him only. Do not kill him."

Alexander, who had been watching the fight with concern and interest, was filled with horror when he heard the command. Before he could utter a word of protest, or even warn Achilles, two archers raised their bows and the arrows went sailing. Achilles, who had his back turned to the archers, was hit in his right calf and his right shoulder. The impact of the arrows was enough to launch him off of Susanna and onto the ground.

Susanna's head came out of the dirt, biting off a scream when she saw what had happened. Her first instinct was to run to Achilles and help him, but she knew if she did that, de Meynell would realize that their battle had all been for show.

She couldn't take the chance.

So, she remained where she was, tears filling her eyes as Achilles sat up, his face contorted with pain. The first thing he did was rip the arrow in his leg free. It came out in one piece and the blood flowed from the puncture wound, streaming down his leg. But the one his shoulder was embedded deep and he couldn't get to it. He tried, but he simply didn't have the reach.

And she couldn't help him.

Biting off choking sobs, Susanna stood up and marched over to him, kicking him in the chest and sending him onto his left side. When Achilles looked up at her, looming over him, he could see the rivers of tears down her face, streaked with dirt. With as much pain as he was experiencing, all he could think of was her. He didn't want de Meynell to see her breakdown.

"Nay, Sparks," he whispered. "Do not weep. I want you to kick me now. Go ahead; he has to think that I am badly injured. Kick me and mean it. It will be all right, sweetheart. I promise."

She didn't want to obey him. God help her, she didn't want to, but she knew she had to. She had to kick and cause pain to the man she loved. She would have become sick over it had there been something in her stomach, but there was nothing. Instead, she sobbed quietly and gagged as she kicked him in the left thigh and then in the gut.

Her distress was overwhelming her.

Achilles grunted, trying to move away from her, but she came around behind him and kicked him in the kidneys. It wasn't hard, but hard enough. Then she fell to her knees, took hold of the arrow shaft, and twisted.

Achilles screamed with pain.

Susanna was a mess. She was no longer attempting to hide her sorrow. She was sobbing openly now, throwing her arm across his neck as if trying to strangle him and putting her hand on the arrow, moving it just enough to cause him excruciating pain. It was quite agonizing but above the searing pain, Achilles could feel her sobbing against him. He knew this was worse on her than it was on him.

God, it broke his heart.

When she barely touched the arrow, he yelled as loud as he could so de Meynell would think she was really hurting him. With her arm across his neck, she was simply holding him fast while she jostled the arrow to cause him pain.

In truth, he wasn't sure how much more he could take. The fight was dragging on and the sun was rising now, but there seemed to be no Richmond army on the horizon. Achilles wondered if they had fled when Caius was released, but he couldn't honestly believe that. He would never believe that The Britannia Viper would leave his friends behind, but the fact that there had been no army sighted concerned him greatly. He wasn't sure how much longer he and Susanna could continue to fight each other, to hurt each other. The sounds of her sobs in his ear was just about killing him, more painful that any arrow could ever be. He thought that, perhaps, this was really the end of things.

It seemed the situation was quickly becoming hopeless.

But then, he began to smell smoke. Not that smoke was unusual in and of itself, but just as he got a strong whiff of it, men began to rush towards the gatehouse. He could hear soldiers shouting to de Meynell.

"The training encampment!" they were saying. "It is on fire!"

As Susanna and Achilles struggled in their life and death fight, the rickety gates of the gatehouse were pulled open, the ropes creaking on their wheels as the panels were rolled back. Susanna stopped touching the arrow as both she and Achilles came to a halt, watching as de Meynell's men began running towards the gatehouse. Everyone seemed to be running in that direction except for de Meynell, Samuel, and Alexander.

In fact, de Meynell appeared shocked by it all. He was confused, watching his men as they rushed through the gatehouse. Servants were ordered to the training field carrying buckets and blankets. Everyone seemed to be moving to fight the fire, but de Meynell wasn't moving. He seemed to be frustrated that his punishment for his spies had been interrupted. In the chaos, he turned to Achilles and Susanna to demand they continue but, in that moment, something extraordinary happened.

Samuel, who had been standing silent and meek at de Meynell's side, portraying every inch of the submissive vassal, suddenly lifted his hand. There was something in it, something gleaming, and he plunged it straight into de Meynell's chest.

Alexander, who was standing closest to Samuel and de Meynell, watched in amazement as Samuel removed the dagger from de Meynell and plunged it into him twice more before the man fell onto his back, his eyes wide with shock.

"De Tiegh!" he gasped. "I will have you executed for this! I will have you killed! I will –!"

Samuel, in a frenzy, fell on the man and stabbed him repeatedly, until he stopped moving, until Alexander bent over and hauled him to his feet, away from de Meynell's bloodied corpse. By that time, a great roar could be heard as the Richmond army began to pour in through the gatehouse, slashing everything that moved.

Leading the charge were Caius and Kevin.

With Samuel still in his grip, Alexander raced over to Susanna and Achilles, who were still on the ground, stunned and muddled from the beating they'd given each other.

"Achilles!" Alexander hissed. "Get up! We must get out of here!"

He reached down, pulling Achilles to his feet as Susanna tried to help. She was shaken and beaten, and as she tried to help Achilles, Samuel reached down and pulled her to her feet as well.

"What happened?" Susanna looked at her brother in utter shock. "Sammy, you... you *killed* him!"

Samuel still had the man's blood on his hands and realized he didn't feel badly about it at all. That Blackchurch knight, that ghost of what he'd once been, had come back to life. He could feel the familiar fire of battle surging through his veins, something he thought he'd lost a long time ago.

But it hadn't been lost... it was only sleeping.

Sir Samuel de Tiegh had made a return.

"I know," he said, smiling weakly at her. "I had to. For you, I had to."

Susanna could hardly believe it. For a moment, the brother and sister shared something, something warm and bonding, as strong as the birthright between them. For Samuel, it was his courage reaffirmed. For

Susanna, it was the brother she'd once had such faith in.

He was back.

"Come on," Alexander said. "We must get out of here while Richmond is taking care of de Meynell's men. We must get Achilles to a safety."

Susanna kissed her brother on the cheek before rushing to Achilles' side, holding on to him to support him. With Alexander on the other side, and Samuel covering their rear, they ran towards the open gates as fast as Achilles could move.

Caius, a massive broadsword in hand, was waiting for them. He had walked out of Aysgarth and straight into his army, who were hiding in the trees. Now armed, he had returned for his friends.

He wasn't going to leave without them.

"You'll have to cross the river, but there are horses waiting," he told them. "Head back to Richmond. We'll secure Aysgarth."

But Samuel shook his head. "This is my castle," he said. "With your help, I will regain it."

Caius could see the light of determination in Samuel's eyes. De Meynell was lying dead over in the middle of the bailey, which told Caius that Samuel had done what he'd been told to do. That weak, beaten man had finally found his courage. With that realization, a smile crossed Caius' lips.

"Well done, my lord," he said. "You have made me proud. I am happy to help you regain your fortress."

It had been a long time since Samuel had heard those words. It had been forever since someone had shown confidence in him. Feeling fortified with Caius' approval, he took a broadsword that had been stripped from one of de Meynell's gatehouse guards and headed back into the fray.

"I do not mean to interrupt any of these important moments we seem to be having, but I would appreciate it if someone would please remove this arrow from my shoulder," Achilles said, distracting the focus from Samuel. "I would ask Sparks, but she did not remove it when she had the chance. I think she rammed it deeper."

They all turned to look at him, standing there pale and bloodied, his eyes red from having had dirt rubbed into them. Susanna's mouth popped open in outrage.

"I was supposed to look like I was hurting you," she insisted. "How would it look if I had ripped it out? He probably would have put another one in you out of spite!"

Achilles smiled weakly at her to let her know he was jesting. "I know, old girl," he said. "You did a good job of it."

Her outraged softened, replaced by an expression of great remorse. "I am very sorry," she said. "I know I hurt you. I am so sorry."

He shushed her. "It was a tickle."

"You were not yelling as if it were a tickle."

"How do you know? You have never tickled me."

She couldn't argue with that. As Susanna went around to the front of him, putting her arms around him and holding him tightly, Alexander and Caius were able to remove the arrow in one piece. It had hit his shoulder blade, but it hadn't broken off. Once it was removed, Achilles was able to move his shoulder without any searing pain, so they assumed nothing was broken.

It wasn't as bad as it could have been.

"Go," Caius said again. "I will do what needs to be done. Yorkshire and her dales are my responsibility. I will ensure Samuel's rule is returned to him and I will further ensure that those mercenaries are sent back where they came from. Sherry, when you return to The Marshal, make sure he knows that. Yorkshire, and Richmond, are secure."

Alexander put his hand on Caius' cheek. "I will," he said fondly. "Thank you, Cai. We are in your debt."

Caius waved them off, watching Alexander and Susanna help Achilles down to the river where they crossed the water to the other side. The last he saw of the trio, they were heading at breakneck speed in the direction of Richmond Castle.

Caius knew it wouldn't be the last he saw of his friends.

For the third member of the Unholy Trinity and the Blackchurch-trained lady knight, it had been a harrowing adventure since the beginning of their association. From personal battles to unending love, the story of Achilles and Susanna was something to be whispered about with smiles for years to come in William Marshal's inner circle. Friends and family alike would speak of them fondly. Certainly, they had faced their greatest adversaries – each other – and they had lived to tell the tale.

Theirs was a love story for the ages.

EPILOGUE

Year of Our Lord 1212 A.D.
The Month of May
Caversham Manor, Berkshire
A demesne of William Marshal, Earl of Pembroke

CALLED TO THE gatehouse by one of his men, Achilles could see the rider on the horizon, approaching Caversham. His men were nervous but he was not. They'd had some trouble from a warring neighbor as of late, trouble that had seen some raids on the village nearby, but Achilles, who had never had a command in his life until five years ago, had quelled the trouble very quickly.

As it turned out, Achilles had learned much from Maxton and Kress and Alexander. They were natural commanders and more than he realized had rubbed off on him. He had taken to command natural-ly. He was still quick to anger, and the first one into a fight, but he'd learned to temper that with military tactics and sound decisions that he never even knew he was capable of.

Of course, his wife had helped a great deal.

In fact, to the four hundred soldiers and four knights who lived and served at Caversham, William Marshal's premier property in Oxford-shire, Lady Susanna de Dere was the true commander of Caversham. She always made it seem that Achilles was in charge, and she deferred to him, but more often than not, she was the seed of his decisions.

But no one cared.

A Blackchurch-trained knight was worth his weight, or her, weight in gold.

But Susanna was with the children now as Achilles stood on the walls of the very large and very fortified manse, more of a castle than a true manse, watching the rider approach. A single rider wasn't of any concern but his men feared it was a ruse.

Achilles didn't think so, especially when he saw who it was.

Kevin de Lara entered Caversham's gates astride his big bay war-horse, pulling the sweating animal to a halt in the middle of the ward as Achilles came off the wall. Kevin was just dismounting his horse when he saw Achilles approach.

"Welcome to Caversham," Achilles said, a grin on his face. "What brings you out into the country, de Lara?"

Kevin was smiling, but there was no real joy behind it. "I have just come from a journey north," he said. "Samuel sends you and his sister his salutations."

"And how is Baron Coverdale these days?"

"Allied with William Marshal and enjoying the protection and cooperation of Richmond Castle, as he has been for the past few years," he said. "Morgan de Wolfe is stationed at Aysgarth now, just to ensure Coverdale has all the help he needs. I have also come to tell Lady de Dere that her brother may be getting married. It seems there is a local lass he has his eye on and she seems most agreeable."

Achilles was very interested. "Is that so? Susanna will be quite happy to hear that." He suddenly grew serious. "But you did not come just to speak on Sammy and his marital status. Why are you really here?"

Kevin began to pull off his gloves. "The Marshal's wife has sent me," he said. "I have been all over England over the past few weeks, personally relaying her message to various allies. Show me your hospitality and I shall tell you, too."

Achilles had suspected as much. The past several years had seen William Marshal and King John fall out of favor with one another through a series of major events and, even now, William was in his lands in Ireland, essentially staying clear of the king, while his wife and his men – Achilles and Kevin included – kept vigilant watch of his English properties. Men like Christopher de Lohr, David de Lohr, Bric MacRohan, Caius d'Avignon, and Maxton of Loxbeare were holding fast, trying to keep peace in a land that seemed to want to tear itself apart.

That included Richmond and Aysgarth. Though the Duke of Brittany never made it to English shores those years ago, thanks in large part to Caius d'Avignon and other Yorkshire barons, the threat was still there.

England, in so many ways, was still a country in turmoil.

"Then let us find my wife," Achilles said as they headed for the manse. "Susanna will want to greet you. But you had better give me the gist of why you've come so I can stave off any fits she might have if your news has anything to do with taking me away from Caversham."

"It does."

"I thought as much. What does Isabel say?"

"William is recalling several of his commanders to Ireland," he said. "It is not Irish lords tearing up the place, but English ones. De Lacy and de Broase among them. They are targeting William's properties and he intends to chase them out of Leinster for good."

"So we will be going to war," Achilles grunted softly. "Who else has he summoned?"

"Maxton and Caius," he said. "Christopher de Lohr is sending his sons and a thousand men. De Russe and de Winter are committing men as well. It will be a very big army, Achilles. The Marshal needs your battle skills."

"And you?"

"I am going as well."

"What about Kress? You know that he and his wife have come back to England. The Marshal has given him command of Tutbury Castle in Staffordshire. Susanna and I have been to see him and Cadie, in fact."

"I know where Kress is," Kevin said. "A man has been sent to summon him. We are all to rendezvous at de Lohr's seat of Lioncross Abbey for further instructions."

"How soon?"

"Within the month."

They were heading in the direction of the manse but Achilles took a slight detour, heading around the side of it to the kitchen yards to the rear. When he heard the time frame, he sighed heavily.

"My wife is not going to like this," he said. "She will want to go."

Kevin shook his head. "I have specific orders for her, too. She is to remain in command of Caversham in your stead."

Achilles looked at him. "She is more capable in a fight than most."

"Of that, I have no doubt. But who will watch over your children?"

Achilles had to laugh. Shaking his head, he crooked a finger at Kevin. "My children can take care of themselves," he said. "Already, my wife trains them. Come with me."

Kevin did. They rounded the manse and headed into the kitchen yard where servants were moving about and animals were corralled. It was mild spring weather, with the sun shining, so it was a more pleasant day than most. As Achilles and Kevin moved deeper into the yard, they came upon a woman and three small girls.

Only, it was no ordinary woman.

Susanna, her long, curly hair piled on the back of her head and held there by big, iron pins, stood with her three daughters. Susanna was dressed in fairly normal clothing; a shift, a durable surcoat, both hiked up to her knees, and underneath she wore leather breeches and boots. That was usual attire for Susanna. In her hand, she held a small wooden sword and, as Kevin noted, all three girls had little swords, too.

Mother was giving her daughters a lesson.

"... Brigit, you are not to hit your sisters with the sword," she was saying as the men walked up. "We are learning how to defend ourselves, not slap people around. Now, let us try again. Hold your sword the way I taught you."

Brigit de Dere, the oldest child at five years of age, was eager to learn what her mother was teaching. She turned to her younger sister by a year, Elisabeth, whom they called Libby, and held out her sword the way her mother had instructed.

But Libby didn't like the sword stuck in her face like that and pushed it away, while the youngest girl, two-year-old Alis, sat on the ground and tried to dig a hole with her wooden weapon.

But that all changed when they caught sight of their father. Immediately, there were squeals all around and Achilles found himself being charged by his three cherubic daughters, all of them with various shades of their mother's red hair. They rammed into him, he roared, and they all went down in a pile.

Susanna stood over them, grinning as she watched Achilles tickle and growl. The girls adored him, perhaps even more than they did their mother, who could be strict with them at times. But not their father – he had been their slave since the moment they opened their eyes and saw him for the first time.

And Achilles didn't care a lick.

"You have just ruined everything I have been working for today," Susanna said. "We were having a fine lesson."

Achilles had baby Alis in his grip, kissing her fat cheeks. "I know you were," he said. "But Kevin has come to visit."

Susanna looked at Kevin, the smile still on her face. "He does this constantly, you know," she said. "Ruining what I have started with the girls."

Kevin laughed softly. "I do not think he cares, my lady."

Susanna shook her head. "He does not," she said, putting her hand on her slightly rounded belly. "I do not even think he will care with this one."

Kevin's smile grew. "Another de Dere offspring," he said. "Congratulations. May this one be a son to balance out the girls."

Achilles stood up with Libby in one arm and Alis in the other. "It will be another girl," he said flatly. "Three pregnancies, three girls. I forbade her to have girls, but that is all she has done. I am sure she will defy me with this child as well."

Kevin gestured to the redheaded children. "But you shall have an army that all men will envy," he said. "Already, their mother trains them. 'Twill be an army of Valkyries."

"I am going to be broke from paying their dowries," Achilles countered. "Worse still, my prospects are diminished because Maxton also has girls. *Too* many of them. We will all be hunting for the same husbands for our children, which will be Kress' sons because he has four. He will be a rich man from all of the bargains he will strike with me and Maxton."

Kevin thought it was all quite comical as Achilles headed for the house, taking his daughters with him. Susanna came to stand next to Kevin, watching Achilles and her brood walk away.

"You have some news, don't you?" she asked quietly.

Kevin looked at her. "I came to tell you that I have recently seen your brother and there is a lady he is fond of. You may be invited to a wedding soon."

That brought a big grin. "I am glad to hear it," she said. "I have been meaning to take the girls up to Aysgarth, but I simply have not had the time. The days seem to go by so quickly."

"That is true."

"My brother aside, why else are you here?"

"What makes you think this is not a social call?"

Her smile faded. "Because you have been holding together The Marshal's alliance here in the south of England while Pembroke has been off in Ireland," she said. "Christopher de Lohr is in command, but you are at the head of the network of allies and spies. I have come to think that you do not sleep and you most definitely do not have a world outside of The Marshal's politics. What is going on that you have come to Caversham?"

Kevin looked at her. "Achilles should tell you."

"*You* tell me."

He hesitated. "If I do, then you must act surprised when Achilles informs you."

"I will. What is it?"

"The Marshal has called Achilles to Ireland," he said. "He is intent to drive out the English forces that are threatening his lands. Maxton and Kress have been summoned, too. It is not just Achilles."

Susanna's expression sank somewhat but she steeled herself. Not only was she a warrior's wife, but she was a warrior herself. She understood how the world of battles worked.

"When will he leave?" she asked.

"He must be at Lioncross Abbey within the month," Kevin said quietly. "Sherry will be staging the forces from there. De Lohr has put Sherry in charge."

"That is because the man married de Lohr's eldest daughter."

"Another story for another time."

"This summons does not include me, I take it?"

"You are to have command of Caversham in your husband's absence."

Achilles was nearly to the kitchen door, pausing to call to Kevin and his wife, urging them to follow. While Kevin obeyed, Susanna was a little slower. She took a moment to look around her, to drink it all in, to appreciate these halcyon days that would soon change because The Marshal was in need of her husband. He would soon be heading off to war.

The Executioner Knights were being called to duty once again.

It shouldn't bother her, but it did. Though she and Achilles had returned to William Marshal those years ago after their narrow escape from Aysgarth Castle, they'd been fortunate enough to serve The Marshal together, as they once swore that they would. It was an unusual situation and The Marshal knew it, but he also found it quite agreeable to have Achilles and Susanna together on tasks. Susanna kept Achilles from becoming too uncontrollable, and Achilles let his wife's talent shine through when required.

It had been an excellent arrangement.

But then came the birth of Brigit, named for the Celtic goddess of fire in homage to Achilles' nickname for his wife – Sparks. Once Susanna became heavily pregnant, The Marshal sent her, along with her husband, to Caversham Castle, where Achilles became the garrison commander. It had worked out splendidly for five years and this was the first time Achilles would be called away, separated from the family he so deeply adored.

Susanna knew it was going to be hard on him.

Therefore, she waved to her husband as he and Kevin headed into the manse, knowing she was going to have to put on a brave face or Achilles might very well not go. Already, she ached for the man who had once told her that without her, his nights were starless. Her nights were starless without him, too.

But sometimes, sacrifices had to be made.

In this case, Achilles had to answer the call of the very man they owed their happiness to, so it was never a question of Achilles not going. He would most definitely go. It would be a simple matter of convincing him he needed to.

As always, she was the more reasonable one between them but, even so, he was her rock.

She was going to miss him horribly.

Heading into the manse, Susanna spent the evening feasting with Achilles and Kevin, and when Kevin left a couple of days later, she spent the next two weeks helping Achilles prepare for the journey to come. They had no idea how long he would be away, because some battle campaigns had been known to take years. So on a misty spring morning in late May, Achilles and Susanna gazed into each other's eyes and spoke words of love that were deeper than any ocean, higher than any mountain.

It was such a painful parting, but a necessary one, and in the end, it was Susanna who pulled away and forced Achilles to go. She watched him ride off into that foggy morning, remaining strong until he was out of sight.

Later, in the privacy of her chamber, she wept her lonely tears.

But God was good to them.

Six months after Achilles departed, his first son was born on a cold autumn night, a big lad who was doted on by his mother and sisters. Little Tiegh de Dere didn't meet his father until he was almost eight months of age, but it didn't matter. Achilles looked into the handsome face of his first son, a lad who looked exactly like him, and it was as if the time and separation had never been.

He loved him more with every beat of his heart.

Achilles knew what love was because, before Susanna, he'd learned to love his fellow knights, men he had experienced life and death with. But nothing compared to the love of one beautiful woman, three adoring daughters, and a healthy son to carry on his name. Achilles had worried, long ago, that the sins of his past would catch up to him, but in the joy of his family, he could only see blessings and rewards.

The youngest member of the Unholy Trinity, like his two brethren before him, had finally learned what true contentment was because his love for his family had made Achilles de Dere, and all of the Execution-er Knights, immortal.

ℭ THE END ℗

Children of Achilles and Susanna

Brigit

Elisabeth

Alis

Tiegh

William

Cormac

ABOUT KATHRYN LE VEQUE

Medieval Just Got Real.

KATHRYN LE VEQUE is a USA TODAY Bestselling author, an Amazon All-Star author, and a #1 bestselling, award-winning, multi-published author in Medieval Historical Romance and Historical Fiction. She has been featured in the NEW YORK TIMES and on USA TODAY's HEA blog. In March 2015, Kathryn was the featured cover story for the March issue of InD'Tale Magazine, the premier Indie author magazine. She was also a quadruple nominee (a record!) for the prestigious RONE awards for 2015.

Kathryn's Medieval Romance novels have been called 'detailed', 'highly romantic', and 'character-rich'. She crafts great adventures of love, battles, passion, and romance in the High Middle Ages. More than that, she writes for both women AND men – an unusual crossover for a romance author – and Kathryn has many male readers who enjoy her stories because of the male perspective, the action, and the adventure.

On October 29, 2015, Amazon launched Kathryn's Kindle Worlds Fan Fiction site WORLD OF DE WOLFE PACK. Please visit Kindle Worlds for Kathryn Le Veque's World of de Wolfe Pack and find many action-packed adventures written by some of the top authors in their genre using Kathryn's characters from the de Wolfe Pack series. As Kindle World's FIRST Historical Romance fan fiction world, Kathryn Le Veque's World of de Wolfe Pack will contain all of the great story-telling you have come to expect.

Kathryn loves to hear from her readers. Please find Kathryn on Facebook at Kathryn Le Veque, Author, or join her on Twitter @kathrynleveque, and don't forget to visit her website and sign up for her blog at www.kathrynleveque.com.

Please follow Kathryn on Bookbub for the latest releases and sales: bookbub.com/authors/kathryn-le-veque.

Made in United States
Orlando, FL
02 May 2022

17432731R00134